W9-BCB-050

JOYCE CAROL OATES *ALL THE GOOD PEOPLE I'VE LEFT BEHIND*

SANTA BARBARA
BLACK SPARROW PRESS
1979

Acknowledgements: *Atlantic Monthly* for "The Tryst"; *Boston University Journal* for "Intoxication"; *Chicago Review* for "The Hallucination"; *Confrontation* for "The Leap"; *Michigan Quarterly Review* for "Eye-Witness"; *Queen's Quarterly* for "Walled City"; *Redbook* for "All the Good People I've Left Behind"; *South Carolina Quarterly* for "Sentimental Journey"; *Southern Review* for "High" and "Blood-Swollen Landscape".

Oates, Joyce Carol, 1938-
    All the good people I've left behind.

    CONTENTS. The leap.—High.—Intoxication. [etc.]
    I. Title.
PZ4.O122Al [PS3565.A8]   813'.5'4   78-22110
ISBN 0-87685-394-7
ISBN 0-87685-395-5 signed
ISBN 0-87685-393-9 pbk.

for Herb Yellin

ALL THE GOOD PEOPLE I'VE LEFT BEHIND

The Leap

Could escape by way of the window. Could climb out onto the
ledge . . . take hold of one of the vines . . . shake it to test its
strength . . . rotten? no? . . . and climb cautiously down the side of
the building . . . slowly, slowly. Four storeys. New unsuspected
strength in the fingers, in the muscles of the arms and shoulders.
Feet grasping prayerlike. Splinters? Thorns? Sudden breaking of
the vine? Below, people have gathered to stare. *Look! There's one of
them escaping! Escaping her own death!*

But Annie was not dying, wasn't the one who was dying.

Ah, so restless! She could not bear it. She left the hospital room
and half-ran to the lavatory and there, alone, fortunately alone, she
paced from one end of the room to the other, panting softly, back and
forth, back and forth, like an animal in a cage, thinking now about
nothing . . . not about the dying woman . . . not about death, about
the constant odor of death . . . but about nothing, nothing, except
the need to exercise her body, the hunger for motion, movement,
even for strain. Keen as sexual desire was this hunger: must move
her legs, her arms, must rouse herself to motion. She wanted to run,
wanted to swim. Wanted to feel her heart pound. She loved her
body, her strong legs and arms and lungs, she loved even the ache of
weariness after exertion, and it frightened her that she seemed to be
sinking inside her body . . . drifting, falling, subsiding . . . her
consciousness growing dimmer in sympathy with the dying woman,
retreating from the surface of her body . . . retreating from the point
of contact with the physical world, which was the only world that
mattered.

Unconsciously, she had been pacing in the shape of a figure eight. Must be the pattern all confined animals take, Annie thought.

—◆—◆—

When I was alive I had good days and bad days and neutral one-dimensional days that were forgotten as soon as they slid away. I regret nothing. I have lost nothing. My life was a good life as such lives go. . . . I remember a china leopard nine or ten inches long, black with gorgeous yellow-orange spots like eyes. A long tail that curled upward, bright green glassy eyes, a birthday present from my niece's little girl, the red-headed one. . . . Is Annie here? Where is Annie? I thought she was in the room with me, a minute ago. . . .

"Who are they? Are they coming closer?"

"I can't see. No—they're going back down. They're stopping by a picnic table down there."

Annie had been dressing hurriedly. Now she bent forward and slipped her arm beneath the heavy weight of her hair and lifted it free of the collar of her dress, moving slowly. She had not been with him: her mind had been elsewhere.

"Two boys and a girl," he said. "They didn't see us. . . . They're no one we would know."

He looked back at her anxiously. His expression was distorted, as if someone had given him a good hard shake.

"Are you all right? You're not upset?" he asked.

"Of course not," Annie said irritably.

She lay back against an outcropping of rock, her arms behind her head, her leg crossed at the knee. Though he hovered by her, solicitous, flushed, she looked past him—at the pines on the other side of the river, at the immense boulders and rock-strewn beach. What had she been thinking of? Whose voice, whose words? She half-resented the intrusion of the real world; there was something urgent she must learn, in that other world.

Her lover sat awkwardly beside her, laughing at his own agitation. He did not like himself, much of the time. He made small savage quizzical remarks. "I'm a mess, a wreck," he would say, smiling into Annie's face. "I'm not good enough for you." She never replied, dreading the direction he might take; she did not trust him. "Do you really love me, Annie? Dear Annie?" He was anxious and merry at once at such times; he jingled car keys or coins in his hand, not knowing what he did. "I can't imagine why but it's lovely—it's lovely," he said. "I hope it never ends."

"It won't end," Annie said. "Why should it?"

"You seem so distracted these days. You're not with me at all."

"That isn't true," Annie said at once.

"All right, then, it isn't true," he said amiably. He took her hand and kissed the knuckles. He touched the inside of her bare foot; drew his forefinger along the blue veins, one after another, as if counting them. Annie shivered. "Fascinating," he said.

"My feet aren't clean," Annie said uncomfortably.

"—it's fascinating, your foot. Look. Have you ever—? So many veins, so delicate, lovely, unexpected. There must be ten or more of them, in this one place. Have you ever noticed?"

"Noticed what?" Annie said.

She stared at her own foot, flinching at the sight of it. Her feet were too big: too long and narrow and pale. Her toes were too long. Ugly. She had always hated the size of her feet, as a young girl, had been very self-conscious, sullen and miserable and stubborn about going to buy shoes.

"How carefully you're constructed," her lover said. "Yes, you're a work of art. Have you ever noticed?"

Annie stared at the veins. There were quite a few of them: was that normal? So many slender, bluish veins, subtle as erasure marks against the soft, unaccountably shiny skin of her instep. For a moment she felt alarmed, disoriented, really not knowing if she had ever seen them before . . . if she had ever looked at her own foot before. A work of art, was it? She saw, yes, that the network of veins was incredibly delicate; the foot itself not as ugly as she believed. But she did not want her lover to look at it.

He leaned forward playfully and seized her foot and kissed it.

"Forgive me for everything," he muttered.

—◆—◆—

Annie? she says and Annie replies at once Yes, yes: she hasn't left. Hasn't gone anywhere. By the bedside, in the rocking chair, here sits Annie with her nervous damp big-knuckled hands in her lap.

Annie?

Yes, she says, clearing her throat, Annie is still here, hasn't left. What time is it? Two o'clock. Afternoon. Not Sunday—not today. Tuesday. The afternoon off from work, Annie hears herself explain, glad to have something to say, something to explain, everything so logical, plausible. Her great-aunt is dying: lies there dying a few feet away: watching Annie with love, always with love, though they say she must be in great pain. Even with the morphine, the stepped-up dosages. Pain? Love? She is only sixty-six years old and is dying unfairly, unfairly, Annie wants to scream and smash and throw her body around, cracking her own backbone like a whip, she is murderously angry, she would shout in the corridors of the hospital *Unfair, unfair! How can this happen!*—except it would do no good, no good at all. And it would embarrass her great-aunt who does not seem to mind dying.

Ah, the ugly injustice of it! Cirrhosis of the liver, sixty-six years old, the sweet-faced uncomplaining schoolteacher aunt of Annie's mother, a widow in 1944 and never remarried; a woman who never drank. Champagne at weddings, maybe. A glass of wine. Ugly ugly injustice, Annie wants to jump up from the rocking chair, wants to throw herself across the woman's legs—wants to break into tears, to sob angrily as a child might sob, wants, even, to make a fool of herself. She is an adult now, twenty-seven years old. She no longer makes a fool of herself in public. That is forbidden; that is the one forbidden thing.

I want to talk to you, she whispers in her lover's arms, *I want to tell you about the injustice, the loss . . . about how much people love her, how much I love her . . . without being able to help her. It doesn't do any good, hasn't any power to help, our love.*

She began once to speak of it and faltered and went silent, hearing the words go wrong; inadequate, they were, and cheap—cheap. Commonplace. Her lover was a nervous jesting man. A guilty man. He loved her, loved her very much, and his love for Annie made him miserable with guilt, so in her presence, even in her arms, he liked to joke; he was witty, ironic, playful. When they were together they were playful and the words that passed between them were playful. Annie began to tell him about her great-aunt but the words failed, she failed, her lover stared at her, embarrassed, not knowing what she meant, thinking perhaps she was making a desperate statement of love—or about to break off with him?—and she went silent finally and a long terrible space of time passed. She could not talk to him, not about this. The first death of someone close to her, someone she loved very much. She could not talk to him or to anyone.

—◆—◆—

One afternoon in mid-summer they drove fifty miles north of the city, into the state park, and at the far end of the park, on a hill above the river, they made love for the first time in nearly two weeks; and though Annie loved him she was not thinking of him, was not able to think of him. She thought: *Death. Dying. A puzzle. An absence. Nothing matters.*

He lay in her arms and pressed his face against her breasts. He never spoke now of his family: only alluded to his children from time to time, incidentally. Of his wife he said nothing. In the first weeks of their relationship, a year ago, he had wanted to divorce his wife and marry Annie; had come to her apartment, drunk; had insisted that it was inevitable—they must marry, they loved each other, anything less than marriage was out of the question. He was too old for anything else. But Annie had protested. Had talked him out of it. He loved his children too much, didn't he realize?—it was not possible for him to leave them yet. In a few years, maybe. In a few years.

It was fairly hot in the sun. Annie wished she had brought her swimming suit along; she would have liked to try the river here, in spite of the pebbly beach. It sounded as if the young people were swimming. From time to time there was splashing, and shouting, and a girl's high giggle.

The river was swift-flowing, quite wide at this point, not very clean. Unless Annie was imagining it, the water looked much dirtier than she remembered from other years. As a young girl she had come out to the state park, with friends, and the river had been rather cold for swimming, but clear; she was certain it had been clear. Now it looked almost muddy, especially close to shore. . . . Still, she would have liked to swim in it. She would dive from one of the big rocks and surface halfway out and her lover, standing fully-clothed on shore, would applaud.

To the right there was a hill higher than the one they were on, and jutting over the river there was a narrow outcropping of rock, a natural ledge: from that she would dive twenty feet to the water below. It was quite a distance but she would dive. She imagined her lover watching her, pleading with her not to try it. *That's dangerous, Annie. Please don't.* Driving his car not long ago on the expressway she had pressed the accelerator down, down, gripping the steering wheel hard, and the speedometer had registered 95 miles an hour before he spoke: the words torn from him, harsh, panicked. *Annie, please. No.* She had turned to him as if in surprise, startled by his reaction; had slowed the car at once; had laughed at him. It was perfectly safe, she said. Why was he so distressed?

Afterward she realized it was because they could not be found together—not even in death. He feared discovery as much as he feared death itself.

So he would plead with her not to dive. But she would ignore him. She pictured herself out there, on the ledge. Tall, on tip-toes, measuring the distance, measuring the current of the river, unhurried, unalarmed, moving to the edge, her knees bending, arms swinging, body perfectly coordinated. . . . And so she would dive. But was the water deep enough? It looked dark there, almost black. Could be shadow. Could be hidden rocks. A reckless thing to do, a stupid thing to do; Annie knew she would never attempt it, not even with her lover watching. But how lovely it would be!—and the sky so perfectly blue as she hurtled herself into space.

Am I dead yet? Why aren't I dead yet? Haven't I earned it— death—as fully as anyone else? It will be too great a struggle to return, from where I am. . . .

"What is that?" Annie said, aloud. "Is someone—?"

"Those kids," her lover said, sitting up.

Annie got to her feet and brushed at her clothes. The air was cool here above the river, deceptively cool; the sun was powerful, however, and they had been lying in it too long. Her head ached a little. She could see the boys and the girl now and the sight of them was jarring. They were obviously drunk or drugged. One of them was sitting on a picnic table with his feet, his bare feet, hanging over the top of a wire trash can. The other boy was wrestling with the girl and both were laughing shrilly.

"We can go down the other side of the hill," Annie's lover said. "We can avoid them."

"Yes," Annie said. But she stood watching them. The boys wore cut-off jeans and were bare-chested; they must have been about sixteen or seventeen years old. The girl was much younger, no more than fourteen. Perhaps younger. She wore a yellow bathing suit. Her hair was cropped short, shorter than the boys'. She giggled so shrilly, made such exaggerated gestures of merriment—bending her body nearly double, shaking her head from side to side—that Annie was certain she must be out of her mind.

"They're just fooling around," her lover said. "They're not going to hurt her. Come on."

"Wait," Annie said.

One of the boys half-ran the girl to the river bank and pushed her in and she fell clumsily, a few feet out. It took her a while to get her footing. She laughed. The boys laughed. The boy at the table tossed a beer can at her—it struck her shoulder and fell into the water.

"What are they doing?" Annie said. "Why are they so loud?"

"They're just fooling around."

"That girl is— She doesn't know what she's doing," Annie said.

The boy who had shoved her into the river now jumped beside her, knees against chest, tanned arms gripping legs—a dive bomb, it was called; it splashed a lot of water. The girl staggered away. She escaped him and climbed onto one of the big rocks, clumsily, and Annie saw with a tiny thrill of dismay that her halter top had come partly undone. The girl did not seem to notice that one small pale breast was exposed.

"Let's leave," Annie's lover said. He slipped his hand beneath her hair and gripped the back of her neck lightly; it was a customary gesture of his. "We don't want them to look over here and see us—all right?"

"Maybe if they see us they'll let her alone," Annie said. "Maybe they'll stop tormenting her."

"She doesn't mind—she likes it. See? She's laughing. She's asking for it, she likes it."

"She's frightened."

"She *loves* it."

"She doesn't know what's happening," Annie said angrily. "They're going to hurt her. We can't walk away and leave her."

"Annie, for Christ's sake—"

The girl adjusted her halter top, fixing the strap as she waded back to shore. It was true that she was laughing. But her laughter was frantic, her thin body frantic. Staring at her, Annie felt the same chilling helpless terror she had felt in the hospital, a sense that nothing could be done—*she* could do nothing—must only watch, her blood gone cold. What was happening, she asked herself wildly, what did the world mean, so hurtful, so perplexing?—would it always frighten her so?

"They're just playing," her lover said. "They're not serious."

"Do you think so . . . ?" Annie said uncertainly.

"Of course, honey. Let's go."

But both boys were after the girl now. Jeering, clapping their hands, they chased her up the hill . . . toward the rocky ledge. Annie could not believe what she saw. She could not believe it. The girl's scrambling figure, her child-like arms and legs . . . the boys' blunt tanned backs, their shaggy heads, their loud mocking voices. . . . It was eerie, dream-like, terrible. The boys were shouting and clapping at the girl as if driving an animal before them.

"Annie, we'd better go—"

"Tell them to stop," Annie said. "Go over there—tell them to stop."

"They're only playing—"

"Please tell them to stop!"

Now the girl was trapped on the ledge, at least twenty feet above the water. The boys were wrestling with her. Annie could hear their crazy laughter. Didn't they realize the danger, didn't they know the girl could slip and fall and hurt herself very badly?—could be killed?

"They're only playing," Annie's lover said nervously.

Annie pulled away from him. She cupped her hands to her mouth and shouted for them to stop. But they did not hear—did not even glance around.

She shouted again in a hoarse, desperate, ugly voice.

And then it happened: while she watched, helpless, the girl wrestled free of the boys and jumped out into space, her legs kicking, arms flailing. She fell straight as a shot and hit the water at an angle, bent slightly to the left.

"Oh God—" Annie cried.

But in a moment the girl surfaced. Head and shoulders appeared. She must have been dazed because she slipped under the water again, thrashing. Annie ran forward. "Get her—save her— Don't let her drown—" she cried. One of the boys dive-bombed beside the girl, who had surfaced again; he plummeted that distance as if he were accustomed to it, missing the girl by only a few inches. The other boy made a yodeling noise and jumped off the rock feet-first, both arms flapping comically. He did not even bother to hold his nose and he struck the water partly on his back, with a cracking sound that Annie could hear from where she stood.

"They're just playing," Annie's lover said, "see?—just overgrown children playing rough."

Annie watched the three of them swim toward shore. She stared as if transfixed. *I am so lost now. Dizzy. My eyes are failing. I am half out of my body, floating in the air. Annie? Can you help me?* She could see again the girl struggling with the boys, there on the ledge, she could hear their laughter, their shrieks and meaningless shouts, and, again, she could see the girl pushing free of them—jumping free—throwing her body out into space, her small face radiant as she escaped them. What had it been for her, Annie wondered, at that moment of savage freedom?—a strained, glowing, rather mad look to the girl's face, as if everything had vanished for her at that instant, the world reduced to a cascade of bright falling images, and air so steeply falling against her that she could not breathe. The jump into space, into oblivion: a terrible ecstasy in it, beyond all emotion.

"Annie, for Christ's sake," her lover pleaded. "Let's go."

—◆—◆—

"I suppose you think I'm a coward. A selfish bastard."

Annie said nothing.

"I suppose you think—it means nothing to me?—because I'm a man, I can't be hurt?—I don't have feelings?"

"No," Annie said slowly. "I don't think that."

Now it was autumn and the death and the funeral long past, and that day in the park past; and Annie's tears, and the fury with which she had beaten at her knees and thighs with her own fists, and even the storming hot memory of her rage. They were sitting together in his car, not touching, trying to piece together a way of saying goodbye.

"You haven't loved me for a long time," he said. "You know that."

"No."

"You haven't, not since that day by the river—do you remember? After that things were changed."

"No," Annie said.

"You wanted me to intervene—and I couldn't, it just wasn't possible— Don't you see, Annie, it just wasn't possible? It isn't fair for you to think I'm a coward. There was nothing I could do."

Annie took his hand but did not look at him. She thought of her great-aunt's face at the end, and of the face of the young girl throwing herself from the rock. Oblivion, ecstasy. No words.

"Of course you're not a coward," Annie said. "None of us are."

High

After the hilarity of the Big V drugstore, where they'd wandered up and down aisles beneath flickering mad-humming rows of fluorescent lights, peering over garishly-colored boxes of tissue paper and shampoo in transparent plastic bottles—of such hues!—green, tawny-yellow, scarlet!—and Deanna sprayed Max with the perfume tester, a vile insecticide-odor called "Night Flight," and the only clerk on duty—a scared-looking little black girl with a big Afro hairdo and purple-wine lips and a white plastic Big V badge—approached them and said, "What you two doin'—?" and after they amazed and elicited a flurry of hand-claps from a fellow shopper, a girl with a child strapped to her back, in a cape of mangy light brown squirrel fur, sleeveless, and were even offered some peanuts from the girl out of a dime-sized cellophane bag with a bright blue *Mr. Peanut* on it, and after they rushed out, faint with laughter, through the novelty automatic doors and into the novelty of a glowering, gusty March afternoon, Deanna and Max linked arms to stride along the viaduct, trying to match their steps, but it was hopeless. Max kept lunging ahead. He kept jerking forward. "I'm hungry and I'm never going to get enough to eat," he said. "I'm headed for the A & P over there."

"What A & P?" Deanna cried.

"The A & P over there! Over there!" Max shouted.

Deanna, who lived right around here, wanted to call after him that the A & P over there, on the far side of the expressway, was closed. It had been closed for a long time. But she forgot about this when she saw Max clambering over the wire fence and then jumping down onto the grass, which was very slippery from the rain, and sliding down, in fast helpless jerks, down toward the traffic a hundred feet or so below. Deanna laughed wildly. She had never seen anything so funny and it was even funnier that Max should climb over the fence when there was a way to get through without climbing over anything: you just squeezed by, close against the side of the viaduct. Max hadn't noticed that! There he was sliding in yard-long slides, as if ice skating downhill, his heels digging into the grass and into the soft mud beneath the grass. The marks made by his boots were deep, streaks of red-brown bright wet mud, very deep and skidding and helpless, and as she stared at him he lost his balance and sat down hard. Deanna doubled over with laughter. From farther up the hill, Max's big heavy shaggy head and immense shoulders and torso were very funny, the way a stranger is funny at a distance, especially when he has just sat down hard in the mud.

Beneath Max, the 4:30—5:00—5:30 traffic was moving along slowly like lava. Max waved and shouted at the cars.

Deanna called out for him to watch her, but he didn't hear, and she started her own slide down to join him. Somehow she slid much more easily and gracefully than Max had. She extended her arms, like a sleepwalker, and noted that her body seemed to grow a little lighter, her heels didn't dig into the earth nearly as much as Max's had. She didn't even lose her balance except for a second, and even then she didn't fall down. She thrust her palm out hard against the ground and slid in jump-jerks that way, skidding down, down. Something stabbed at the palm of her hand but she had no time to examine it.

Max, sitting in the mud, was trying to pull off one of his boots.

"Don't do that," Deanna said. "You don't want to do that. That isn't anything you *want to do.*"

She was afraid he might hurt himself, he was struggling so with the boot and his face was so red. He was not a fat man: but he was large. He had difficulty bending his thick thighs. Deanna stared at his hands, amazed—they were so big—chapped and raw and reddened and very frantic. She tried to stop his hands. "You don't want to do this, Max," she pleaded.

"Don't tell me what I want to do!" he whined.

"But Max—"

"Just like my mother and everybody else—and the airplanes—and—and everybody else—"

But he gave up and sat back, exhausted. He was panting. Deanna located a crumpled Kleenex in the pockets of her slacks and dabbed at his face, which was livid with perspiration. He flinched only once, then closed his eyes and allowed her to wipe his face, slowly and lovingly. She stared down at his wavy brown-black hair, each hair individual and stark, and yet part of the entire contour of the waviness of his hair. Staring, she discovered several silver hairs—they seemed to spring into life—first one and then a second, then a third, then a fourth—as if coming to life while she stared— It was strange. She had never really studied her own husband's hair so intently. Her own husband, her ex-husband, had a spade-shaped beard, but she had never stared carefully into it. Max was clean-shaven. He had shaved that morning, even. It was a compulsion with him, he said; he had to shave, otherwise his face itched and felt dirty. Deanna saw how his lips were thin and watchful, resting from all the laughing they had done back in the drugstore. His teeth, inside his lips, were bluish-white and watchful too. There were these layers to Max, layers inside one another. If she stooped to stare she might have been able to see his tongue, hidden behind his teeth.

How she loved him!

"You could commit suicide, jumping from here to there," Max said, pointing down into the traffic. He had begun to cheer up again.

Deanna laughed. "—could commit murder, jumping feet-first on a car windshield," she said. This idea seemed to come out of nowhere. Or maybe it was based on an incident she had read about in the newspaper—some boys dropping a garbage pail onto the expressway and causing an accident?—she couldn't quite remember. But Max seemed to think her remark was funny. He shook his head helplessly and laughed. Deanna felt a tinge of joy, an elation that was new to her. It did not seem to be hers, exactly. . . . There were new ideas, new poetic ideas, that rose in her brain and took shape through her, through her alone; yet they did not seem to belong to her. In the past she had not been so imaginative. She had never been "creative," and hadn't known why when so many creative people were everywhere around her. Her husband had been very creative. He had teased her about being so slow, so poky, about not laughing quickly enough at his ironic jokes. . . . When it was time for him to leave her, he explained sadly that he had already "left her" in his imagination, months before; why hadn't she known?—

sensed something? "Deanna," he had said morosely, "the world itself is leaving you behind."

He left town, and Deanna found out later, through acquaintances, that he'd gone with a young girl student of his to visit her family in a Cleveland suburb, a girl described as "very pretty and very feminine" with "honey-colored hair"—which sounded just like Deanna herself, as she had been ten years before! She had wept for days. All true data of that experience now tended to be confused, in her mind, with the sound of sobbing and the ugliness of a runny stopped-up nose and a stuffed head and a raw, aching throat. So she did not think of it any longer.

Yet once in a while, when Max laughed so appreciatively at her jokes, she half-wished her husband could hear. Her husband had always approved of Max, who had begun as a friend of the husband's and was now a friend, a very close friend, of Deanna's.

"God, I'm so hungry. I'm ravenous," Max said. "I'll never be filled up." He started to slide down the incline, on the seat of his pants. Deanna could see the A & P grocery store across the way, but she didn't think they should go there, because of all the traffic and for another reason she couldn't remember at the moment. She pulled at Max's hair. He thrust her hands away and said, "What's wrong?— what's going on? There's an awful lot of confusion and noise here—" A trailer truck rattled by, with jeeps hiked up on its back, bright green-and-white jeeps that made Deanna think of Boy Scouts for some reason. The jeeps were so clean, so shiny. The cab of the truck was muddy. Max was sliding down the incline and Deanna cried out for him to be careful—was he going to jump down?—it was so strange, so bewildering, to be down here. For three years she had lived around this neighborhood, but she had never *seen* it before, not from this perspective. The drizzle, the cold mud, the roaring of the traffic, the agitated motions of Max's head . . . and overhead a jet or something streaked by so swiftly it was only sound, mere wrenching sound, a splitting of the sky into pieces. Deanna squinted up but could see nothing—only clouds. They were opaque. She squinted through her spread-out fingers but could not see the jet, though she could still hear it.

Max hated planes so it was lucky that he didn't hear it. He *hated* planes. He lay awake, unable to sleep, because of planes droning overhead all night long—big trucks roaring in the sky—overhead in

the sky—motors and engines and the screams of jets—sometimes
mingling with the big trucks on the city streets and all of them
vibrating, roaring, rumbling, rattling, careening through the night
and through his head, so that he gloated when he saw headlines of
plane crashes and even made a few nasty little obscure jokes which
his students didn't seem to get, which was just as well. He had a
plain, high-colored, shy, sometimes-handsome face, though his
eyes were set deep in their sockets and hidden by the thick lenses of
his glasses. His eyes, seen up close, were a deep cunning alert
green. His glasses protected his eyes, but also denied them. . . .
One day someone had snatched his glasses off and Max had stumbled
down a stairway in the university's administration building, and a
stranger rushing up at him had been transformed into an inconsequential blur. Max and this person had screamed at each other.
Colliding, grappling, they had fallen together in a furious embrace
down ten or eleven steps to the landing, where Max had lain gasping
for breath, too stunned to feel pain or any sensation at all. But that
had been the start of his new life: Without his glasses, people and
things were blurred, and inconsequential, and *he did not have to see
them.* This was a revelation to Max. He had never experienced any
revelation quite like that. And in the days that followed—this was
during a student strike in the spring of the previous year—Max
began to discover new parts of himself, new layers, amazing new
fragments of his own life he had never guessed at before. His life had
been mainly shyness, embarrassment, being bossed around, doing
well on examinations and pleasing older people. He had gone to
parochial schools as a child, and then to a costly high school in
Chicago, run by Jesuits, and from there to Fordham University
where he'd remained, for many years, studying for a Ph.D. in
19th-century Western European history. And all along he had never
guessed that he, himself, was historical: that the past feats of history,
the leaping-across-chasms, the setting-afire of cities, the throwing of
bombs, were all in himself, in Max himself, if only he might liberate
them. He was thirty-six years old before he had awakened and now
he knew that he would never drift into sleep again. He wore a
hip-length jacket made of wool the color of khaki; it had a number of
pockets that buttoned shut, and flaps on its sleeves. His hair was
long, flowing over his collar. His boots were from the Army-Navy
store out on Main Street.

But it alarmed him that Deanna was yanking at him like this. She slid her arm inside his jacket—why? She was laughing and scolding him—why? He feared her. He did not really like her. It was just a coincidence, their being alone for these two weeks when most of their friends were out of town, during the semester break. Max had been planning to drive to Oak Park to visit his mother, but he had learned (indirectly, because his mother never told him what was going on if she could help it) that his sister and her three children were there, and he couldn't bear the thought of seeing so many people and enduring the children's noise, he was headachy all the time and depressed, and so he had stayed here, holed up in his apartment, except for one desperate day when he'd gone over to the Art Institute—only three days before!—it seemed like weeks ago— and there he'd run into Deanna, the ex-wife of an ex-friend of his, Jerry Hecht. He had been staring gloomily at a new acquisition in the museum's American Wing, a shiny-surfaced, enormous, very dark oil painting by a painter he'd never heard of before, a still life of a pheasant with a wrung, wrinkled neck, a rabbit with a glowing red breast, several ears of Indian corn, *all hanging upside down,* beside a large object that must have been a transparent vase, which showed blue, bubbly water inside. All this was on a gleaming, polished surface, perhaps the top of a dining room table. The painter's name was Stuart Parrington; he had been born in 1801 and had died in 1886. In a daze, Max had turned around and noticed a woman wandering in his direction, her head slightly bowed, her mouth working silently as if she were sleepwalking and murmuring to herself, guiding herself across the parquet floor from one wall of paintings to another. Impulsively, Max had called out, "Deanna!"

And so it had begun.

He had known Deanna for years, but at a distance. She was one of the prettier wives, the young wives of the young instructors, blond in his memory but brown-haired in fact, and almost drab-looking that day in the American Wing. Her face had thickened though a quick girlish smile could still transform it. She had looked up, sighted him, and the two of them had laughed for no reason—and half an hour later they were in her apartment, which was now *hers,* though the last time Max had been there it had been her husband's and hers. How confused that day had been, a long tortuous after- noon stretching into dusk and into night. . . . All along, embracing and caressing and struggling with Deanna, Max had heard his mind shrieking, *Do I really want this? . . . do I really want this?*

At dawn she lay with her face pressed against his chest, weeping, telling him about her husband Jerry and his cruelty, about her in-laws' gloating over the divorce, about a miscarriage she had had two years ago but hadn't told anyone about—not even her best friends—and Max found himself weeping along with her, out of pity or exhaustion. He kept recalling, involuntarily, stray ironic remarks Deanna's husband had made about her, when he and Max had gone out drinking on Friday afternoons at a local tavern with some other instructors, all male. Half of his mind twitched with anger at the husband, but the other half acquiesced to the husband's judgment. She was so slippery, so damp!—so helpless! But he pitied her. And her apartment overlooked the expressway, it was so depressing, so closed-in, the walls were painted a white that was too white for one's eyes, like white-wash, so Max ended up somehow inviting her over to his apartment for a few days. There, Deanna seemed to cheer up and to take pleasure in cooking for him, padding around barefoot in his kitchen, wearing a terry-cloth bathrobe of his much too large for her, a delighted grinning little wife. It was all very frantic, very unusual. Max kept slipping away to hide in the bathroom, where he stared stupefied at his drawn face, noting his red-rimmed eyes and wondering if it was time to shave again, since he was sometimes a little anxious, a little jumpy, if he didn't shave often enough. And the planes overhead . . . the planes were mixed up with Deanna's singing out in the kitchen, which sometimes dipped low and was hardly more than a murmur, as if she were talking to herself or even scolding herself. Max distinctly heard her say, *Now where did I put that thing?—Deanna, where did you lay it down?* On both mornings she got his mail for him, hurrying down the three flights of stairs to the foyer, in his bathrobe, and Max cringed to think that someone would see her—though, on second thought, what the hell did he care what anyone thought? He tried to laugh at all this, to see it in a blurry inconsequential light. One morning they had a hilarious time leafing through a magazine that Deanna had pulled out of a neighbor's mailbox slot, laughing helplessly at the cartoons, and Deanna had sat primly on his lap and kissed and nuzzled him, so that he was actually grateful to her for coming over to stay with him . . . but the second morning, this morning, had been a disaster.

It wasn't exactly morning, by the time they woke fully and staggered out of the bedroom. Max had snapped on the radio just in time for the noon news broadcast and heard that a jetliner on its way to Miami had crashed, killing 87 passengers, and he had chuckled at the news in his usual manner. Deanna, in his blue terry-cloth bathrobe, standing at the stove trying to scramble some eggs before they burned, said absent-mindedly, "Oh you awful man, that isn't funny! They felt pain, you know." Max had stared at her. Then, feeling a little queasy, he had hurried into the other room. His brain began to wobble. —*They felt pain! They felt pain, you know!* An overwhelming sensation of guilt and nausea hit him in the stomach. *Felt pain, they felt pain!* He had wanted to rush back to Deanna and explain to her that for Christ's sake he hadn't meant anything by chuckling, he never meant anything by anything he said these days, and since his Awakening he knew he was free of guilt, and of depressing guilty thoughts, and of the knowledge of the pain of other people and even of his own pain, he wanted to scream at the dim-brained hectic woman out in his kitchen that it was the airplanes that were to blame, not him!—not Max!—the airplanes and their horrible ceaseless rattling across the skies that had driven him to such desperation that he, Max, a decent human being, a decent kindly shy well-meaning human being, an intellectual, should actually chuckle at the news of 87 people falling from the sky (and he thought with another wave of terror that perhaps children had been among the passengers . . .) and should feel the need, the exquisite overwhelming irresistible need, to get as high as possible with everything he had in stock, before the entire weight of the universe crashed onto his head. . . .

Now Deanna was giggling beside him. "No, don't! Don't cross yet!" He blinked and saw a convoy of cars rushing at them, led by a huge semi-detached truck with no burden to slow it down, so he jumped back onto the grass and Deanna scrambled up beside him. It was hard for him to remember exactly why they were down here. He knew it was necessary to get across the expressway, to get to something on the other side, but he couldn't remember exactly why they were down here and not crossing on the pedestrians' caged-in wire tunnel, and he half-blamed Deanna for this, she was so impulsive and noisy and kept pawing at him. When he pulled away she kept saying, "What? What's wrong? Shouldn't I touch you any more?—

what's wrong?—what's changed between us?" But in the next instant he noticed a break in the traffic, and stepped down eagerly onto
the pavement, preparing to run like hell. Deanna giggled and clung
to his arm. Max's heart pumped itself up to the size of a basketball,
then to the size of a big balloon, then it contracted suddenly when he
caught sight of a truck rattling along toward them out in the left lane,
and once again they scrambled back up on the grass.

Max yelled and waved his fist at the traffic. *What the hell is going
on?* he heard his own voice ask, but it got no answer. He had a
sudden exhilarating vision of himself and Deanna at the side of the
expressway, about to dart across, figures of threat and terror to the
drivers, and he had to laugh because it was so powerful, the vision, it
was so surprising. Could that be Max himself there, frightening the
commuters?—Max in his khaki-colored jacket, his hair wild, an air of
constant dramatic energy about him unlike any Max people knew?
His heart swelled with the vision of this Max and he wondered if his
big nicked hands could sprout claws and if tusks might shoot out of
his grin and his small eyes grow huge with scarlet-rimmed evil. He
flew so high, he was so totally powerful, that anything might happen
and it wouldn't even surprise him, though it would certainly surprise those commuters.

But now there was a genuine break in the traffic and Max pulled
Deanna out and they ran, screaming with laughter, like lovers or like
brother and sister, like children, heading for the median where they
would be safe. Deanna could run fast, it was surprising. She wore
orangish slacks made of a material too thin for this weather, and her
hair was all wild and her eyes opened very wide to take everything
in. She was thinking with part of her mind that she was afraid—
why?—of what?—afraid of what?—but there was no need because
they got to the median safely and Max pulled her up, like a husband
who was very protective of her.

His face was handsome now, gleaming with sweat. His glasses had
slipped down one side of his cheek, the earpiece must have slid up
from his pinkened ear, but Deanna didn't dare adjust it because she
knew he would draw away from her. He loved her, but he would
draw away. She knew it. So she didn't dare. Even when he was high
and joyous he sometimes drew away from her, or his face registered
some sign of dislike, and she knew those signs well, and in a dark
plunge her mind gave her the vision of how surprised Max would

look if she gave him a shove forward and out into the traffic, into the spasms and screeches out there!—how surprised they would all look! Max was pointing out the strange expressions on the faces of people in cars speeding by them, and those expressions really were strange, and ugly, and almost frightening because they showed so much hate for Deanna and Max, who after all were strangers and innocent and had never done them any harm. Deanna felt a prick of terror, not knowing if she should be angry about this or just laugh or maybe stick her tongue out at one of those drivers—there was such illusion in the world, so many pockets of cold dense city air, pockets of illusions weighing everyone down and threatening the love between her and Max—

Then Max yelled and dragged her across the other three lanes, and they got there though Deanna didn't think she had exactly run along the earth itself, had maybe been tugged floating across by Max's grip, and they ran up onto the service lane, gasping in triumph, and up the slippery muddy slope which seemed steeper than the other slope, while people were honking at them and a siren rushed onto them, and when Deanna turned, dazed, she saw a white-and-red vehicle hurtling along with its red light revolving like mad, spinning faster than her own brain, a siren rising and rising to madness, and she was able to get clear in her vision that it was only an ambulance speeding along and nothing for *them*, only an ordinary commonplace ambulance tearing along to the hospital a few blocks north of here. . . . From her apartment she had seen many ambulances speeding along, had seen many firetrucks and police squad cars, had heard many sirens, and knew instinctively that it was nothing that should terrify her, but somehow she felt shaky and needed to clutch at Max, who was climbing up the slope ahead of her, as if he'd forgotten her . . . then, thank God, he remembered her and grabbed onto her bleeding hand, giving her a robust yank. "We're almost there!" he cried.

But at the top they had to contend with the fence again. It was a linked wire fence, about eight feet high, with barbed wire at the top, a vicious deadly thing, slashing at their fingers and clothes and wobbling as if about to topple over. But Max got them over somehow. He dragged Deanna over and she felt something slip and her left leg dug into something, she felt the material of her slacks tear and then the flesh of her calf, oh, oh, the rush of pain, and she cried out in surprise as Max yanked her the rest of the way and caught her in his arms. All arms and legs! They fell to the ground. Max began to laugh helplessly. He was saying something about the police—"The police to the rescue!"—and when Deanna managed to get to her feet again, stunned, gasping for breath, she saw that there *was* a policeman running toward them.

He was shouting at them. But Max was so brave that he strode to meet the man, extending his hand for a handshake, a parody of politeness, Max was so funny that Deanna couldn't help but laugh though she did feel a little frightened . . . and a little embarrassed too, because the cop's shouting pierced the warm liquid sensation of her mind and for an instant she could see him very clearly . . . then Max bowed low and she laughed in delight and everything went warm and wet again.

"What the hell?—what the hell are you two doing?" the cop cried.

He seemed to be shouting at them from a great distance—a tiny head perched on the horizon of smokestacks and buildings—but then as Deanna stared the head grew enormous as the smoke-seared boiling-black head of a baby in a painting she had seen once in some art museum, and the painting had terrified her at the time, but she'd forgotten it until now, and she believed that if the cop did not retreat to the horizon again she would die. But his shouts got raw and ordinary and he turned into a normal-sized man again, and now Max had taken charge completely and was explaining about the A & P and even pointing at it. Deanna looked and saw that the A & P was there, and though it was darkened there were huge posters all across its broad front windows that said in gigantic unmistakable red letters BUY EAT SAVE BUY EAT SAVE BUY EAT SAVE.

"What's going on? What the hell is this?" the cop kept saying.

Deanna thought it was insane, that he should keep asking them a question it was his own responsibility to answer, since he was a policeman, but she supposed he already knew the answer and was only holding it back, to trick them; also, she saw that he was a very young cop, a boy-cop, a child-cop, and it angered her that a cop should actually be younger than she was because it didn't seem right, and why was he shouting at them if he was younger than she was and already knew all the answers? She giggled into her bleeding hand. Max was explaining about the A & P and how he was hungry, and Deanna had a flash of a thought again of shoving him—and then something happened and she *had* shoved Max—ran at him and shoved him right into the cop. The she turned to run, herself. She ran with her hands raised in the air so that people driving by—they were in a street now, parallel to and above the expressway—would have the freaky idea that the cop was going to shoot her. A black woman in a Volkswagen swerved to avoid her. Deanna laughed at that, it was so hilarious, straight black people, *straight black people,* acting like middle-class white people, they were so crazily funny, Deanna doubled over with laughter in the middle of this street— where had another street come from so fast?—and out of a bus's broad flat wall-like front came blasts of a horn, enough to scare Deanna away and over to the A & P. She ran. Behind her Max had to fend for himself.

Panicked, his glasses slipping off, Max had shoved the cop backward, crying, "Oh, what?—what happened? Wait—" The cop staggered, losing his balance, and another city bus rushed out of nowhere and braked and skidded on the wet pavement, but didn't stop in time, and the cop was thumped forward, *thud,* and fell with arms outstretched and an amazed clear expression on his face that Max somehow shared, though he knew at the same time that it was only a joke. "Natural selection! Natural selection!" Max yelled through his cupped hands. He ran back to the fence and clawed at it, hearing a small voice at the back of his skull, a teacher's voice that was somehow his own, coming out of a tiny man standing at a tiny blackboard with a spidery smeared incredible dynasty of an Austrian monarchy sketched on it, hearing this voice calling out to enormous bear-sized Max clawing at the fence, *My God, what has happened?*

Deanna had tried to get in the A & P, but the automatic doors were not working, so she ran around the back and through an alley, panting, beginning to sob, trying to get into the rhythm of running so that it was not this awful pain, trying to get her breath into rhythm, into sane healthy rhythm, trying to channel her breath up into her nose and away from her mouth, so that she wouldn't be so ragged and would have room to release the laughter deep inside her chest, a secret tunneling of laughter that had to get free, and she ran by some people waiting for a bus, black and white startled faces, she saw how amazed and stupid those faces were, like the faces of strangers—how could they know, how could they guess?—how could they know anything at all? She soared past her own weeping and the throbbing of pain that was supposed to belong to her, but which she now disowned, and then she got the laughter loose and began to laugh at last, thinking *God, this is it, I'll never be able to stop—*

Intoxication

This phase of their lives was delirious, unforeseen, an intoxication that swept upon them as if from the outside. They could not have guessed the excitement of planning the near future . . . the weeks and months ahead . . . even the days immediately before them, in which so much had to be accomplished. So much, so much to do! What a frenzy!

And in the middle of it, their friend Darrell telephoned.

He was visiting his family in Chicago, a day's drive away; he hadn't seen them in nearly two years; did they have an evening free?

Cynthia was delighted. Of course they wanted to see him. Of course they had a free evening for him. "You telephoned just in time," she said. "A few days from now . . . it would have been too late."

For a while, for nearly a year, it had been a time of dullness and things gone wrong: small mishaps, colds that developed into flu, Dean's melancholia, Cynthia's helpless miserable nagging. She did not want to say such things to her husband—yet she heard herself saying them, amazed and tearful. Then he would shout at her. And she would stagger, as if about to faint; too weak to reply to him, too stunned; blood rushing to her face, slaps of heat against her cheeks. . . . She would burst into tears. He would comfort her. They would forgive each other: a continual litany. Telling lies, they must have felt, from time to time, strangely united; like guilty children, like conspirators.

Six or eight years ago had been a time of connections, of swift brave alliances. Like many of their friends they had gotten married at that time: relieved that the monotonous complexities of their lives might be pared back, pounded down, into something simple, whole, and marvelous. A time of weddings, of intoxication. Staying up late to plan the future . . . the months and years ahead . . . so many details to be considered and molded, gently or with force, into a whole. Now it was different, the very atmosphere seemed different. Cynthia stumbled through her half of the marriage in a daze, whispering to herself, trying to decipher the meaning of her own symptoms . . . as if she were to blame for them, might be called to account for them, when in fact she was blameless, even Dean might be said to be blameless, and who would point at them and jeer? They had entered a new phase of their lives, that was all.

As soon as they gave a name to what they lived in—*a failed marriage*—and what they were moving toward—*divorce*—their home became peaceful again. The marriage was now temporary, like a holiday; like a ship's crossing begun in good weather, with high spirits, ending dismally but with no one to blame. The weather, the atmosphere: no one to blame. So they found themselves staying up late again, as in the old days, planning a new kind of future . . . telling each other how sane everything seemed, now, not only their own condition but the various separations and divorces among their friends, which had always bewildered them. There had been the simple joys of a kind of adulthood no one seemed to have known about, before sailing into it. But here it was: they were in it. As things flew apart, cracking and fragmenting and flying off, almost daily, at times hourly, it amazed the Renekers that the very center of their relationship—their ability to talk to each other, their respect for each other—held firm. This was sanity; *this*, perhaps, was adulthood. They stepped back out of their desperate embraces to recognize each other as separate, independent people, a man and a woman, two human beings, not necessarily husband and wife.

They had always loved to plan things, rather like children. Each of their vacations—to England, to Italy, to France and Spain—had been a marvelous adventure, an exploration; merely planning for these trips had taken a great deal of time. Visits of relatives; parties and dinners; buying a car, looking for another apartment or for a house; speculation on Dean's future in his profession. . . . It allowed them to discuss, to argue, to make lists of things that must be done, and to assign the proper order in which they must be tackled. *Lawyer. House put on market (no sign out front, if possible). Informing parents. Financial matters: the checking and savings accounts, the insurance policies, the car ownership. . . .* The divorce was a project, a challenge. It forced Cynthia to resume her old, cast-off girlhood cunning; it allowed Dean to be generous once again. How much of this new phase of their marriage must be kept secret, and how much of it might be revealed . . .? There were complications, one or two missteps. A certain amount of secrecy was necessary, and beside secrecy ordinary emotions paled; they were not very interesting.

Cynthia no longer accused him of not loving her; she no longer screamed at him. He did not shout at her. If they embraced, the embrace was friendly and hurried. The real responsibilities of life, Cynthia came to see, are small, trivial, essential chores, a matter of getting things done, not weeping and screaming, raking one's cheeks to draw blood. No, that was over. That phase of the marriage was over. Now they discussed dates . . . columns of figures . . . took turns on the telephone, since so many calls seemed to be necessary. No wonder, in the past, property rights had taken precedence over human rights!—half-seriously, Dean claimed to understand that paradox. "Cursed be he who moves his neighbor's landmark." "Thou shalt not covet thy neighbor's wife . . . goods . . . property." How tangible and sane this dimension of the world seemed, after the fearful, phantasmagoric power of the emotions. . . .

The household must be divided. It would be divided literally: his things, her things. An excellent idea. In making certain that she was not going to appear selfish, Cynthia in fact appeared girlish, naively generous, and charming; Dean, who had paid for most of these things, and at the time of their purchase had been well aware of their price, now felt indifferent and gallant, even a little reckless, as if he were plundering another man's kingdom. There was elation, certainly, in breaking a household in two, such as there had never been in establishing it—so many years of choosing and deliberating, of worry over money, had gone into it, that the pleasure had been somehow lost.

Dean stood on a chair, to reach the highest book shelf. Art books: *The American Landscape, The Impressionists, Art of the Middle*

Ages. So heavy, so costly. . . . Cynthia pulled her own books off the shelves; most of them were paperbacks, bought during her college years. *The Sound and the Fury, The Scarlet Letter, Moby Dick, The Portrait of a Lady* . . . she had not reread them, but meant to, had been meaning to reread them for years; as soon as the divorce was settled and she had moved elsewhere, as soon as she had enough time. . . . *The Complete Works of Chaucer.* A weighty book, well-marked, dusty. She had liked Chaucer very much; at one time she had known Middle English well, and had even thought about taking further courses in it, but something had happened. . . . *Paradise Lost?* It was Dean's college text, heavily annotated and very dusty. He didn't want it. Of course he didn't want it—he hadn't opened it in a decade. "But what should I do?" Cynthia asked helplessly. "Should I throw it out? Just throw it out?"

As it grew later, they were less hesitant to throw things away. Who had bought all these things, who wanted them now, who cared about them? And the dust—! What an embarrassment! They laughed together, joking about Cynthia's housekeeping—how hard she had tried, how anxious she'd been, never knowing that there were certain things, like these books on the very top shelf, that were accumulating years of dust. They joked about Dean's worrying over money—the painful monologues he had delivered, running his hands through his hair, sleepless with irrational fears—and what did it matter now? His job paid him a fairly good salary; he was certain to be promoted in another year, once again; what point had there been in so much worry?

"I thought it was expected of me," Dean admitted. "I thought that men worried, husbands worried . . . it was part of it, of marriage. . . . My father worried about money all the time: I must have been imitating him."

Sorting books became a little tiresome, so they went into the kitchen and opened several bottles of wine: inexpensive California and New York State wines that friends had brought them. They rarely drank wine at home, so the bottles accumulated. Better to drink than to pour it all out—though Cynthia was feeling a little light-headed from the excitement. She was wearing jeans and a soiled red-and-white-striped jersey, she had taken off her shoes, she was laughing, and then she became engrossed leafing through a paperback copy of *To the Lighthouse*—which Dean resented—so he snatched it out of her fingers and threw it onto the floor.

"You bastard!" Cynthia cried. "What are you doing?"

"Going—going—gone," Dean laughed. "Let the Salvation Army pick up all this crap."

They divided the house into areas. Beyond the sofa in the living room were Dean's belongings—carried or dragged over there; in front of the sofa, Cynthia's. The kitchen was mainly hers. Dean didn't want much, really. He accepted the larger of the two cheeseboards, and the stoneware casserole set his mother had given them as a wedding present. But wouldn't he need more things?— Cynthia asked. He intended to rent a house for a year, a completely furnished place with dishes and linen and other boring necessities included, so he said, and he didn't really need much. Still, she insisted he accept a half-dozen crystal goblets. He carried them into the living room and tossed them onto the sofa, and one rolled across a framed lithograph lying there at an angle; it fell to the floor and smashed.

"Okay, don't walk barefoot in here," he said.

"What are you doing? Why are you breaking things? —You're drunk."

They opened a small bottle of crème de menthe; who had given them this? They didn't like crème de menthe, Cynthia really didn't like to drink at all, but she filled a martini glass and sipped from it, as they divided the phonograph records. So many of them, so many things accumulated over the years . . . it was confusing. Cynthia felt a sentimental attachment for the folk songs and protest songs of the Sixties, but she did not want to admit it; Dean seemed contemptuous of them. They decided to throw them all away—give them to the Salvation Army. The serious music was another thing, however. They both wanted the same records.

"You never liked Debussy," Cynthia said passionately.

"Of course I did."

"Never!"

"I certainly did."

They began laughing. What did it matter? It did not matter. Cynthia jumped up and was on her way to the kitchen, when she stepped on a sliver of glass—a tiny sliver—but she didn't cry out. It didn't hurt at all; she picked the glass out and that was that; her

foot hardly bled. "Jesus Christ, did you step on that glass? After I
told you about it?" Dean cried.

Later, they cleared a space on the sofa and sat together, finishing
the crème de menthe. Darrell had telephoned; they would see him
the following evening; he would be the first to know, the first to be
told. Cynthia rehearsed the way she would begin, in her imagination; she would try not to speak dramatically.

Dean leafed through *The Twilight of the Idols*, absent-mindedly,
and came across this quotation as if he had known where to find
it—of course he had not known, it was only an accident: ". . . the
value of a thing sometimes does not lie in that which one attains by it,
but in what one pays for it—what it costs us."

"What it costs us . . ." Cynthia whispered.

She wondered what that meant: she had never understood
Nietzsche.

—◆—◆—

"It's fortunate—fortunate— It's— I mean, that you don't have any
children," Darrell said.

"Yes, it's fortunate," Cynthia said at once.

". . . yes, it is," Dean said.

Darrell kept looking from one of them to the other. He was clearly
agitated, far more nervous than usual; he had hardly touched his
drink. Something was wrong, something was not going well. They
had had a drink at the house, and now they were having dinner at a
seafood restaurant on the lake, but the evening was not going well.
Darrell seemed older than they remembered; his pale hair was
thinning; his boyish glasses, with their flesh-colored frames and
their round lenses, gave him a jaunty, inappropriate look. "I really
find it hard to believe, what you've told me," he said again, trying to
smile.

Dean changed the subject; he asked Darrell how his work was
going. While Darrell spoke without much interest of several pro-
jects he was working on—he was an assistant art editor for a national
news-magazine—Cynthia located the three of them in a distant
mirror, behind a display of corks and netting and foot-high plaster
seahorses. They had taken Darrell to *The Sou'wester* once before, and
the evening had been marvelous; he had said he'd never enjoyed an

evening so much. They had known him for many years; he'd been best man at their wedding; of all their friends, Darrell was the only one to continue to write. The others had faded away, had disappeared into America, though Cynthia dutifully continued to send them Christmas cards and occasional postcards. *I really find it hard to believe, what you've told me.* Darrell's mirror image was not flattering. He had a rather large head in proportion to his thin shoulders and chest, and his habit of continually touching his lips or chin was disconcerting. The appeal of his kindly, sensitive features was lost, in that large dim mirror; Cynthia and Dean appeared more attractive, more vital. Dean was smiling; he wore a yellow sports shirt open at the neck; Cynthia wore a white outfit—fashionable slacks with wide, floppy bell-bottoms, and a tight-fitting blouse cut high on the shoulders, to show her slender, tanned arms. She was thin, but she had never looked prettier. It was obvious, given the scene in the mirror, that she and Dean were married, and Darrell was their bachelor friend, the friend to whom they told intimate news, about whom they were slightly patronising.

Darrell had once entered a monastery in Indiana—a Trappist monastery—but whether he had stayed only briefly, or had been serious about it, Cynthia did not know. Was he religious, even now?—it would have been embarrassing to ask. And why hadn't he married? He was shy, perhaps too solemn, but a very charming person, really; it was unfortunate that he had become so nervous. . . .

"My mother wants me to come back to Chicago to live," he said. "I don't see how I can do it. But since my father died she's been having the most extraordinary bad luck . . . with other tenants in the building . . . little accidents, mishaps, like slipping on an icy sidewalk . . . and she's convinced people are trying to break in her apartment, even when she's there, with the television set turned up high. It's so sad, so depressing. . . . She claims that the son of one of the tenants swore at her, and she says that the cashiers cheat her at the grocery store. . . . And. . . . "

"That's too bad. That makes it difficult for you," Cynthia said.

"It makes it very difficult for me," Darrell said. "But I don't want to talk about myself."

"The paradox about life," Dean said, "is that we want things to stay the same—but things keep changing. And if we managed to keep things from changing, to make our lives absolutely permanent, we couldn't bear it—we'd force changes from the outside."

Cynthia finished her drink. Over her husband's shoulder, out on the lake, were several sailboats, one of them with a handsome yellow-and-blue sail. She would have liked to call the men's attention to the boats—would have liked to change the subject. It had always been her role, throughout the years, to direct conversations in a general sense: to rescue Dean from morbidity, or interpose when he seemed to be speaking too emphatically. He had often thanked her, afterward. But now she allowed her attention to wander about the restaurant, taking in people at other tables . . . the waitresses with their charming nautical outfits, their stockings like fish-net, their tight little jackets made to resemble seamen's jackets . . . the bartender, grave as always, making drinks with a show of professional precision. In the cocktail lounge someone was playing a piano. How pleasant this was, how charming it all was. . . . It struck Cynthia that she might never come here again.

They had ordered lobsters, but service was slow.

Another round of drinks: even Darrell had finished his.

Cynthia felt that things were going poorly—Dean had been led into recounting the ugly, pointless story of a colleague of his whose teenaged son had been arrested recently—manslaughter charges—a hit-and-run accident—and Darrell was nodding, nodding sympathetically, as if this concerned him. She interrupted her husband by putting her hand on his arm; she leaned toward him to whisper, "Which one of us gets Darrell?"

Dean snorted with laughter.

Darrell looked from one of them to the other. "What's wrong?" he asked, smiling.

"Just a joke," Dean said. He was blushing. "We've been—well, you saw the way the house looked—we've— Cynthia meant—"

"It was only a joke," Cynthia said.

For a moment they were silent. Dean's smile had faded, Cynthia herself was not smiling, and Darrell had begun to scratch at his wrist and forearm in an absent-minded compulsive way. Cynthia said, slowly, "There isn't any reason to be so solemn about all this. It's a very amiable undertaking . . . we're both cooperating . . . I mean, Darrell, it isn't like Ron and Maddie, where she sued him for divorce, you know, and there were the children, and she had to hire a detective like someone in a trashy movie and . . . and get evidence against him of. . . . It isn't like that, it's like Richard and Jeannette, in California. . . ."

"Richard and Jeannette?" Darrell asked. He frowned. He seemed not to know what Cynthia was talking about.

"The Masons," Cynthia said.

"Darrell doesn't know the Masons," Dean said flatly. "You've been drinking too much."

"I was only trying to make a point," Cynthia said. "I was trying to assure Darrell that there's nothing contentious about what we've decided to do; it's like the dissolving of a partnership, it's really a legal thing now, and no grudges or aggression involved. . . . Darrell looks like he's at a funeral, for Christ's sake! It's your fault, sitting there with such a smug self-pitying look."

"I don't mean to seem solemn," Darrell said quickly. He adjusted his glasses and smiled at Cynthia. "It's just that my mother, her delusions, her fear of . . . well, frankly, I believe it's a fear of death, some sort of psychological phenomenon, I suppose there's a term for it, imagining . . . projecting . . . these delusions about people trying to break into her apartment. . . . I was very happy to be able to drive over to visit you and Dean, Cynthia, it means a great deal to me, to have friends like you; your letters are so interesting and . . . and have your voice in them, Cynthia, I really mean that. And so, and so . . . the news about the divorce . . . well, I suppose I'm being selfish, *I'm* the one who probably should be accused of being self-pitying, but in fact I feel upset by what you told me. I can't help it. I'm sorry. If I do look like I'm at a funeral it's because I . . . ."

"Do you see?" Dean said angrily. "Cynthia, do you see? You couldn't wait to tell him, you had to make it so goddam dramatic! Now—do you see?"

"I wasn't dramatic," Cynthia said faintly. She looked to Darrell for confirmation. "I thought I was being as casual as possible, as . . . as ordinary as possible."

"She wasn't dramatic about it," Darrell said. "It's just me. I've been under a lot of strain, I really should apologize. . . . But it's wonderful to be here. It is. This restaurant is so cheerful and the service is so professional. . . ."

"The service is slow," Dean said.

"It does seem slower than usual," Cynthia said.

They talked about the restaurant for a while, and reminisced about other restaurants: the three of them had eaten together often, in Ann Arbor, many years ago. And when the Renekers had been at Palo Alto for two years, Darrell had driven to California, had stayed with them for a week, and they had showed him around San Francisco. From restaurants they jumped to the topic of friends and acquaintances, and suddenly they were back talking about disturbing news, small mysteries—why had no one heard from Jerry and Deanna Hecht, for instance?—hadn't he accepted a teaching job somewhere strange—in New Mexico, or maybe Florida?—or Hawaii? Darrell hadn't known the Hechts very well; but he had lost touch with Barbara Schiller, whom Cynthia had known so well, what had happened to her? Everyone had like Barbara so much and of course she was a brilliant woman, a mathematical genius. . . . But she hadn't written to Cynthia for over two years. No, not even a Christmas card. However, Cynthia had run into a mutual acquaintance from Ann Arbor, a man named Gelling, a little older than the rest of them—did Darrell remember?—no?—a small balding man, wonderful sense of humor, getting his Ph. D. in something peculiar, like agricultural chemistry? Yes, she had run into him on the street in a most unlikely place—Toledo—when she was visiting her parents not long ago. She had gone alone, Dean had been too busy to make the trip, and she had happened to notice someone who looked familiar . . . strolling along downtown Toledo, in mid-day, his hands in his pockets, aimless, with a strange cheerful smile. . . . It turned out to be Gelling, and she called his name, but the conversation between them had been a very painful one: he seemed embarrassed, nervous. And she had always liked him so much!

"Probably out of a job," Dean said, shrugging.

"I didn't know him well," Darrell said. "I do remember him, though, from your parties, and he seemed very. . . . It's a pity, isn't it, so much unemployment."

Three large cups of clam chowder were brought; Cynthia was relieved, since her husband had been getting increasingly restless. Darrell seemed happier too.

"I'm sorry I was critical of you, Cynthia," Dean said. ". . . I didn't mean it."

Cynthia blushed. "I. . . . Well, I might have been too melodramatic. . . ."

"No, not at all. You weren't."

"It's just that divorce can be an entirely amiable affair, and there's no reason to always assume that . . . to assume . . ."

"You're right," Darrell said quickly. "It was very stupid of me."

"For instance, we're dividing everything equally. No fuss. When something can't be divided, like the car, we're subtracting half the cost from the other things. Dean and I can't understand, really, why people have to fight. Even if we had children I think we'd be far more rational about it, don't you think so, Dean?"

He nodded. But he wasn't giving her his fullest attention; he was eating quickly, his gaze lowered to the soup. A broad-shouldered, handsome man, with a ruddy complexion. . . . He had been her husband for years; now he sat apart from her, eating clam chowder hungrily, nodding as he had nodded so often at home, at the dining room table, not quite listening. She had selected his fine-knit shirt herself; that shade of yellow was very attractive.

"Neither one of us has plans to remarry," Cynthia said carefully. "It isn't that sort of thing at all."

"Cynthia might go back to art school," Dean said. He tapped Darrell's arm, enthusiastically. ". . . might go to England, to London."

"Yes, my younger sister is in London," Cynthia said.

"I don't think I've met her," Darrell said. "But London is marvelous, you're very fortunate. I wish I . . ."

"I've been suffocating here, in this awful city," Cynthia said. "It isn't Dean's fault, of course. I never accused him of holding me back. But it will be a relief to leave. You see," she said warmly, leaning forward, "we each have our own lives, and we want the other to be happy. That's the only important thing. I want Dean to be happy, to be free and happy, and he wants me to be happy. . . . But did you know, Darrell, about his little predicament a few years ago?"

Darrell looked bewildered.

"Oh Christ! Don't bring that up," Dean sighed.

"You know, don't you?" Cynthia smiled at him, flirtatiously. "I'm sure he told you, or hinted . . .?"

"I don't know what you mean," Darrell said.

"You do!"

"He doesn't know, Cynthia."

"He doesn't? You mean you didn't tell him? You didn't brag about it?"

"It wasn't that important, honey. We've gone over this. . . ."

Darrell took off his glasses, rubbed his eyes, and put his glasses back on. His voice was strained: "You know, I really think the two of you are joking. It sounds like a joke. The last time I saw you, you seemed to be making plans to start a family . . . you certainly were, I wasn't imagining it. I remember feeling envious, even a little hurt . . . absurdly hurt . . . the way I do sometimes, without being able to help myself . . . jealous of other people, of married people. And now . . . . You are joking, aren't you?"

Cynthia giggled. "Suppose you have to choose between us?"

"What do you mean, choose between you?"

"Between Dean and me—between us. Suppose you had to choose, who would you choose?"

"Choose in what way? Why?"

"Cynthia, you're being rude," Dean said irritably.

"You're just worried he won't choose *you*," Cynthia laughed.

"The two of you aren't getting a divorce, are you," Darrell said slowly. "You're just teasing me. Is that it?"

"First we're separating; Dean is moving out next week," Cynthia said. "But the divorce proceedings have already begun. I mean, the consultations with the lawyer, that sort of thing. The law has been changed, it's so much simpler now, we can use the same lawyer as long as neither of us wants more than his share. It's wonderful, the way the laws have been reformed. When Maddy divorced Ron, it was sickening. . . . But of course he was guilty of adultery; it was stupid of him to contest it."

"*Guilty of adultery*," Dean laughed.

"Guilty according to the law at that time," Cynthia said quickly. "I know it sounds absurd . . . the word *guilty* sounds absurd. . . ."

"Why did you use it, then? You like the sound of it," Dean said.

"And you don't like the sound of it. Why is that?"

"Who are you interrogating?"

Cynthia turned to Darrell. "It isn't even a case of him wanting to marry someone else. He doesn't want to marry her. In fact, I think he stayed married to me as long as he did, so he would be protected from marrying his girls. So he could tell them about his wife, his neurotic wife! Afraid she might commit suicide!—what a laugh, what a slanderous laugh! Eventually it all got back to me."

"It didn't get back to you," Dean said, reddening. "I told you, myself."

"You told me some very general, wispy stories," Cynthia laughed. "The details came from other sources."

"Yes, and I know about those other sources, that lying little bitch!"

Cynthia felt groggy. It seemed to her that something was hopeful about the situation—something—it had to do with Dean's baffled anger. He was hateful, he was bitter, but not because of *her*. She resisted the impulse to console him, however, and turned back to Darrell. "You haven't answered my question, you haven't said which one of us you choose."

"Choose?"

She saw that he was pretending not to understand.

"If you can't have us both, if you have to choose one of us—which one?" Cynthia said. She was joking, yet her voice did not sound quite right. It had become strained and throaty.

Dean had finished his chowder; he pushed the heavy cup an inch or so away from his place—a habit that infuriated Cynthia. That he should eat like that, so noisily, and behave like a man eating at a lunch-counter!—she had always detested him. But he caught her glance, he smiled. Occasionally the two of them had exchanged glances, in Darrell's presence, when Darrell seemed particularly obtuse or naively charming. "Yes," Dean said. "Which one do you choose?"

"This isn't funny to me," Darrell said. ". . . drove all the way from Chicago, and my mother is so unhappy. . . . Death, divorce, none of these things are funny."

"What do you mean?" Cynthia said. She stared at him. "Death, divorce? *Death?* Death and divorce are two very different things."

"Yes, they're completely different," Dean said.

"Death is death, the end of life, the end of everything," Cynthia said irritably. "Divorce is . . . the freedom to begin again, to start over."

"Look, none of this is particularly funny to me," Darrell said.

"Why won't you answer my question?" Cynthia said. "Are you afraid?—Make him answer, honey. He's such a coward."

"We're dividing the world between us," Dean said, his elbows on the table now. He had an easy, expansive manner—he did as he liked, and had the personality to bring anything off. That was why she detested him, why she had to stare in helpless admiration at him. Even when he told the truth he spoke bluntly and arrogantly, presenting the truth as a probable lie, daring people to disbelieve. "She gets half, I get half. Two mutually exclusive territories. We promise to stay out of each other's zone. That's sanity, isn't it? Common sense. . . ? I'm not finished with my life just yet."

"*Your life!*" Cynthia laughed.

Darrell was shaking his head. He made a movement to stand.

"What are you doing? What's wrong?" Cynthia asked.

"I really think . . . I think I'd better leave," Darrell said softly.

"What, leave? Leave. . . ? But we're only joking," Cynthia said.

"You might never see us again," Dean said.

"Don't leave, we were only joking! Look—"

"I really think—"

"Hey, don't leave us like this," Dean said. "Are you serious?"

"Don't leave me with *him*," Cynthia said, seizing Darrell's wrist. "You don't know what he's like when he's disappointed. . . . Darrell, please, if you walk out of here and leave us, if you. . . . Look at his face, look how angry he is! He can't stand to be betrayed. Anyway, we were only joking; it was just a silly joke. We didn't mean anything by it."

"I'm not hungry," Darrell said tonelessly. "This visit was a mistake."

"Dean will be so angry," Cynthia whispered. "Please. Wait. . . . Once he was so angry, after a party we gave, after the guests went home he was so *angry* . . . because the party hadn't gone right, people had left early, and he blamed me, he was furious with me. It wasn't my fault. It was his own fault, for drinking so much. He ruins everything, he ruins our friendships, then he blames me and says he has to escape, has to get out before it's too late, but how is it my fault? Once he said he'd like to kill me, and then himself—"

"Shut up! That's ridiculous!"

"All because his lies were exposed, and he was terrified they would find out at the office, there was a girl blackmailing him—a fifteen-year-old girl—claimed she'd had an abortion he arranged, and had almost bled to death in a cab—"

"Which turned out to be a lie," Dean said hotly. "And she wasn't fifteen. She wasn't fifteen! And you know it very well, you lying bitch—why are you saying these things?"

But Darrell had stood, pushing his chair back. His face had gone pale.

Cynthia tugged at his wrist, angrily. "What? No. No, you don't. Where do you think you're going? You're not—"

Dean took his other arm. He rose from his chair, grinning.

"For Christ's sake, sit down. What's the problem? Why are you so . . .? Our dinner is here, look, it's finally here. What the hell's the problem, Darrell? You look sick."

"We were only joking, Darrell," Cynthia said. "My God."

"Look, why are you exaggerating this? Just sit down. Sit down."

"You can't leave us," Cynthia said.

As if her living self were somehow bound up in him, in this mild, anxious man whose arm she held, she half-rose from her seat, as her husband had from his. "*You can't leave us,*" she whispered.

The Tryst

She was laughing. At first he thought she might be crying, but she was laughing.

Raggedy Ann, she said. You asked about nicknames—I've forgotten about it for years—but Raggedy Ann, it was, for a while. They called me Raggedy Ann.

She lay sprawled on her stomach, her face pressed into the damp pillow, one arm loose and gangly, falling over the edge of the bed. Her hair was red-orange and since it had the texture of straw he had thought it was probably dyed. The bed jiggled, she was laughing silently. Her arms and shoulders were freckled and pale, her long legs were unevenly tanned, the flesh of her young body not so soft as it appeared but rather tough, ungiving. She was in an exuberant mood; her laughter was child-like, bright, brittle.

What were you called?—when you were a boy? she asked. Her voice was muffled by the pillow. She did not turn to look at him.

John, he said.

What! John! Never a nickname, never Johnny or Jack or Jackie? I don't think so, he said.

She found that very funny. She laughed and kicked her legs and gave off an air, an odor, of intense fleshy heat. I won't survive this one, she giggled.

He was one of the adults of the world now. He was in charge of the world.

Sometimes he stood at the bedroom window and surveyed the handsome sloping lawn, the houses of his neighbors and their hand-

49

some lawns, his eye moving slowly along the memorized street. Day or night it was memorized. He knew it. *The Tilsons . . . the Dwyers . . . the Pitkers . . . the Reddingers . . . the Schells.* Like beads on a string were the houses, solid and baronial, each inhabited, each protected. Day or night he knew them and the knowledge made him pleasurably intoxicated.

He was Reddinger. Reddinger, John.

Last Saturday night, late, his wife asked: Why are you standing there, why aren't you undressing? It's after two.

He was not thinking of Annie. That long restless rangy body, that rather angular, bony face, her fingers stained with ink, her fingernails never very clean, the throaty mocking voice: he had pushed her out of his mind. He was breathing the night air and the sharp autumnal odor of pine needles stirred him, moved him deeply. He was in charge of the world but why should he not shiver with delight of the world? For he did love it. He loved it.

I love it—this—all of you—

He spoke impulsively. She did not hear. Advancing upon him, her elbows raised as she labored to unfasten a hook at the back of her neck, she did not look at him; she spoke with a sleepy absent-mindedness, as if they had had this conversation before. Were you drunk, when you were laughing so much? she asked. It wasn't like you. Then, at dinner, you were practically mute. Poor Frances Casey, trying to talk to you! That wasn't like you either, John.

There must have been a party at the Buhls', across the way. Voices lifted. Car doors were slammed. John Reddinger felt his spirit stirred by the acrid smell of the pines and the chilly bright-starred night and his wife's warm, perfumed, familiar closeness. His senses leaped, his eyes blinked rapidly as if he might burst into tears. In the autumn of the year he dwelt upon boyhood and death and pleasures of a harsh, sensual nature, the kind that are torn out of human beings, like cries; he dwelt upon the mystery of his own existence, that teasing riddle. The world itself was an intoxicant to him.

Wasn't it like me? he asked seriously. What am I like, then?

I don't ask you about your family, the girl pointed out. Why should you ask me about other men?

He admired her brusque, comic manner, the tomboyish wag of her foot.

Natural curiosity, he said.

Your wife! Your children! —I don't ask, do I?

They were silent and he had the idea she was waiting for him to speak, to volunteer information. But he was disingenuous. Her frankness made him uncharacteristically passive; for once he was letting a woman take the lead, never quite prepared for what happened. It was a novelty, a delight. It was sometimes unnerving.

You think I'm too proud to ask for money, I mean for a loan—for my rent, Annie said. I'm not, though. I'm not too proud.

Are you asking for it, then?

No. But not because I'm proud or because I'm afraid of altering our relationship. You understand? Because I want you to know I could have asked and I didn't—you understand?

I think so, John said, though in fact he did not.

At Christmas, somehow, they lost contact with each other. Days passed. Twelve days. Fifteen. His widowed mother came to visit them in the big red-brick colonial in Lathrup Park, and his wife's sister and her husband and two young children, and his oldest boy, a freshman at Swarthmore, brought his Japanese roommate home with him; life grew dense, robustly complicated. He telephoned her at the apartment but no one answered. He telephoned the gallery where she worked but the other girl answered and when he said softly and hopefully, Annie? Is that Annie? the girl told him that it was not Annie; it was Cynthia Brauer; and the gallery owner, Mr. Helnutt, disapproved strongly of personal calls. She was certain Annie knew about this policy and surprised that Annie had not told him about it.

He hung up guiltily, like a boy.

A previous autumn, years ago, he had made a terrible mistake. What a blunder!

The worst blunder of my life, he said.

What was it? Annie asked at once.

But his mood changed. A fly was buzzing somewhere in her small, untidy apartment, which smelled of cats. His mood changed. His spirit changed.

He did not reply. After a while Annie yawned. I've never made any really bad mistakes, she said. Unless I've forgotten.

You're perfect, he said.

She laughed, irritated.

. . . Perfect. So beautiful, so confident. . . . So much at home in your body. . . .

He carressed her and forced himself to think of her, only of her. It was not true that she was beautiful but she was striking—red hair, brown eyes, a quick tense dancer's body—and he saw how other people looked at her, women as well as men. It was a fact. He loved her, he was silly and dizzy and sickened with love for her, and he did not wish to think of his reckless mistake of that other autumn. It had had its comic aspects, but it had been humiliating. And dangerous. While on a business trip to Atlanta he had strolled downtown and in a dimly-lit bar had drifted into a conversation with a girl, a beautiful blond in her twenties, soft-spoken and sweet and very shy. She agreed to come back with him to his hotel room for a nightcap, but partway back, on the street, John sensed something wrong, something terribly wrong, he heard his voice rattling on about the marvelous view from his room on the twentieth floor of the hotel and about how fine an impression Atlanta was making on him—then in mid-sentence he stopped, staring at the girl's heavily made-up face and at the blond hair which was certainly a wig—he stammered that he had made a mistake, he would have to say goodnight now; he couldn't bring her back to the room after all. She stared at him belligerently. She asked what was wrong, just what in hell was wrong?—her voice cracking slightly so that he knew she wasn't a girl, a woman, at all. It was a boy of about twenty-five. He backed away and the creature asked why he had changed his mind, wasn't she good enough for him, who did he think he was? Bastard! Shouting after John as he hurried away: Who did he think he was?

I never think about the past, Annie said lazily. She was smoking in bed, her long bare legs crossed, at the knee. I mean what the hell?—it's all over with.

He had not loved any of the others as he loved Annie. He was sure of that.

He thought of her, raking leaves. A lawn crew serviced the Reddingers' immense lawn but he sometimes raked leaves on the weekend, for the pleasure of it. He worked until his arm and shoulder muscles ached. Remarkable, he thought. Life, living. In this body. Now.

She crowded out older memories. Ah, she was ruthless! An Amazon, a Valkyrie maiden. Beautiful. Unpredictable. She obliterated other women, other sweetly painful memories of women. That was her power.

Remarkable, he murmured.

Daddy!

He looked around. His eleven-year-old daughter Sally was screaming at him.

Daddy I've been calling and calling you from the porch, couldn't you hear me?—Mamma wants you for something! A big grin. Amused, she was, at her father's absent-mindedness; and she had a certain sly, knowing look as well, as if she could read his thoughts.

But of course that was only his imagination.

He's just a friend of mine, an old friend, Annie said vaguely. He doesn't count.

A friend from where?

From around town.

Meaning—?

From around town.

A girl in a raw, unfinished painting. Like the crude canvases on exhibit at the gallery, that day he had drifted by: something vulgar and exciting about the mere droop of a shoulder, the indifference of a strand of hair blown into her eyes. And the dirt-edged fingernails. And the shoes with the run-over heels. She was raw, unfinished, lazy, slangy, vulgar, crude, mouthing in her cheerful insouciant voice certain words and phrases John Reddinger would never have said aloud, in the presence of a member of the opposite sex; but at the same time it excited him to know that she was highly intelligent, and really well-educated, with a Master's degree in art history and a studied, if rather flippant, familiarity with the monstrousness of contemporary art. He could not determine whether she was as impoverished as she appeared or whether it was a pose, an act. Certain items of clothing, he knew, were expensive. A suede leather coat, a pair of knee-high boots, a long skirt of black soft wool. And one of her rings might have been genuine. But much of the time she looked shabby—ratty. She nearly fainted once, at the airport; she had confessed she hadn't eaten for awhile; had run out of money that week. In San Francisco, where she spent three days with him, she had eaten hungrily enough and it had pleased him to feed her, to nourish her on so elementary a level.

Who bought you this? he asked, fingering the sleeve of her coat.

What? This? I bought it myself.

It's very beautiful.

Yes?

He supposed, beforehand, that they would lose contact with each other when Christmas approached. The routine of life was upset, schedules were radically altered, obligations increased. He disliked holidays; yet in a way he liked them, craved them. Something wonderful must happen! Something wonderful must happen soon.

He was going to miss her, he knew.

She chattered about something he wasn't following. A sculptor she knew, his odd relationship with his wife. A friend. A former friend. She paused and he realized it was a conversation and he must reply, must take his turn. What was she talking about? Why did these girls talk so, when he wanted nothing so much as to stare at them, in silence, in pained awe? —I don't really have friends any longer, he said slowly. It was a topic he and his wife had discussed recently. She had read an article on the subject in a woman's magazine: American men of middle-age, especially in the higher income brackets, tended to have very few close friends, very few indeed. It was sad. It was unfortunate. I had friends in high school and college, he said, but I've lost touch . . . we've lost touch. It doesn't seem to happen afterward, after you grow up. Friendship, I mean.

God, that's sad. That's really sad. She shivered, staring at him. Her eyes were darkly brown and lustrous, at times almost too lustrous. They reminded him of a puppy's eyes.

Yes, I suppose it is, he said.

On New Year's Eve, driving from a party in Lathrup Park to another party in Wausau Heights, he happened to see a young woman who resembled Annie—in mink to mid-calf, her red hair fastened in a bun, being helped out of a sports car by a young man. That girl! Annie! His senses leapt, though he knew it wasn't Annie.

For some reason the connection between them had broken. He didn't know why. He had had to fly to London; and then it was mid-December and the holiday season; then it was early January. He had tried to telephone two or three times, without success. His

feeling for her ebbed. It was curious—other faces got in the way of
hers, distracting him. Over the holidays there were innumerable
parties: brunches and luncheons and cocktail parties and open
houses and formal dinner parties and informal evening parties, a
press of people, friends and acquaintances and strangers, all de-
manding his attention. He meant to telephone her, meant to send a
small gift, but time passed quickly and he forgot.

After seeing the girl on New Year's Eve, however, he found
himself thinking again of Annie. He lay in bed, sleepless, a little
feverish, thinking of her. They had done certain things together and
now he tried to picture them, from a distance. How he had adored
her! Bold, silly, gawky, beautiful, not afraid to sit slumped in a
kitchen chair, naked, pale, her uncombed hair in her eyes, drinking
coffee with him as he prepared to leave. Not afraid of him—not afraid
of anyone. That had been her power.

His imagination dwelt upon her. The close, stale, half-pleasant
odor of her apartment, the messy bed, the lipstick- and mascara-
smeared pillows, the ghostly presence of other men, strangers to
him and yet brothers of a kind: brothers. He wondered if any of them
knew about *him*. Asked her about *him*. (And what would she
say?—what would her words be, describing him?) It excited him to
imagine her haphazard, promiscuous life; he knew she was entirely
without guilt or shame or self-consciousness, as if, born of a different
generation, she were of a different species as well.

At the same time, however, he was slightly jealous. When he
thought at length about the situation he was slightly jealous.
Perhaps, if he returned to her, he would ask her not to see any of the
others. . . .

What have you been doing? What is your life, now?
Why do you want to know?
I miss you—missed you.
Did you really?
In early March he saw her again, but only for lunch. She insisted
he return to the gallery to see their current show—ugly, frantic,
oversized hunks of sheet metal and aluminum, seemingly thrown at
will onto the floor. She was strident, talkative from the several
glasses of wine she had had at lunch, a lovely girl, really, whose
nearness seemed to constrict his chest, so that he breathed with

difficulty. And so tall—five feet ten, at least. With her long red hair and her dark, intense eyes and her habit of raising her chin, as if in a gesture of hostility, she was wonderfully attractive; and she knew it. But she would not allow him to touch her.

I think this is just something you're doing, she said. I mean—something you're watching yourself do.

When can I see you?

I don't know. I don't want to.

What?

I'm afraid.

They talked for a while, pointlessly. He felt his face redden. She was backing away, with that pose of self-confidence, and he could not stop her. But I love you! I love you! —Had he said these words aloud? She looked so frightened, he could not be certain.

Afraid! he laughed. Don't be ridiculous.

One day in early summer he came to her, in a new summer suit of pale blue, a lover, his spirit young and gay and light as dandelion seed. She was waiting for him in a downtown square. She rose from the park bench as he appeared, the sun gleaming in her hair, her legs long and elegant in a pair of cream-colored trousers. They smiled. They touched hands. Was it reckless, to meet the girl here, where people might see him?—at mid-day? He found that he did not care.

We can't go to my apartment—

We can go somewhere else.

He led her to his car. They were both smiling.

Where are we going? she asked.

For the past several weeks a girl cousin of hers had been staying with her in the apartment, so they had been going to motels; the motels around the airport were the most convenient. But today he drove to the expressway and out of the city, out along the lake, through the suburban villages north of the city: Elmwood Farms, Spring Arbor, Wausau Heights, Lathrup Park. He exited at Lathrup Park.

Where are we going? she asked.

He watched her face as he drove along Washburn Lane, which was gravelled and tranquil and hilly. Is this—? Do you live—? she asked. He brought her to the big red-brick colonial he had bought nearly fifteen years ago; it seemed to him that the house had never looked more handsome, and the surrounding trees and blossoming shrubs had never looked more beautiful.

Do you like it? he asked.

He watched her face. He was very excited.

But— Where is— Aren't you afraid—?

There's no one home, he said.

He led her through the foyer, into the living room with its thick wine-colored rug, its gleaming furniture, its many windows. He led her through the formal dining room and into the walnut-panelled recreation room where his wife had hung lithographs and had arranged innumerable plants, some of them hanging from the ceiling in clay pots, spidery-leafed, lovely. He saw the girl's eyes dart from place to place.

You live here, she said softly.

In an alcove he kissed her and made them each a drink. He kissed her again. She shook her hair from her eyes and pressed her forehead against his face and made a small convulsive movement—a shudder, or perhaps it was suppressed laughter. He could not tell.

You live here, she said.

What do you mean by that? he asked.

She shrugged her shoulders and moved away. Outside, birds were calling to one another excitedly. It was early summer. It was summer again. The world renewed itself and was beautiful. Annie wore the cream-colored trousers and a red jersey blouse that fitted her tightly and a number of bracelets that jingled as she walked. Her ears were pierced: she wore tiny loop earrings. On her feet, however, were shoes that pleased him less—scruffy sandals, once black, now faded to no color at all.

Give me a little more of this, she said, holding out the glass.

My beauty, he said. My beautiful girl.

She asked him why he had brought her here and he said he didn't know. Why had he taken the risk?—was taking it at this moment, still? He said he didn't know, really; he didn't usually analyze his own motives.

Maybe because it's here in this room, in this bed, that I think about you so much, he said.

She was silent for a while. Then she kicked about, and laughed,

and chattered. He was sleepy, pleasantly sleepy. He did not mind
her chatter, her high spirits. While she spoke of one thing or
another—of childhood memories, of nicknames—Raggedy Ann
they had called her, and it fitted her, he thought, bright red hair like
straw and a certain ungainly but charming manner—what had been
the boy's name, the companion to Raggedy Ann?—Andy?—he
watched through half-closed eyes the play of shadows on the ceiling,
imagining that he could smell the pines, the sunshine, the rich thick
grass, remembering himself at the window of this room not long ago,
staring out into the night, moved almost to tears by an emotion he
could not have named. You're beautiful, he told Annie, there's no
one like you. No one. He heard his mother's voice: Arthritis, you
don't know what it's like—you don't *know!* A woman approached
him, both hands held out, palms up, appealing to him, the expanse
of bare pale flesh troubling to him because he did not know what it
meant. You don't know, don't *know.* He tried to protest but no
words came to him. Don't know, don't know. Don't *know.* His
snoring disturbed him. For an instant he woke, then sank again into
a warm grayish ether. His wife was weeping. The sound of her
weeping was angry. You brought that creature here—that filthy sick
thing—you brought her to our bed to soil it, to spoil me—to kill
me— Again he wanted to protest. He raised his hands in a gesture of
innocence and helplessness. But instead of speaking he began to
laugh. His torso and belly shook with laughter. The bed shook. It
was mixed suddenly with a gigantic fly that hovered over the bed, a
few inches from his face; then his snoring woke him again and he sat
up.

Annie?

Her things were still lying on the floor. The red blouse lay draped
across a chintz-covered easy chair whose bright red and orange
flowers, glazed, dramatic, seemed to be throbbing with energy.
Annie? Are you in the bathroom?

The bathroom door was ajar, the light was not on. He got up. He
saw that it was after 2. A mild sensation of panic rose in his chest, for
no reason. He was safe. They were safe here. No one would be home
for hours—the first person to come home, at about 3:30, would be
Sally. His wife had driven with several other women to a bridge
luncheon halfway across the state and would not be home, probably,
until after 6. The house was silent. It was empty.

He thought: What if she steals something?

But that was ridiculous and cruel. Annie would never do anything like that.

No one was in this bathroom, which was his wife's. He went to a closet and got a robe and put it on, and went out into the hallway, calling Annie?—honey?—and knew, before he turned the knob to his own bathroom that she was in there and that she would not respond. Annie? What's wrong?

The light switch to the bathroom operated a fan; the fan was on; he pressed his ear against the door and listened. Had she taken a shower? He didn't think so. Had not heard any noises. Annie, he said, rattling the knob, are you in there, is anything wrong? He waited. He heard the fan whirring. Annie? His voice was edged with impatience. Annie, will you unlock the door? Is anything wrong?

She said something—the words were sharp and unintelligible.

Annie? What? What did you say?

He rattled the knob again, angrily.

What did you say? I couldn't—

Again her high, sharp voice. It sounded like an animal's shriek. But the words were unintelligible.

Annie? Honey? Is something wrong?

He tried to fight his panic. He knew, he knew. Must get the bitch out of there. Out of the house. He knew. But if he smashed the panelling on the door?—how could he explain it? He began to plead with her, in the voice he used on Sally, asking her to please be good, be good, don't make trouble, don't make a fuss, why did she want to ruin everything? Why did she want to worry him?

He heard the lock being turned, suddenly.

He opened the door.

She must have taken the razor blade out of his razor, which she had found in the medicine cabinet. Must have leaned over the sink and made one quick, deft, hard slash with it—cutting the fingers of her right hand also. The razor blade slipped from her then and fell into the sink. There was blood on the powder blue porcelain of the sink and the toilet, and the fluffy black rug, and on the mirror, and on the blue and white tiled walls. When he opened the door and saw her, she screamed, made a move as if to strike him with her bleeding arm, and for an instant he could not think: could not think: what had happened, what was happening, what had this girl done to him? Her face was wet and distorted. Ugly. She was sobbing, whimpering. There was blood, bright blood, smeared on her breasts and belly and thighs: he had never seen anything so repulsive in his life.

My God—

He was paralyzed. Yet, in the next instant, a part of him came to life. He grabbed a towel and wrapped it around her arm, struggling with her. Stop! Stand still! For God's sake! He held her; she went limp; her head fell forward. He wrapped the towel tight around her arm. Tight, tight. They were both panting.

Why did you do it? Why? Why? You're crazy! You're sick! This is a—this is a terrible, terrible—a terrible thing, a crazy thing—

Her teeth were chattering. She had begun to shiver convulsively.

Did you think you could get away with it? With this? he cried.

I hate you—

Stop, be still!

I hate you—I don't want to live—

She pushed past him, she staggered into the bedroom. The towel came loose. He ran after her and grabbed her and held the towel against the wound again, wrapping it tight, so tight she flinched. His brain reeled. He saw blood, splotches of blood, star-like splashes on the carpet, on the yellow satin bedspread that had been pulled onto the floor. Stop. Don't fight. Annie, stop. God damn you, stop!

I don't want to live—

You're crazy, you're sick! Shut up!

The towel was soaked. He stooped to get something else—his shirt—he wrapped that around the outside the towel, trembling so badly himself that he could hardly hold it in place. The girl's teeth were chattering. His own teeth were chattering.

Why did you do it! Oh you bitch, you bitch!

After some time the bleeding was under control. He got another towel, from his wife's bathroom, and wrapped it around her arm again. It stained, but not so quickly. The bleeding was under control; she was not going to die.

He had forced her to sit down. He crouched over her, breathing hard, holding her in place. What if she sprang up, what if she ran away?—through the house? He held her still. She was spiritless, weak. Her eyes were closed. In a softer voice he said, as if speaking to a child: Poor Annie, poor sweet girl, why did you do it, why, why

[handwritten margin notes: She wanted to be in control. Control of bleeding sumb]

did you want to hurt yourself, why did you do something so ugly. . . ?
It was an ugly, ugly thing to do. . . .

Her head slumped against her arm.

He walked her to the cab, holding her steady. She was white-faced, haggard, subdued. Beneath the sleeve of her blouse, wound tightly and expertly, were strips of gauze and adhesive tape. The bleeding had stopped. The wound was probably not too deep—had probably not severed an important vein.

Seeing her, the taxi driver got out and offered to help. But there was no need. John waved him away.

Slide in, he told Annie. Can you make it? Watch out for your head.

He told the driver her address in the city. He gave the man a fifty-dollar bill, folded.

Thanks, the man said gravely.

It was 2:55.

From the living room, behind one of the windows, he watched the cab descend the drive—watched it turn right on Washburn Lane—watched its careful progress along the narrow street. He was still trembling. He watched the blue and yellow cab wind its way along Washburn Lane until it was out of sight. Then there was nothing more to see: grass, trees, foliage, blossoms, his neighbors' homes.

Tilsons . . . Dwyers . . . Pitkers . . . Reddingers . . . Schells.

Blood-swollen Landscape

Approaching him was a person he hated: he wished dead.

In and out of his eyesight floated that thought. *Die. Be dead.* It was weightless, it couldn't be stopped. Couldn't be unsaid. It was a wish that sprang to life somehow in his vision, in his eyes; as soon as he saw that man the thought wished itself to completion and. . . .

And so he was a murderer in his heart.

Martin was coming out of the Science Building, hurrying, upset about some news he had just received, news of a friend's wife, and so his control was shaky, he really was not himself—Martin Hershfield, 26, an Instructor in the Physics Department of this comfortable little college—and perhaps not to blame. He happened to glance up and saw, approaching him, one of his enemies: also a young man of 26, with a bony, grim, tense face, wearing a suit that looked cheaper than Martin's, bought off the rack probably at the Norban's Discount Store at the shopping mall. He and Martin were moving like missiles in a head-on collision course. Would they collide? No. Martin stared at him and a thought flashed into his head that terrified him: He wished that young man dead.

Martin veered guiltily off to the right and crossed a patch of soil—walked right through a fragile barricade of white string, which twisted around his ankles, oh damn it, oh my God, surely other people had noticed, and not just his enemy?—but it was too late, he had to keep walking right through the new-planted grass. In a daze he kept on walking. He regained the sidewalk and made his way deftly through the packs and swarms of students, staring past them, over their heads and shoulders, trying not to register the effect of their smiles and grins and occasional bright hellos—*Hello, Dr. Hershfield!* If he didn't make eye contact with them they would not exist and he would not exist.

His beige wool-and-dacron suit was too warm for this mild day. Too warm. And his face was too warm; he was afraid he would burst into tears. He was a young man six feet two inches tall, carrying a valise stuffed with books and examination papers and mail and the paper bag he had brought his lunch in, and was taking back home so it could be used again, and his height and appearance and position and age made it necessary for him to get to a private place, so that he could cry. Otherwise, shame.

He took a short-cut behind the library, not a sidewalk but only a dirt-and-gravel path, not much used. This would take him away from the center of the campus. If Merrill, back there, was also wishing him dead, it would take him away from Merrill as well; he detested, dreaded Merrill and the others, he was overcome by the snaky uncanny confidence of his enemies, which looked, on the surface, like his own nervousness, but which was really a deathly strength he could not comprehend. . . . Yet he did not wish anyone dead, not really. Not dead. Dead. Absent but not dead . . . "dead" but not dying-dead, the state of being that comes after the throes of active dying. . . . No. It wasn't in Martin's heart to wish anyone dead, not even his deadly enemies.

And yet. . . .

Martin had reached in the pigeonhole assigned to him in the row of instructors' mailboxes, the row nearest the floor, and pulled out a handful of letters. He pawed through them, hoping as always for good news. Hoping. Hoping for something. But the important letters—the Confidential Letters—the letters that might, might mean he had a future, he wasn't going to be finished at 26, would be at home, waiting for him, and at school he usually received advertising brochures and other impersonal professional mail, envelopes with his name stamped on them. Occasionally he received a real letter, from a friend: but the friends' letters had become dangerous, since if they contained bad news they would depress him and if they contained good news they would depress him also. Good news meant, now, that someone had a job for next year or a postdoctoral grant or a fellowship, and since

Martin had been tentatively scheduled for "non-renewal" of his contract here at Tull College, he dreaded hearing about his friends' good/bad luck. So, when he found Marie McGahern's letter he should not have opened it, but taken it home to his wife, and opened it with her, or in front of her, or handed it wordlessly over to her to be opened. . . . But he had torn it open anyway, recklessly. He had read:

> . . . feel very out of touch . . . floating-free, detached . . . not really concerned with my own feelings, it's strange. . . . Wanted to call you one night, just to talk. But your wife would not understand. So. Wondered about you & her. Is she precious-sacred to you? does she allow you to touch her? or? Or do you allow her to touch you? We all got married too young. . . . Haven't been in contact with Bob for 4-5 weeks now. Over with? It dies hard. He kept saying to me & maybe wrote you heart-breaking letters on the subject, kept saying "You do what is best for you. . . ." And: "You do what is best for you . . . for you. . . ." So I did. So I arranged it. The method used on me has a very illustrative name your wife would know . . . since she is a scientist, like you & Bob & others . . . but I have forgotten the name (suppressed it?) . . . a kind of suction, vacuum-suction. . . . I recommend it. It all shoots out, dense clotted blood, in five minutes it just comes out . . . which saves a lot of time, you must admit: five minutes vs. the usual five days. . . . And you don't know if you're really pregnant or not. You think well maybe I am . . . but . . . but maybe I'm not . . . you're terrified & think yes maybe . . . but the doctor himself doesn't know (doctor = intern on duty) & you don't, of course . . . & there's no mess & you walk home after 30 min. in the usual way, not dizzy or stumbling or hemorrhaging & if anyone glances at you on the street that person does not see a vicious murderer or even a panicked blood-drained woman or. . . .

He had stopped reading. He had stuffed this letter into his shabby valise and walked away.

Walking out of the building he had thought of Marie, his friend's wife, and of his own wife, and of himself and others, and in a queer panicked instant he had felt himself drained of blood, wobbling, unwell, doomed—wondering where he was—so far from Boston,

from home— He stared in front of him. Confused. His suit was too
warm for this surprise of a day, a pre-spring day. Very far from
Boston and his eight years of advanced schooling, very far. In fact he
was in a town called Mason, Ohio. *Mason, Ohio*. He always had to
force himself to remember it, it was not a place anyone knew; but
Tull College was located here, founded 1850, a liberal arts college
with a small enrollment and a fine solid reputation. . . . Mason,
Ohio was Martin's home, temporarily. Therefore he should acknowledge it, not dread it. He should acknowledge all facets of reality,
benign and evil, so as to order it, and out of order would come clarity
and happiness. Clarity and happiness. So he walked out of the
handsome brick-and-aluminum Science Building (built 1966) and
saw his enemy—one of his several enemies—and fled from that
enemy and from everyone else, cutting across a plot of fragile green
grass, quarter-inch grass, getting string entangled in his shoes,
making a fool of himself, perhaps destroying what remained of his
future, all in an effort to get away somewhere so that he could
cry. . . .

 Mid-April sunshine. A morning of forsythia and opened windows
in classrooms and bare-armed students swarming everywhere, a
tide of smiles Martin could not handle, even when he was in a
normal state; he fled blindly. He thought: *Oh Jesus, we're being
punished . . . it's starting . . . but why?*

 As soon as he got out back in a field, and then in a sparse woods, he
began to cry. He had not cried for ten or twelve years.

 Martin's wife Rosalind, forty miles away in Columbus, took down
notes as one of the professors dictated to her, strolling between the
rows of caged white rats. The experiment—"Aggression-Inducing
Factors in White Rats"—was similar to one Rosalind had helped
with back at Harvard, the year before, but of course she said nothing
about this.

 "Okay," the professor said, "have one of the girls type it up. But
be sure she can read your handwriting—otherwise it will be a mess.
They're all moronic, they can't spell."

 "Yes," Rosalind said.

 She changed out of the lab coat and handed the papers in to one of
the secretaries, helped the girl read through the statistics and notes,
and paused before going home; wanting somehow to talk with the

girl, to exchange simple, trivial news, to laugh about something. The typist was about twenty years old and Rosalind was a few years older. But the girl smiled only courteously, shyly, at Rosalind, and would not venture anything further. So Rosalind gave up.

. . . might as well go home.

She was a laboratory assistant in the Psychology Department here, not officially admitted into the doctoral program—as the chairman of the Graduate Committee had explained to her, bitterly, their doctoral studies program had been cut back by the university, the university budget had been cut back by the state, and— Her credentials were excellent, of course. She had a B+ average from Harvard, a Master's Degree in experimental psychology. Excellent. But the doctoral program here was being cut back, severely, and no new candidates could be admitted at present; of course, as soon as the budget was restored, they would be delighted to accept her as a candidate. . . .

Rosalind had told the chairman of the committee that this was fine; she would be happy to wait.

She understood.

The chairman had smiled, relieved. "You understand, Mrs. Hershfield . . . ?"

Yes, she understood.

And so she had smiled that day, and she smiled most days. She knew the value of a smile, unlike her husband, whose smile had turned jagged and ironic. . . . In high school all the popular girls had smiled, at everyone; perhaps they smiled because they were popular, or were popular because they smiled.

So she smiled. And the Department had hired her, over countless other applicants, as a laboratory assistant on the part-time salary scale. Martin had been shocked at the salary and had said, "Is this a misprint?" And Rosalind had said cheerfully, "Honey, this is just a phase in our life together, a temporary phase."

Martin's mouth shaped itself into that jagged smile. "Everything is temporary," he said.

She dreaded driving back to Mason, returning to the duplex they rented, unlocking the door, looking down to see what mail had come. . . . She dreaded it, but there was nothing else to do.

You spend your life walking in straight lines, turn sharply left/

right, following the direction of sidewalks and other necessary guides. In this way you create certain human routes. The natural human route, in civilization, is straight, sharp-angled, perpendicular to its goal. This does create tensions in civilization. *Tensions are possible. Probable.* So one morning in Ohio a young man felt the containment of his former life begin to shift out of shape.

He crossed through the faculty parking lot, walked along the edge of the bulldozed hill, on muddy planks, and on, out, until he was in a field and safe and his face shifted into a face of anguish, a boy's face. He wiped at his eyes angrily. Then he was in a woods and crying and at the same time shamefully aware of himself crying, angry at himself, not yet frightened at what was happening to him. He felt very warm and itchy; this suit was a mistake. It was his only good suit. In Massachusetts April would not be so warm, not even on a freakish spring day. He could not always remember where he was but he knew he wasn't home.

He stopped crying. It had lasted only a minute. It was over.

From this hill he could look back down toward the campus. In the foreground was the partly-excavated hill. He couldn't remember what had been planned for this side of the campus, but he knew it had come to an abrupt end, just as the "Expansion Program" itself had ended abruptly. A financial disaster of secret proportions had struck Tull College; everyone used that expression, saying that disaster had "struck." Like lightning, something had rushed in from the outside. Don't ask from where. Don't ask why. Don't.

And therefore Martin had four enemies, three of them young men and one a woman of about thirty. They were all on the lower faculty, they did not have tenure, they had all received the same letters informing them of "non-renewal" of contract. . . . But it was not such a simple matter. Their letters had been waiting for them on the first Monday after the official start of the fall semester; a shock from which Martin had yet to recover, but he had performed his duties this year as if he had recovered; after all, he was an adult and he had a degree from M. I. T. Weeks passed. Then, on October 20, Martin had been called into the chairman's office and was told that the non-renewals were the result of tragic financial set-backs, *not* meant to be personal, not personal at all. But there was hope, the chairman said. The faculty association was engaged in a struggle with the college senate, and with the Chancellor himself, in an effort to regain

10% of the budget, and if this struggle were won, the Physics Department would, or might, or would like to, re-hire one of them.

Martin had stared. "One of us?" he asked.

"We hope very, very much to re-hire one of you," the chairman said, smiling his nervous smile. He was a pleasant man in his fifties, from M. I. T. also, but unfortunately too old to have known Martin's advisor.

"That's. . . ." But Martin had fallen silent, staring at the older man's face. It was a peculiar, difficult moment. He had wanted very much to say *That's good*, but he could not quite say it. So the moment passed, awkwardly.

The winter had passed and now it was April and Martin knew no more; no one knew any more. He had four enemies, four rivals. One of them was the gaunt-faced Merrill Pritchard, whom he had just avoided—neurotic, brilliant, with his degree from Michigan. He was unmarried, though. That might count against him. He was also very shaky, he smoked a great deal, he dressed badly. The most serious rival was a big red-headed kid from the University of Wisconsin, with his ex-football player's manliness and stamina and a reputed I. Q. of 190, married, and with a pregnant young wife; he was an assistant professor, however, which meant his salary was higher than Martin's, and would cost the department more to re-hire. Another assistant professor, a blond woman Martin especially disliked, had come here from M. I. T. five years before, but no one seemed to like her very much, or to defend her, and Martin had heard rumors about her missing classes. So perhaps she was out of the running. His fourth rival was an instructor who had been hired along with him, new to Tull, a sweet-faced young man who suffered from asthma and whose family was reputed to be wealthy—he even had a last name which was a famous brand-name in the United States, though this might have been simply a coincidence—and whom Martin for some reason did not take seriously, always forgetting to worry about him. *Don't forget Ralph*, part of his brain would shout.

He wished them all dead.

He had walked into a clearing and he began to hear noises somewhere. His head was heavy, leaden, as if there were something inside it he could not get clear. The sound of someone walking nearby irritated him; but it distracted him. So he thought: *A simul-*

taneous phenomenon. He followed a path slick with mud and saw someone ahead of him, a figure moving slowly. The person seemed to be trudging. It wore boots and slacks and its arms were bare.

It was a woman: but her body was not womanly. Martin paused for a moment, watching her. She looked familiar. She stopped to reach inside her boot, clumsily, as if she were trying to pull up a sock that had ridden down inside it. Her boots were made of a shiny synthetic material and were splotched with mud. Martin saw that she had gotten mud on her hand and seemed not to know what to do . . . then she wiped it, carefully, on the back of her thighs, out of her own range of vision.

A quick hot flash of a thought entered Martin's brain, through his eyes—

But he did not allow himself to think it.

A sudden knocking in the car made Rosalind accelerate. The car was a five-year-old Pontiac, bought second-hand, and each drive to and back from Columbus she considered a risk, then an accomplishment; the car had lasted the winter and might last out their term in Mason. Now she was entering Mason, passing a denuded strip of land advertised as *Parkway Estates: A Planned Residential Community.* None of the foundations for the houses had yet been laid, though the land had been stripped for as long as she had lived here.

Mason was a small city, with a downtown of typical Midwestern stores, grim and old-fashioned, a single movie house which was open only on weekends, and one large AAA-approved hotel; Rosalind avoided it, and did her shopping at the mall outside town, where the new, fluorescent-lit stores sometimes cheered her up. Now she thought suddenly of the duplex apartment, the unlocking of the door, the mail lying inside, and she did not want to go home. Not yet. So she parked at the mall and ran into the drugstore to buy a few things—she did not want to go home—instead she would walk through this enormous store and take notice of the wide, clean aisles, the merchandise displayed—terrace tables with fringed, green plastic tops, lawn chairs, inflatable rubber rafts, a Diet-Counter that displayed bottles and boxes and foot-long candy bars made of "Chokolate"—and the cosmetics counter, with a wide accusing mirror behind it in which Rosalind always happened to catch sight of herself, guiltily, seeing that small, unstriking, unsurprising face of hers, and realizing once again that it wasn't a face that belonged in that mirror.

She stared at the magazines on display, her eye drifting without effort from cover to cover, from the face of one beautiful woman to another, moving on . . . skipping the sports and detective magazines . . . coming to a stop on another face: that of an Asian child, whose features were twisted with pain. Rosalind stared. She saw that his lips were edged with sores, reddened and angry as boils. . . . She touched her own lips, involuntarily.

In that instant she felt a terrible premonition: *We are all going to be punished.*

Martin walked through things that resisted him. Bushes, limbs that were elastic, healthy, with the greening of this April day. . . . He did not pay attention to them. Sharp little hooks caught at his trousers but he ignored them. Spongy springy wet earth: his shoes would be muddy, muddy as that woman's boots, but he did not think about it. *Dear Sir: I am inquiring about a possible position in your department, beginning in September of this year. At present I am an instructor in. . . . My Ph. D. degree is from. . . . I studied with Dr. A. G. Cordoba and. . . . If you are interested, my credentials and transcripts (undergraduate and graduate) and letters of recommendation are on file at the Placement Bureau. . . . If you are interested in my application. . . . If you are. . . .* His wife had typed that letter and its variants out 240 separate times, but Martin was not thinking of her either; he was thinking of possibility-probability factors. Genes. The barometer. A too-warm suit. The pattern of clouds in the sky if you bothered to look (like a quilt, various shades of white and gray and darker gray). Healthy instincts of blood and muscle and eyes, directing the scene. Staring at the woman ahead of him Martin thought freely of all these factors, feeling himself a machine programmed in infinite patterns of complexities. He recalled Cordoba in a lecture, "What we know is likely to happen, but what we don't know is also likely to happen—" Martin had not understood. Now he thought he might understand.

"Hello?" he called to the woman. "Hello—?"

She stopped and looked back at him, cringing. Her face was broad, pale, doughy. Her eyes had a dead-dull lustre to them and were slightly bulging . . . her lips were parted in a silent astonished scream. . . . Martin saw at once that there was something wrong with her. He stared, he stumbled against something. He brushed out of his way a branch covered with small white bell-shaped blossoms. He said again, softly, "Hello."

The woman might have been any age—twenty-nine, forty. He had seen her a few times around town, always dressed in slacks, always with her hair cropped short and curly, the curls stiff with grease. Her body was slightly misshapen, especially ungainly in the shoulders and torso; but her face, apart from the staring eyes and the working, shapeless mouth, was almost attractive. Dull-thoughtful, dull-meditative. Brain-damaged. Martin was staring into the eyes and into the brain of a damaged person.

"Hello," Martin said, "where are you going? What's your name? Are you afraid of me? Do you walk out here very often? Do you know me? Why are you staring at me like that?"

Rosalind tore open the first of the letters. Her heart pounded sickeningly. She saw the extremely smooth sheet folded inside the envelope, recognized it as the kind of paper used for mimeographing, and, yes, when she unfolded the letter it was another mimeographed reply: *We are very sorry to inform you that.* . . . She crumpled it and threw it aside, it bounced off the kitchen table and onto the floor, she opened the next letter, more carefully, and noted that there were the impressions made of typing on this piece of paper, she could feel them beneath her fingers, unmistakable, and for a long moment she held herself back from unfolding it. . . . It was so important, a typed-out letter on authentic stationery! Finally she unfolded it and her eye, practised and cynical, skimmed the paragraph for crucial phrases: *we are interested in your application, we hope to, our budget has not yet, if, if you are still, following year.* . . . She put this letter down and opened the third, which was from a college she hardly remembered writing to, somewhere in Alabama. *We regret that.* . . . She threw it down. Then she snatched it up again, trembling. Something had thrown her off: yes, the letter was a form letter, but her husband's name and address had been typed in, as well as the date, and there was a salutation: *Dear Dr. Herchfeild.* . . .

"Dear Dr. Herchfeild," she laughed. "Go to hell, Dr. Herchfeild."

She threw away an advertisement and came upon the last of the letters, from friends they had known in Boston. The return address said just McGahern. Rosalind believed it was the wife's handwriting. She opened the letter and began to read it, with that helpless, flinching, cringing anti-hope, the hope not to read good news, her eye skimming the close-packed handwritten paragraphs. Then she began to read:

> . . . something is happening like rashes or bumps on the face
> . . . that are mysterious patterns . . . things trying to get said by
> the blood? the corpuscles in the blood? . . . Well you & Martin
> & Bob are the scientists & make the statistics. . . . I don't hate
> you. I don't even hate Bob. We're out of touch since 4-5 weeks
> ago . . . did he write you? . . . how I got rid of the baby . . .?
> Try Martin & see what he will do . . . he will make you do the
> same . . . it's a vacuum suction method very safe & efficient &
> not very painful so they say . . . I was out of my head anyway &
> couldn't feel or focus & I might have missed important parts of
> the scientific procedure. . . .

Rosalind dropped the letter. Her fingers had gone cold. She picked it up again, walked quickly into the bedroom with it, as if to read it in secret. She read it through twice, then a third time . . . then she put it in a drawer, beneath some things, so that Martin would not find it. She stood for a while, staring at the rented bureau, the rented bed with its slick-pine headboard, the bedspread she had pulled hurriedly up that morning to cover the rumpled bedclothes. . . . She lifted the bedspread, drew it back; looked at the bedclothes; did not focus upon anything; drew the bedspread back up again and tucked it in. . . . They did not make love any longer. It did seem to be over but she had not really thought about it until now. . . . *I couldn't feel or focus & I might have missed important parts of the procedure.* . . .

The woman walked away from him, her head bent.

Martin followed her. "What's wrong? Why are you leaving? Why are you afraid of me? Is something wrong? What do you know? Do you know something I don't know?"

She hurried. Her shoulders were hunched. Martin saw dizzily the quivering flesh of her upper arms, very pale, dough-like, the loose flabby flesh. It was ugly. It irritated him. He dropped what he had been carrying so that he wasn't weighed down, and he said, irritably, "Where are you going? Why are you running away? Wait—" He was willing. Watchful, heated, cautious. His body was drenched with heat. *Wait*. It was his body that remembered, not Martin himself, how he had once been in love . . . *in love* . . . how he had told his friends excitedly that he was in love and now he realized . . . oh God, he realized what it was, what it was to be *in love* . . . he had never guessed at it before. . . . Had never guessed at it. Had never guessed. There were things you could not guess at. They existed, but in a dimension not yet opened to you. Like a book you can't read because its printed words are in a language you don't know, or because your eyes are filmed over with something opaque, blood-tinted, a throbbing membrane like the membrane that covers the soul. . . .

"Don't run. Don't do it. Don't run, please, don't," Martin said. He grabbed at the woman's arm. His fingers closed around her forearm, she jerked violently away from him, his fingers slid down around her wrist and held. Out of his body came a strength, concentrated in those fingers, that he had not noticed before.

She cringed away from him, her body bent. Her eyes were narrowed now, the lids nearly closed, as if she were staring into a bright light. She was breathing laboriously. Panic. He too felt it: the mucous-like coating of panic on the tongue. His own breathing was audible. It was a dense ungainly rhythm—her breath, his breath—a pumping of lungs and hearts, the two of them standing in a strange equilibrium, Martin holding her body straining and yet balanced perfectly against his own, the bulk and weight of a body that belonged to him. . . .

Then her face twisted violently and she began to cry. She sobbed. Her eyes narrowed to cracks and he saw in terror the way the tears came out of them: liquid springing out of those ugly eyes, streaming down that coarse-skinned face. . . . It was something too ugly to experience. He said, "Don't—" But the word was choked off, his throat felt paralyzed. He felt his own eyes narrowing and the hot pressure of tears behind the lids, stinging like salt. Like salt rubbed against a flimsy membrane. *Don't. Wait. Please.*

He saw a man's face lunging at his, and he saw the length of his own arm dragged out hard, he saw the bulk of his body out of the blinded lower half of his eyes. He heard the man cry, "Don't—"

The visible and invisible world was swollen tight with blood.

He felt his body hunch, grow taut and stiffened with terror, he felt the man's hard fingers closed about his wrist—

He felt the rhythm of their gasping for breath—

He felt the man's terror, the salt-stinging of tears against that man's eyes—

Then the fingers released the wrist: the fingers let go, the wrist and the arm and the springing panicked body jerked free. It was free. The pulsation in his head, concentrated in his eyes, drew back into his own head now, released her, drew back sharp and delicate as a gesture, flowed back into his own being and released her. . . .

The woman ran from him. He half-heard the crashing of her flight. Then he heard nothing, he was not hearing any sounds, anything; he stood, still, in that posture of balance, his arm outstretched, his fingers outstretched, as if for a long frozen moment he were still holding the woman.

It had been a balance, an equilibrium.

He had seen himself.

He saw.

At four-thirty Rosalind called her husband's office. The telephone was answered on the first ring, by another instructor—Merrill, who shared Martin's office—who told her, brusquely, that he did not know where Martin was. No. He had not seen Martin all day. In fact, Martin had not showed up for his three o'clock freshman class and students had been milling around for fifteen minutes or more, causing a commotion, and it had been very irresponsible of Martin, to say the least—

"He didn't teach his class?" Rosalind asked, shocked.

"I just told you," he said.

"But—but— Haven't you seen him all day?"

"I really don't remember," Merrill said.

He hung up.

Rosalind hurried out of the house, out the front walk. She did not know what to do. For a while she stood on the sidewalk, staring down the road. It was a paved road but its shoulders were wide, made of gravel that had been partly washed away, and the dark-hued mud gave a peculiar countrified look to the area. The newsboy appeared on his bicycle; that meant it was late in the afternoon.

He handed her the paper, hand to hand. He must have said hello, or "Here's your paper," some phrase that also involved her name, *Mrs. Hershfield,* but she could not quite comprehend it.

He rode by. She turned slowly and walked into the house. She was observing herself now, almost against her own desire, as she had observed the behavior and often the death agonies of experimental animals—rats, guinea pigs, cats, even a few dogs. All these creatures had lived and had lived out certain procedures, within her range of observation. And now she herself was living out a certain procedure.

He came home some time later. It must have been after six. She went to the door and he stepped inside, staring at her; his face was Martin's face, and yet it was altered. She was going to say, "Where were—" but she only stared at him.

"There's nothing to be afraid of," Martin said.

She saw that he was trying to smile. His lips looked dry and awkward. It was not his own smile, but something else; she saw the queer straining of his facial muscles, and the straining of his eyes to get in focus.

"Why—what— What happened to you?" Rosalind whispered.

"Nothing. Nothing to be afraid of," he said.

He walked past her like a sleepwalker. He seemed to be favoring one side of his body, as if he were in pain. Rosalind followed him but did not touch him. His hair was uncombed, there were burrs and streaks of mud on his clothes, his shoes were muddy and wet—he was empty-handed—

"What happened? What happened to you?" Rosalind cried.

He went into the bedroom. Slowly, lowering himself with great effort, he lay on top of the wrinkled bedspread; the way he moved, so timidly, so carefully, made Rosalind realize that this was a man she no longer knew. But she forced herself to call him by name: "Martin—" She forced herself to ask what was wrong, what had happened, something of course had happened at the college and she had a right to know, she was his wife, he must explain all this to her—

Martin interrupted. "Let's sleep," he said softly. "Sleep. Sleep with me. Help me. Hold me. Sleep with me, please."

She stared at him. "What—?"

"Everything is refuted," Martin said. He closed his eyes and lay very still. "So help me, sleep with me. I'm so sleepy . . . help me. . . ."

"What do you mean? *Everything is refuted*—what does that mean?" Rosalind asked. He lay still, his eyes shut. His face seemed nearly abstract with exhaustion. The skin on his nose and forehead was slightly sunburned; his lips were partly open, motionless. She wanted to scream at him—*What does that mean? What have you done to yourself?* But she was too frightened to speak. She felt the space between them turning solid, turning into an almost tangible element she would never penetrate. . . .

He lay on his back, his arms and legs flung out as if with exhaustion, his face strange to her, unreadable. Without opening his eyes he said hoarsely, "There's nothing to be afraid of. . . ."

She walked quickly out of the bedroom.

She was very frightened.

Eye-Witness

Annie, you bitch: listen to your ugly nasal whining voice, listen to your lies. You're so pathetic—pitiful—transparent. So absurd. *I'm not sick. There's nothing wrong with me.* Just listen . . . ! Trying eagerly to make conversation with any vague shadowy shape that appears. You don't know who they are. You don't know if they're human or not. *I'm not sick. Not. There's nothing wrong with . . .*

A creature in a nearby bed. Another creature in a wheel-chair. Nurses. Orderlies. (One of them your own age, with dark curly hair and a foreign accent—Italian? Greek?) Listen to your tinny voice echoing inside your head, listen to your ludicrous faltering attempts at "conversation": *The weather. It's a rainy day isn't it. It's been raining a long time hasn't it. I can't wait for summer. I like fall too. When the leaves change. And spring. But I like winter too—I like the snow—some people don't but I do—I like everything, really.*

Grinning and blinking and squinting. A cute little girl. You bitch, you liar: don't you know everyone is laughing at you?—jeering? Ugly gawky Annie, it's no use your slouching and letting your arms dangle, you're tall, big as a horse, your feet are enormous and it's no wonder the salesmen are always surprised and make little jokes—can you blame them? Your sister is older than you and her shoe size is 6½ and she is embarrassed, she is always complaining, in a voice that is high-pitched and nervous and very girlish—complaining about her big feet which are nevertheless far smaller than yours. It's no wonder she laughs at you. It's no wonder everyone laughs.

Annie, you bitch, why don't you shut up?

Opening your eyes wide to show you aren't groggy. Blinking.

79

Your lashes blinking. *I'm not sick now. I feel fine. I've been feeling fine for days.* Directing your voice past your visitors' heads, hoping for attention, praise. Hoping that one of the nurses will report your progress to the doctor: *Annie Quirt is ready to be discharged.* Hoping the doctor himself will hear, leaning in the doorway of the room.

Annie, am I Annie? I think so. Yes. . . . Yes. I'm not sick: I'm fine. I have never felt better in my life.

Listen to them laughing at you!

Not even bothering to hide their smiles. Not raising their hands to their mouths, not turning aside. The way they laughed at your grandfather, down at the train depot that morning. 7:30 in the morning and the old man staggering on the platform, disheveled, muttering to himself, his clothes partly unbuttoned. You wanted to hide, you wanted to pull him away, so that the two of you could hide together. But he wouldn't leave the platform. He was cranky, he jerked away from your hand, he told you to go home if you didn't want to stay with him—he'd get on the train alone—he didn't need you. People were watching. Listening. One or two or three laughed. The old man was drunk, they thought—just another silly old drunken man—but with a waspish temper, eh? White hair, patches of a white beard, stained shirt front and one trouser leg ripped at the knee, must have fallen, ridiculous bad-tempered senile old drunk—shouldn't someone call the police?—there was a little girl with him—what was the little girl doing with him? Not that she was so little!—eleven years old and already at least five feet three or four. Big-boned, with a wide squarish jaw, coarse red hair, big feet. Jeans, a cotton pull-over shirt, a windbreaker. Ugly little creature. What—

There you go again, just listen to you. Making "conversation" like your mother and her sisters. Like the girls you hated in high school. Your lips numb, your face curiously hot. Something is wrong, something is wrong, which is why people stare pityingly at you, even the orderly with the dark hair stares at you, not attracted by your frantic grins or your emaciated shoulders and chest and arms. *It's a lovely day isn't it. The sun. The blue sky. I want to walk outside—I love to walk—I was very athletic in high school—played basketball and field hockey and tennis and—*

Annie, you are such a pathetic liar, such an awkward liar! The stale stink of your lies is disgusting. The way you lick your lips is disgusting. (Your lips are cracked, aren't they? You must look a sight!) Annie, it's enough to make a person nauseous, listening to your silly lies: *Doctor, it was a mistake. I was nervous and I made a mistake. It's nobody's fault. If I mentioned anyone's name it was a mistake. I got nervous, I couldn't sleep, I lost count of the pills. I don't know how I got here. I must have hit my head, crawling on the floor— bumped against the edge of the refrigerator, I think. I was nervous. My mind was upset. I took a Kleenex and wiped off all the make-up that was left but some of the mascara got into my eyes—there were tears in my eyes and the mascara ran—do I look like an owl?—a silly owl? Smudged and bruised. My God. I can't stop laughing, can I? I didn't mean to frighten the cats—my pet cats—I didn't mean to frighten anyone— But I'm well now. It's all over.*

—◆—◆—

A friend arrived, a friend pounded on the door, a friend's voice was raised in alarm. Yes, we know all about you, Annie—we know far more than we wish to know. Slovenly, selfish, stupid Annie. What's one more death?—or life? But someone must clean up the mess. If you slash your wrist (ineptly) with someone's razor blade there will be a considerable mess which, of course, *you* won't clean up; if you vomit your guts onto the floor of your tiny kitchen you can be reasonably certain that *you* won't be stuck with the job of mopping it up. And polishing the linoleum afterward.

Annie, shut up. And stop grinning. It makes us all nervous.

Annie, are you falling asleep? Isn't that rude, to fall asleep when someone is talking to you?

And your self-pity, Annie—isn't it disgusting—one of the women in this room with you is very, very sick—don't you know?—or care?—very, very sick—legitimately sick. Post-Caesarian complications, malfunctioning kidneys. But she doesn't complain, does she? You don't hear her whining and telling outrageous lies, do you? Of course not. She's dying quietly. She isn't causing a fuss; she isn't grinning and chattering, keeping everyone awake.

Grandfather Quirt: eighty-two years old when he ran away from home. Stole fifty dollars from his daughter-in-law's pocket book and, with Annie, took a Greyhound bus to the city, declaring he was never coming back. He too was dying but possibly didn't know. Or did he? Dreams, they say, sometimes prophesy death. And death itself casts a shadow backward from the future.

Whispering with Annie. Secrets. Plans. A train to Chicago and another train out West, to the Pacific Coast. (He had taken a trip to California once, decades ago. Had been very impressed by the proximity of the ocean, the mountains, and the desert. Land of wonders!—waiting for him all these years.) Our secret, Annie, he had said, and she had shivered with delight, helping him count the money. Again and again—fifty dollars. It seemed like so much! And four dollars and thirty-five cents of her own, saved, kept in her uppermost bureau drawer; mostly change. It seemed like so much.

Fifty dollars?

Chicago?—and California?

People laughed, jeered. Pointed. Annie's hair hung in her eyes. She gnawed at her fingers, miserable. The old man drew away from her, mumbling to himself. He walked off-balance. He was no one she knew. The station-master asked her questions and she brought her sticky hands to her face, to hide. But she must have told him her name because her father arrived before long in the station-wagon and there were raised voices and she heard her own voice, raised in a terrible scream. (She didn't *want* to go back home. She didn't *want* her and Grandpa to go back home.)

There were many witnesses that morning. At 7:50 the train pulled into the station and crowds of people moved back and forth, staring at Annie and her grandfather and her father and the station-master and a patrolman, staring and listening, laughing openly. An old drunk. An old fool. Crazy, wasn't he?—alcoholic too. Probably alcoholic. Wouldn't go back home with his son; wanted to run away, off to California; off to the Pacific Coast—!

Annie stuck her fingers in her mouth, gnawing and sucking. She didn't know the old man now. He bellowed something about being nobody's father—nobody's business but his own—his own *self*, he was—and free to do whatever he goddam pleased. Did they understand, the nosey bastards? Did they? Eighty-two years of answering to other people's demands—eighty-two years of confinement—and now he was free, he wasn't going back, nobody could make him go back—

White-haired, wild-eyed. A wreck. They had spent most of the night in a park, sleeping on newspapers beneath a low, sprawling juniper tree, and Annie had slept, strangely enough, quite well; though of course she had been very excited. In the morning, however, she was tired. Deathly tired. She began to cry because her grandfather was shouting and throwing his arms about and they would have to stop him, would have to hurt him, and there was nothing she could do about it—nothing she could do except watch.

Annie, what a bitch you are: telling that story about your pathetic dying grandfather, just to get sympathy for yourself. For yourself. Always. Lying in a lover's arms, whispering of your disappointments and sorrows and befuddlements, expecting to be loved. But who will love you, once he knows your innermost self?

I don't want to live, you whimpered, *I'm not sick,* you claim; I did something very very ugly and must be punished; *I'm not sick, I've never felt better: When can I go home?* What a sneaky lying bitch, how sly, how shameless. It would have been a blessing had you died. Your father would be grief-stricken, your mother astonished, your sister shocked and embarrassed, and your lover—your former lover—irritated, perhaps: or angry: angry and indifferent at once. You wished to die merely to punish him, don't bother to lie about not wanting to live, about hating yourself, loathing yourself. *You have always loathed yourself.* Yet you lived, didn't you, for twenty-six years, you enjoyed getting drunk occasionally and you certainly enjoyed eating—gorging yourself, in fact—and you enjoyed, or pretended to enjoy, the company of other people. All along, however, you detested yourself. But you made no move to die, you were too lazy, too distracted. And foolishly hopeful. (The blackheads on your nose—maybe they would go away, as most of your pimples went away; maybe you would be beautiful soon? It wasn't impossible!) Too cowardly, perhaps.

It isn't necessary to locate my parents, you said, smiling your hopeful demented smile. *We don't keep in close touch and I'm so much better now, I'll be out of the hospital by the end of this week—*

When she woke the first time she was hooked up to something: a tube. Tubes. Her waking was experimental—she was not certain, really, if she was alive.

There were needles. There were sharp stinging injections, like insect bites. Her mouth was numb; when she cried out, the sound came from somewhere else in the room.

Something dripped into her, rhythmically.

I want to die, she whispered. I don't want to die.

Clatter of wheels in the corridor. Doors opening and closing. Voices, exclamations. Occasional laughter. The drone of a television set, the swelling and fading drone of an airplane overhead. I don't want to die, Annie thought. Her head ached where she had banged it. Cracked the bone? An ugly bruise. They had turned her stomach inside-out of course, as punishment; it was part of the punishment, too, that there were so many people around. Shadowy figures, passing near. Staring at her. Whispering. *Who is that—? Is that the one—?*

In second grade, a sudden attack of nausea just before her turn to read. *The Wind in the Willows*, it was; a book she loved. But she had eaten her lunch too quickly and had played too hard on the playground and suddenly, incredibly, she was sick—gagging and retching while the others stared. Someone giggled behind her. Messy Annie, bad Annie, look what you're doing! Just look! All over the front of your dress and splattered onto the floor! Aren't you ashamed? Aren't you *ashamed?*

Grandpa, she whispered, reaching for his hand. Grandpa? —They would go away together after all. Buy the tickets, get on the train, crouch together at the rear of the car until the train started and they were safe. He wouldn't die, then; wouldn't collapse suddenly while Annie's father argued with him; wouldn't shrivel up in the nursing home, toothless and foul-smelling. It wasn't too late, Annie cried. If only he would forgive her. . . . She must have answered the questions that man asked, otherwise how would he have known who to call? She must have given her name. Her grandfather's name. *Must* have.

Waking, she knew she would be punished. Was being punished all along.

(Out in the corridor a young nurse giggled and a man's voice rose flirtatiously and it was part of Annie's punishment to lie there, a few yards away, a witness. Her hair was straggly and unwashed, her eye-sockets were hollow, she was very very ugly, she had almost died and smelled now of perspiration, vomit, and despair. No one would ever love her again—would ever glance at her again—and it was her punishment, to witness the love-play of others. *I have become pain,* she thought.)

Your friend Marcia eyes you suspiciously. You talk and talk. Occasionally you explode in a small scream of laughter. It's ridiculous, the hospital's rule about twelve days' observation—you've never felt more rational, more sane in your entire life. No danger of trying again—absolutely not! Never! You didn't "try," really, it was an accident, you had wanted only to sleep and kept waking throughout the night and got edgy and anxious and angry with yourself, and . . . You didn't "try" to destroy yourself, not at all. Not at all! Marcia smiles faintly but does not join your laughter.

" . . . anyone you want me to contact?" she asks.

"What do you mean? No."

"Anyone you were, you know, close to . . . involved with. . . . I mean . . . There was someone, wasn't there, you were getting serious about . . . ?"

"No."

"No?"

"No."

Twelve days' observation.

Fortunately it isn't thirty.

Annie, listen to your wheedling little-girl voice, listen to your shameless lying: Open-eyed, licking your lips, explaining to Dr. Pruitt that you have never felt better in your life, that you're ready to resume your career, maybe return to art school, take courses in print-making and photography. Dr. Pruitt's face is creased and wise, he is one of the Fathers of the world, like your own father patient and a little ironic, possibly a little bitter. He listens to your outrageous lies, he manages a smile, he is really very kind. (Though harassed. Distracted.) A word from him and you are free; a wrong word from him and you are committed for further observation. (Two suicide attempts in a single week—after all!)

What do you remember, Annie?

What?—when?

Of being *there.*

I remember nothing except swirls of light: clouds of light.

Did you climb up out of your body?

Yes. Yes. I climbed up out of it—I looked down and saw that it was dying, it was twitching with death—it was foul, ludicrous, shameful. An error. I vowed that I would never descend into it again but something drew me back, pulled me back, and I woke in tears, I woke gagging and sobbing—

Is that all you remember?

Gagging—sobbing—screaming.

Do you regret—?

Everything.

Even the yawning is a pretense. You don't want your visitors to know how you dread their judging you, their assessing you. And they notice, of course, that *he* is not here. (Those flowers?—from your employer at the gallery. Yes, it was very thoughtful of him. He had a girl arrange for them, no doubt, but it was thoughtful just the same.)

Long-legged, sullen, a bit contemptuous of the hospital staff. You make jokes. You ask Terry for a cigarette and he gives you one, gladly. Then there is Varian, growing a beard, gunmetal-gray, ascetic, an ex-lover of yours, never really a lover but quite a good friend, in the sense in which you have "friends" now. Sitting on the windowsill, arms crossed, talking mainly about his former wife and the child support payments he is forced to make though his wife has a fiancé now and they are living together. Don't marry anyone, Annie: it isn't worth it. You come to wish you were both dead if it fails.

I can't believe that, you say, smiling your demented smile and licking your lips.

Someone taps on a metal arm-rest and begins to hum and you would like to hum along with him but your throat aches. You are thinking of . . . You are *not* thinking of . . . (But he loved you so! Groaned against your body, loving you, sick with love for you!) You are thinking instead of . . . of old friends . . . a letter from Maxine Mandel you never answered, a year ago now or more . . . must remember to write, must remember to write; must remember to telephone your sister when you're discharged. . . . What is Varian mumbling about? Always his wife, his precious wife! Whom he detests. Loves. Can't stop thinking about.

. . . Yes, Annie, you can look at me like that if you want but I know what I'm talking about: marriage is too much of a risk. Love is too much of a risk. (He makes a gesture which she rather resents, taking in her, the bed, the room, the whole of the hospital. *Bastard.*)

No, I don't believe that, you say, smiling still. I'm an incurable romantic, after all.

The Hallucination

Her husband's voice lifted through the floorboards of the old house.

She was awake, suddenly. She couldn't remember having fallen asleep—what time was it?—she sat up, shivering, and heard now the voice from downstairs, familiar, but too loud, as if Alan were on the telephone. But it was too late for him to be talking to anyone: it was nearly two o'clock in the morning.

. . . she could hear her husband's voice, but could not distinguish any words.

She got out of bed, slowly.

On the landing she heard the anger in his voice. And the pleading.

" . . . why don't you go home? . . . go somewhere else?"

The lights were out downstairs. Alan stood at the front door, in the darkened hallway, talking to someone out on the porch. Joanne was fully awake now: she stared at her husband's shadowy figure, wondering if the frightened anger in his voice, in his tense body, would be enough to protect them. She could not see who was there—only a blurred form, on the porch, pushed in close in the space between the door and the screen door, which he had opened. They never bothered to latch the screen door.

" . . . why don't you go home? I'm not going to let you in. What do you want? Look, I can't help you," Alan was saying. He spoke quickly, yet gave to the final words of each sentence a peculiar dragging weight, almost a plea, the way one might speak to a child. "I said I can't help you. . . . What do you want?"

Outside, a man's voice—high and thin—the words unintelligible. Then a burst of laughter.

Joanne was at the foot of the stairs now, and she could see the intruder more clearly—a head of long blond hair, a face in continual movement, youthful and creased, sunburned, the mouth contorted in a wide grin. He kept jerking his head from side to side, furiously. He was arguing with Alan through the door but his words were only plunges and leaps of noise. In Joanne's panic she seemed to see him as someone come back to reclaim the farm, the old farm-house she and Alan had just moved into—six miles outside Beulah, Vermont, and a quarter-mile from the interstate highway to the south—but that was because the boy was wearing denim jeans and a vest or jacket of denim, and because of the bleached, haylike look of his wild hair.

"Alan, who is it? What does he want?" Joanne said.

He turned to her, startled. His blond, greyish-blond hair looked dishevelled; she had never seen him so distraught—tense, alarmed, yet irritable too, and a little embarrassed—as if she had come upon him when he had believed himself alone, totally alone. The face on the other side of the door bobbed like a mirror's reflection, broken loose. Joanne had taken down the old, dust-yellowed white curtains that had framed the door's window, and in their place she had put up fireproof curtains of a gauzy beige material, transparent from inside, from the darkened hallway. The boy on the porch was exposed by the overhead light. He brought his face up close to the window, pressing it against the pane, while Alan, turned to her, signalled for her to stay away. "Joanne, don't let him see you! Stay back!"

"But what is it—?"

"I don't know, I don't have any idea," Alan said. He spoke in a low, distracted mutter. The boy was rapping on the door in a series of quick, shallow knocks, so rapid they sounded like a single wave, a sequence of vibrations. ". . . I was just coming up to bed, I was just putting my things away, when he knocked on the door," Alan said. In his tone, now, was a sound of innocent perplexity, a slightly accusatory note, as if he were explaining this for the second or third time, to someone who did not quite believe him. "He's in his twenties, just a kid . . . I don't know what the hell he wants or where he came from . . . unless he wandered over here from the express-way, and . . ."

"What does he want?" Joanne whispered. "Does he want to use the telephone, or . . .? Does he want help?"

"Joanne, stand back out of the light, will you? I don't want him to see you, please, for Christ's sake. I'm hoping he'll just go away—but maybe I should call the police—"

Joanne did not quite hear him, she was so distracted by the boy on the porch. He was now holding onto the doorknob with both hands, turning it from side to side, and rubbing the forehead and the crown of his head against the window. Laughing, giggling, crooning and interrupting himself with a sudden jerk of his head, a strangled shout—his shoulders were raised high and narrow, his body seemed constricted, somehow deformed—he was a stranger, he had a stranger's face, yet Joanne experienced once again the fleeting mad thought that he had come back home, back to this restored nineteenth-century farmhouse, that he had not wandered back the driveway by accident. "The police," Joanne repeated. "The police. I wonder if—I think— Did you call them yet?"

"Honey, no, I've been afraid to leave the door," Alan said.

"Is he drunk? Is he crazy?"

"I think he's high on drugs," Alan said. "He must be hallucinating. Just don't let him see you—he's out of his mind, obviously, and if he wanted to he could smash the window and get in here. He doesn't seem to know what he's doing—he doesn't seem to hear me—he's arguing with someone, but it isn't me, this is the strangest thing that's ever—that's ever—"

"How long has he been out there?" Joanne asked.

"Maybe ten minutes."

The figure out there lurched away from the window, backward. But the thatch of blond hair reappeared, almost immediately, and there was a heavier pounding on the door and the doorframe, and a sudden banging of the screendoor against the side of the house, as if he were kicking it, impatiently, having just discovered it.

"Didn't you call the police?" Joanne said faintly.

"Go away! Get out of here!" Alan shouted.

The boy jumped backward.

"We're going to call the police if you don't get out of here— Go on, get out! Go home!" Alan said. His voice climbed, angrily. Joanne felt a moment of intense relief, hope, an absurd pinprick of relief, thinking that her husband's anger had driven the boy away. But he had only stumbled backward, bumping into something on the veranda—one of the old wicker rocking-chairs that had come with

the farm, that Alan had recently repainted a bright hunter green—
and this made him more furious, so that he ran to one of the windows
and began scratching at it, drawing his fingernails wildly against the
glass, up and down and around in crazy desperate circles. Alan and
Joanne went into the room Alan used as a kind of study, a big,
cluttered, handsome room with built-in bookshelves, so that they
could see what he was doing. Despite the frenzy of his head and
shoulders and torso, the dancer-like contortions of his body, he
seemed oddly helpless—he only clawed at the window-pane, as if he
did not dare to smash it. Yet he was very angry—crazily angry—
shouting something that sounded like *You, y'no, yah*— But really it
was nothing at all, strangled screams in a foreign language.

"Go upstairs and call the police, Joanne," Alan said. "I'll watch
him to make sure he doesn't break in."

"But— But I—"

"Look at him, look at his eyes— His eyes are rolling back up into
his head," Alan whispered. "Jesus, look! Have you ever seen anything like it? He's out of his mind. He's completely out of his mind."

"But why did he come here? Do you think he knows us? Is he one
of your students?"

"No, I'm sure he isn't. No. He's too old. No."

"He isn't very old—he could be eighteen or nineteen—"

"No, he's older than that."

"It looks like he's crying—"

"Why don't you go upstairs and call the police?"

"What is that, on his face? Is he crying? Is he sweating, like that?"

"He's sweating."

"His mouth is all wet—"

Joanne was clutching at the collar of the robe she'd put on, an old
blue flannel bathrobe from her girlhood, years ago. She was confused but part of her mind functioned with an odd over-bright
clarity: the porch light was bright, very bright, and around it moths
and gnats fluttered, in the early-summer mildness of a June night,
and she felt isolated and observed and eerily, inexplicably girlish,
standing barefoot in her husband's study, a few feet away from a
maddened boy. Something like this must have happened many
years ago—otherwise, why did she seem to remember it?—and why
a gradual slowing of her heartbeat, a gradual conviction that she was
in no danger, really, that the frenzied boy would not harm them?

Her fingers relaxed. She flexed them, they were numb, the nails had dug into the flesh of her palm, tiny pricks of pain too remote to be real. Alan was instructing her to go upstairs, to call the Beulah police or the highway patrol or, if she was too nervous, to dial the operator and tell her what was wrong. An emergency. Send police out. Send help. Maybe an ambulance . . . yes, an ambulance . . . a boy out of his mind, probably on drugs. Not a drunk. "Tell them it's a boy on drugs, hallucinating," Alan whispered. "And that it's quite serious. He could really go crazy at any moment and break in here and—"

The boy had stopped clawing at the window. He backed away, slowly, until he collided with the porch railing. He turned, surprised, and yet slowly, with the mechanical, faintly ludicrous alarm of a cartoon figure. *What? What? Oh.* He touched the railing. With his left hand he stroked the uneven surface of the railing, as if he were trying to see it better. His head drooped. Joanne could see his profile—a boy's face, the jaw dropping slackly, threads of saliva on his chin.

"Isn't it terrible . . . ?" Joanne said. "Oh, it's terrible . . . terrible."

"He was trying to talk to me through the door, but he couldn't understand anything I said," Alan said. He spoke now in a more normal voice. He and Joanne stood side by side, not touching. The boy was only a few yards away, but he seemed less dangerous. He was stroking and caressing the porch railing, his head bent attentively toward it. The laughter had stopped. Evidently the railing had taken on some important meaning to him . . . very slowly, painstakingly, he drew his fingertips along it, with a delicate precision that seemed to open, in Joanne, a swift pragmatic pity. Alan was describing how he had been clearing his desk, had just switched off his desk lamp, when the rapping began; it had not been ordinary rapping, there had been no possibility of its being someone in his right mind, but from the start exaggerated and hysterical—so Alan had acted quickly, turning off the hall light so that the boy could not see him, though he had left the porch light on, in order to see what the boy was doing. A friend of theirs had visited, earlier that evening, and they had forgotten to turn the porch light off; that must have been what had attracted the boy, Alan thought, he must have seen the light from the highway, and. . . . But Joanne felt pity for him, she

interrupted her husband and said: "Alan, please. I don't think it's so
serious. I think he just wants to use the telephone . . . look at him,
he doesn't seem dangerous, does he? I think . . . I think that . . ."

"Still, we'd better call the police."

"He must be from around here. He must have wandered over
here by accident . . . maybe he was with some friends, boys his age,
and they let him out, as a joke? . . . or maybe he lives nearby. . . ? If
we call the police they'll arrest him, won't they? Won't they take him
to jail?"

"Joanne, I think we should call the police."

"Maybe he'll just decide to leave. . . ."

"He's out of his mind," Alan said irritably. "He could do anything.
Right now he seems harmless, yes, but. . . . Can you hear what he's
saying? What is he saying?"

"Should we open the window a little?"

"But don't let him— No, wait. Wait," Alan said, pushing her back.
"No, don't open it, go on upstairs and call the police, will you? I
think it's serious enough for the police. I'm not afraid of him, I don't
think there's any danger—he's so skinny—I don't think there's any
real danger to us, but maybe we should call the police just the
same— It might be that— He could go wild and—"

"He's saying something, isn't he?"

"I can't make any sense out of it."

"Maybe we should try to help him," Joanne said uncertainly. "I
mean— I mean— What can you do for someone in his condition,
hallucinating? . . . or whatever it is? Is it like being drunk, or is it
different? I've read so much about drugs but I don't know what to do.
Do you think we should call the police, Alan? Why don't we try to
help him? . . . Maybe," she said, taking Alan's arm, squeezing it,
"maybe he just wants us to help him, maybe call his parents for him
. . . or maybe he thinks this is his house, he's just trying to get back
home, and . . ."

The boy was rocking back and forth now, his body twisted, but-
tocks pressed against the railing. How pale his hair was, platinum-
blond hair, amazing!—like a wig that was almost glamorous. The
denim jacket and jeans were filthy, streaked with mud and grease or
black paint, and he wore a shirt without buttons, opened upon his
sunburnt, bare chest, that looked as if it were made of some thick,
canvas-like material, crude scarlet and bright green, like an Indian

blanket. Out there, he was somehow over-exposed, magnified. Joanne saw clearly the foot-long tear in the left pant-leg of his jeans and even the wet bloody wound inside, a child's accident; and she saw the tension in his feet, the strain of tendons and muscles as he rocked slowly back and forth, as if the great, mysterious effort, pushing himself against an element that opposed him. He had lost his shoes somewhere: he wore thick white socks, like gym or hiking socks, with tiny diamonds of black and red in them, the socks torn and filthy, one of them—the one on his left foot—ridden down to his heel. Now that he was only crooning to himself, straining his body in and out of a posture that must have hurt his spine, he seemed only pitiful; Joanne wanted to open the window a few inches and talk to him, console him. Like her husband she would tell him to go home, but gently, gently. *Go home where you belong, don't stay here, don't force us to call the police and turn you in.* . . . She even made a motion toward the window, but hesitated. She was afraid. And Alan seized her by the wrist and asked her what she thought she was doing? . . . she had better stay back out of the light, in case he looked this way.

"Are you sure he isn't one of your students?" Joanne whispered.

"I'm fairly sure," Alan said.

"But what if . . . what if he's one of your students?"

"Joanne, I'm sure he isn't. I'm sure he isn't. I've never seen him before. He must be from Beulah, or one of the farms around here . . . no, honey, he isn't from the college. He just doesn't look as if he would be." Alan was Dean of Humanities at a small college in Beulah, an excellent liberal arts college that had originally been affiliated with the Anglican church, but was now a secular institution; a young dean—Alan was only thirty-nine—he tried to become acquainted with all six hundred of the boys and girls he dealt with, and he even taught an honors course, a seminar in American Civilization, though the three-hour course was not part of his regular workload as an administrator. He and Joanne had moved to Vermont two years before, and had moved out to this farmhouse only a few months ago; it looked larger than it really was, like so many of the older houses in Vermont, but it was spacious downstairs, with a big living room, a closed-in porch Alan used as a study, and a high-ceilinged, drafty kitchen. Made partly of wood and partly of stone, it gave the appearance of being a small fortress, rather sombre and

crypt-like in overcast light, half-buried beneath elms and the
spreading, sprawling branches of an enormous willow tree . . .
hardly visible from the road, back a long cinder-strewn lane that was
itself lined with elms and smaller trees. When they turned in from
the narrow country road, coming back from an evening in town,
Joanne experienced a faint shock of surprise, sometimes even of
dread—as if they had turned up an unpaved road by mistake, leaving
the public road behind. The house could hardly be seen from the
road. And then it emerged slowly, reluctantly: handsome enough if
you knew what to look for, but over-priced, drafty, with a cellar that
leaked and a furnace that must soon be replaced and an attic in which
wasps and bees had lived for decades. Friends from school had
dropped in a few times, but only after having been invited to drop in,
to "stop by" if they happened to be in the neighborhood . . . and
only once had a student come out, to see Alan about financial
difficulties concerning the college newspaper; other than that, no
one had ever visited them except as party or dinner guests, and no
one had ever wandered up the driveway from the road, like this boy,
to take them by surprise.

"He could be from Burlington," Joanne said. "He could be far
from home. Oh God . . . look at him, look at his eyes. . . . Maybe we
should let him in. . . ."

"You want to let him in?" Alan said sharply. "You want to let him
in," he repeated.

" . . . maybe give him something to drink, cold water, let him run
some water over his head . . . a cold cloth . . . I could soak a towel in
cold water and . . ."

"You want to let a madman in our house," Alan said.

" . . . his face is all wet, that's saliva hanging down his chin, onto
his chest," Joanne said. "He must be seeing things. Right there, in
front of us, standing right out there . . . he's seeing things, isn't he?
He's hallucinating, isn't he? I wonder what he's seeing."

"Would you like to ask him?" Alan said. "You can ask him. Invite
him in, have a conversation with him. . . . Get the tape-recorder.
You could record it. Go ahead."

"But I . . . I . . ."

She fell silent, hurt.

"I only want to help him," she said.

Alan pulled her back from the window. He walked her into the
hall. "I'm going to call the police. The sheriff's office."

"But . . ."

"Do you want to come upstairs with me, or what? I'm going to call them," he said angrily. "I don't trust you down here. I'm afraid you'll open the door to him."

"I won't open the door to him, but . . ."

" . . . and if he sees you, what if he goes crazy? How can you tell what he's really seeing, when he looks at us or at anything?" Alan spoke in an urgent, reasonable voice. He was a man of moderate height, Joanne's own height, though with his shoes on—she was barefoot—he seemed much taller. He still wore the dark green shirt he had worn to school that day, and the dark flannel trousers, though he had taken his tie off; in the dim, blurred light that came through the gauze curtains his face was shadowy, almost secretive, diminished. The boy, so exposed, drew Joanne's attention back that way, though her husband was arguing with her and gripping her shoulder, hard. She knew she must listen to him. She must pay attention. He rarely spoke like this, rarely with that note of drama, of warning—most of the time he was low-keyed, like Joanne himself, smoothed by early, consistent success (his in his profession, Joanne's in terms of beauty, social achievement, her very womanhood itself) and a sense of rightness, of being and inhabiting what was right. They had both been praised for their ability to be competent, but predictably competent; now, Alan's words seemed to Joanne exactly the words that must be said, that had already been said, in the past, but she balked at hearing them, a small neutral smile interrupting him: " . . . Well, what do you want me to do, then?" he said.

"I don't know. Nothing."

"I still think he's dangerous. What can we do, go to bed? . . . with him out there on the porch singing to himself?"

"He hasn't tried to break in the house."

"What do you want me to do?" Alan asked.

"Nothing."

He paused, staring at her. She saw a complex fusion of dislike, impatience, bewilderment in his face—the eyes narrowed, focussed directly upon her. In the last year or so he had begun to look his age; before that, he'd always seemed like one of his own students, a graduate student, perhaps, though more courteous and alert than the average student. "Nothing?" he said. "Go to bed and leave him out there, and try to sleep? . . . knowing he might break in at any minute?"

"I don't know," Joanne said slowly.

The after-effect of the panic spread through her now: a sensation of chill, the clarity sharp-edged, without emotion. She peered through the door window and there he was, still, yes, still out there, leaning back against the railing, his legs outspread, his head now lowered. His arms hung down limply. Moths fluttered about him but he did not seem to notice. Joanne remembered an incident she had not told Alan about: in Cambridge, down there for a visit not long ago, she had seen a nice-looking boy talking to a parking meter, then yelling at it, trying to strangle it . . . and, only a few hours later, somewhere up the turnpike where she had stopped for gas, she'd seen another boy gesticulating, pleading with, trying to get into a conversation with an ice-cube machine outside a Texaco station. The two incidents returned to her now, gracefully fused. She had half-wished the boys had been in the same dimension with her, not so that they might be sane again—what value had that, when everyone was sane!—but so that they might interpret her. How did she look, to them? What contours had her face, what elegant ghastly proportions her slender body? And her eyes—transformed weirdly by a power she would never dare take on, herself—what beauty might they have, not known to her, and certainly not to her husband? This handsome, alarmed, impatient man who argued with her, this sensitive man whom responsibility had touched so subtly—only a few silvery, curly hairs, only a few slight indentations between his eyebrows—he too was transformed, something quite exotic and unknowable, but there was no way of seeing him, no way in.

"I don't know," she repeated, staring.

Alan pushed her away, in disgust, and started up the stairs. "I'll call the sheriff's office," he said. "I've had enough of this for one night, God damn it—"

Joanne saw the boy lurch forward. He took a few steps toward the door, as if to call Alan back, then he reeled around and faced the opposite way, mumbling to himself. He was still rocking, not quite forward and back; not from right to left, either; but in a clumsy, uncertain, but stubborn rhythm, like a child imitating someone he is watching closely, trying to get the movements correct. Then he bounded off the veranda, down the steps, and ran away—across the weedy front yard, toward the driveway. Joanne could see his blond hair several seconds after the rest of him seemed to disintegrate.

"Alan," she called. "Alan. . . . Alan, wait. Alan? He's gone."

At first Alan did not reply; she was afraid he had called the sheriff.
"Alan . . .? Alan, he's gone," she said triumphantly. "He's gone."
"Is he gone?" Alan asked.

He stood at the top of the stairs, crouching in order to look down.
He sounded a little embarrassed. "Is he gone?"

"He ran out toward the road."

"What did he . . . ? What did he do, just run away suddenly?"
Alan asked, doubtfully. "Out toward the road?"

"Yes, he's gone."

Alan came back downstairs, cautiously. He opened the front door,
leaned out, looked from side to side. Joanne pushed past him.
Barefoot, she stood on the veranda, looking out into the darkness.
She waved a moth away from her face. Alan muttered something
about the surprise of it, the shock of someone banging on the door
like that . . . at one-thirty in the morning . . . and he'd been so tired,
so exhausted, from committee meetings that day . . . what could you
expect of him, what had she expected? She did not make sense of
this, but was watching to see if the boy might appear: first the
glimmer of the hair, she would catch sight of that first. Running back
the driveway, from the road. Running in his stockinged feet. Crying,
gesturing, exploding into laughter . . . so mysterious, the bearer of
so mysterious a message, and now so hopelessly lost!

"What did you care if he was dangerous or not," Alan said sullenly.
"You had nothing to lose."

" . . . It's all right," Joanne said. She had begun to shiver. Still,
she felt no emotion, only that clarity, as if someone had struck her
and she had not fallen, but remained upright, watchful. "He's gone.
There isn't even anything to show he was here."

Alan straightened the wicker chair, as if to correct her. But he said
nothing.

"Had you dialed the sheriff?" she asked.

"What difference does it make?"

"When we were in London that time, and walking through the
subway, at Hyde Park Corner, you were afraid of that old woman,"
Joanne said softly. "Remember? That old alcoholic woman with the
market bags, and the scarves tied around her neck. . . ."

"I don't remember any woman," Alan said.

"She asked us for something, we couldn't understand what she
was saying."

"She wanted money."

"Did she? I don't know, I don't know what she wanted," Joanne said. "You were afraid of her. . . ."

Alan went back inside, and after a few minutes she followed him. She latched the screen door and locked the inside door.

She switched off the porch light. Now she could see clearly across the grassy front lawn to the ridge of trees that lined the driveway. First she would catch sight of the blond hair, a glowing patch of light . . . then the body would take shape out of the confused shadows. . . .

A visitation out of the night. A ghostly lover.

"How can we know what any of them want from us?" she called out to her husband.

But Alan had gone upstairs. He had turned on the creaky hot-water faucet in the bathroom and could not possibly have heard her.

She went to bed and slept, and dreamt fitfully about the boy. The rolling eyes, the agonized expression, the shrill jabbering in a language she could not comprehend: and the strange beauty in him. Only she could see it, that beauty. Alan could not see it, the boy himself could not . . . only she understood.

The next day she was haunted by his image. She did not think of him, the young man himself; in a sense he had not existed. She saw in her mind's eye his ghostly image, she tried to summon it back, tried to see it more clearly. Her heart raced. He had come out of the night to her . . . to her and Alan. Had it meant anything? What had it meant?

She wondered, once again, how she might have appeared to him—whether he had caught sight of her.

But she did not really think about him. And just before dinner Alan came into the kitchen and thrust something at her—the Burlington newspaper, which he had folded back. His hands were shaking.

"What? What is it?" Joanne asked sharply.

She found herself staring at the familiar print of the newspaper, at first not understanding what the headline meant. The news item was on page 9, headlined HITCH-HIKER IN CRITICAL CONDITION. An unidentified young man, about twenty-one years old, weighing about 140 pounds, had been hit by a truck heading south on the turnpike near Beulah, early that morning—he had evidently wandered onto the turnpike in a daze. *Not yet identified. Believed to have been under the influence of drugs.* Joanne read the brief article twice, began it a third time, then broke off and stared at the dancing newsprint. Had it been real, her dream of a boy, her forlorn pitying rush of love . . . ?

Alan took the paper from her. His face was flushed with a peculiar triumph. "There," he said. "*There.* You had your way, didn't you?"

Joanne stared at him. "Why did you show this to me?" she said. "What has this got to do with me?—with either of us?"

He let the paper fall and walked away; she heard his footsteps overhead. After a long moment Joanne picked the paper up, turned it back to page one, and lay it on the cane-back chair by the rear door, where they kept the papers until Alan got rid of them each week. She was reasonably sure he would not accuse her of anything— would not, probably, ever speak of the boy again.

sentimental Journey

Dear Warren, wrote Annie Quirt on the eve of her thirty-first birthday, *I wonder if you remember me . . . ? I don't really care, I think I am writing to you because I can't sleep tonight, because I have been thinking of you, almost obsessed with memories of you.* . . . Obsessed? Annie wondered if that did not sound too extreme; even pathological. But it was true. She crushed out her cigarette and wrote: *I remember you so vividly . . . the khaki jacket from Army Surplus, worn at the elbows . . . those tennis shoes of yours that came to your ankles and were sometimes unlaced, or was it that the laces had broken and you'd knotted them . . . ? I remember you hunched over your desk, taking notes in a big loose-leaf notebook like the kind high school students use. . . . You were so earnest, so serious, so hard-working, unlike the others, unlike certain friends of* `` *yours who didn't deserve your friendship and who took advantage of you.* Annie was writing on plain sheets of paper, hurriedly, almost feverishly, not stopping to read what she had written. She felt rather sick but such feelings did not count: she had vowed, in this new phase of her life, to transcend and to obliterate the merely physical. *You were so good, Warren. I think that was it. So good. Innocent . . . loyal . . . sweet . . . funny. . . . You had a temper, I remember that, I remember how angry you got with Tony, once, when he was drunk and arguing stupidly about . . . about what? . . . how the great philosophers were only expressing the prejudices of their eras? . . . and you rejected what he said, you were truly angry, and passionate, and I realized for the first time the depth of your character. . . .* How crude, how pathetic! Annie lit another cigarette and turned over the page and continued the letter. She knew her words were absurd, grotesquely sentimental; she knew that Warren, even sweet little Warren Breck, would probably laugh at them; she knew, even as she wrote, her hand aching, that she would not dare mail the letter. Nevertheless she wrote, as quickly as possible, not allowing herself time to think. The emotion that was coursing through her was too powerful to contain. It was like grief, somehow concentrated in her eyes and throat and upper chest. She felt like crying. She had been crying, earlier. Ugly wracking sobs, dry sobs, that were incomprehensible. *I knew so little about life then, about the value of a genuine friendship . . . I didn't have time for such things . . . I was always in a hurry, in a rush, it took me a long time to see how shallow a person Tony was, and how I had wasted. . . .* Ten years ago! A decade! Could it be possible, a decade had passed and Annie Quirt, who had always imagined herself so tough and sly and independent, who had been enormously self-confident because of her looks, and the great good luck of her girlhood, was writing to a boy she hardly remembered, a friend of the boy she had loved in college, or had deluded herself into believing she loved . . . ? Annie laughed aloud. She was bent over the kitchen table, a cigarette burning in her left hand, her hair falling into her eyes. The light was poor; she hadn't wanted to put the over-head light on, for fear of attracting her sister's attention; as she wrote a fluid, dancing blur followed her words. *It's 2 AM and I've given up trying to sleep. Earlier tonight I was leafing through some of my college books, paperbacks I hadn't looked at for a decade, and I came across something you had written . . . at the back of* The Republic. . . *you couldn't remember, couldn't possibly remember . . . we must have been joking around. . . . That 8 AM class on the top floor of Brennan Hall, us in the back row, Dr. Hotchkiss with his yellow-white hair like a wig and his stammer when he got excited . . . remember, you and he argued, you were the only person in the class he respected, I think. I know. I was too ignorant to appreciate. . . .* She looked up, startled. A footstep? A soft thudding sound of some kind? She made a gesture to crush out the cigarette; it would put her at a disadvantage, if Jean saw her smoking when she had stated her intention to quit. But the kitchen was smoky anyway. . . . *I remember a day in early spring, at that ugly Victorian mansion you and the others rented rooms in, remember? . . . it was four storeys high, painted a ghastly red-orange, the brick was crumbling, most of the windows in the basement were broken. . . . Tony and Dave and that girl with the braids, the nursing student, and I, do you remember? . . . knocked on your door and disturbed you studying . . . you had an exam in organic chemistry the next morning, you sitting at your desk bare-chested . . . so pale! . . . I remember how pale you were! it was hot in the room, the radiators couldn't be turned off. We wanted you to come with us out to, what was that place, Erlich's, for a beer. . . . You seemed so lonely then, so alone. I knew you wanted to come with us but at the same time you had to study, I could see how torn you were, I told Tony to leave you alone, to stop bullying you. . . . And then it was the end of the semester: then it was graduation: every-thing was over and we never saw each other again.* What if Warren were married? It was entirely possible. It was even rather likely. He had been shy, almost to the point of pain; but he had been quite normal. At one of the rare parties he'd attended, once, he had danced with Annie and had engaged her in a long earnest confused conversation, and his feeling for her had been plain, almost embar-rassingly obvious. She had liked him well enough, as a minor per-sonage in the exciting drama of her life; but she had not felt, really, any affection for him at the time. All her energies had gone into love: into that relationship with Tony. She had not even valued her friendships with girls she had known for years, during that time. How she disliked herself, that earlier self !—how richly she de-served the various disappointments that had followed! *I think I am writing, Warren, just to reach out to you, to say hello, I don't expect you to reply, I want only . . . I would like . . . what do I want? . . . just to know if you're alive, and happy, and if your plans for medical school worked out. . . . I assume they did. Of course they did. You are probably established now and practicing medicine and probably you are married also, and your wife will resent this letter; I advise you just to scan it and think of me, of Annie Quirt, the red-head, remember? . . . Tony Engel's girl? . . . and then rip the letter up, throw it away. . . .*

"Annie?"

She looked around, startled. It was Jean in her night-gown, barefooted; her older sister Jean blinking at her. Annie saw, but chose not to interpret, her sister's look of apprehension.

"What are you—? Are you writing something? I saw the light on, I noticed your bed was empty—"

"I'm writing a letter," Annie said quietly.

"A letter?"

"Yes, a letter. To a friend. I have friends, I write letters to them occasionally; do you mind? I didn't think I was disturbing you."

Jean relaxed visibly. She tried to smile.

"Of course you weren't disturbing me, Annie, I just woke up and wondered and for a moment . . . for a moment I was, you know, a little worried."

"You were worried," Annie repeated. She and Jean stared at each other for a long moment. At such times Annie kept her expression stiff and neutral: she was Jean's baby sister, she and Jean had always liked each other, it was not Jean she disliked. In fact, in a way, she rather liked Jean's sisterliness—she liked being fussed over, worried over, grieved over, to a certain extent. She did appreciate Jean's generosity, leaving her husband and three children for more than a week, just to stay with Annie in Annie's small, crowded, depressing apartment. But if she thought of Jean and of Jean's love, if she thought of Jean's undisguised sorrow that first day, she might break down; she might succumb to those dry wracking sobs. And this would distress her sister all the more. "But why should you be worried?" she said calmly. "We've been over this already. I am perfectly well now . . . I've regained my old sense of, what was it? . . . not humor but skepticism, cynicism . . . or sin? My sense of sin," she said, smiling broadly. "Yes. I've regained it. So you can stop worrying. You can go back home to your loving husband and your beautiful children, you can dismiss the babysitter, you can move back into your enviable life . . . right? Because Annie has regained her sense of sin and knows right from wrong now and has learnt her lesson well."

"Who are you writing to, Annie?" Jean asked. She stepped forward though she must have known Annie would cover the sheets of paper with her arms, to hide them; Annie did this without really thinking, as a reflex. It was an insulting gesture but Jean did not appear to mind. " . . . To *him?*"

"No," Annie said quickly, curtly.

"Well, I. . . . As long as. . . . I'm glad, I mean, that . . ."

"Of course I'm not writing to *him*," Annie said angrily. Her voice was trembling. "He's gone, he's forgotten. He's dead. To me he's dead. *Dead.* . . . No, I'm writing to a friend, an old friend. I'm writing to someone you don't know. A friend. From college. One of the few worthwhile . . . one of the . . . He doesn't know about my life now but if he did he wouldn't judge, he liked me for myself, for . . . for myself . . . he wouldn't judge. . . . Just a friend, Jean, nobody you know or have to concern yourself with. All right?"

"Yes. All right," Jean said softly.

—◆—◆—

Priscilla Ann Quirt, she was: in her innermost heart did she love herself too dearly, or despise herself ? An urbane, courteous young doctor at the Mental Health Clinic of the university where Annie had done graduate work, some years ago, had spoken of her poor *self-image.* She did not value herself enough, he believed. Wasn't it a pity, he said, covertly eying her, or pretending to covertly eye her in order to flatter her, when she was obviously very intelligent?— and very attractive as well. Wasn't it a pity, he said, that she could not adjust her inner vision of herself, to bring it more in line with reality?

" . . . bring it more in line with reality," Annie repeated. She frowned. She was not playing the role of a near-mute, disingenuous girl; she was consciously playing at playing a role, in order to show this wise bastard what she thought of him. "Yes. I will try. *Bring my inner vision more in line with reality.*"

"You don't approve of yourself," he said, reddening. "There's nothing wrong with you—with your mind. The drugs scared you and that's quite natural, in fact that's a good thing—you're too sensitive for anything so crude. Your system can't take it. But there's nothing wrong with your mind, with your sanity; with what we call sanity. Do you understand? It's almost as if you have a problem of vision, of measurement . . . from the inside you see one image of yourself, but no one else sees that image. You have to work hard, don't you?—to make other people see that image."

"Yes," Annie said. "All right."

"All right what?"

"I agree, I see your point, I'm impressed with your insight and kindliness and wisdom. I'm very grateful," Annie said.

He stared at her. For a while he said nothing.

"I'm very grateful but I have to leave now," Annie said. "I have a class. I'm teaching a class. If you won't give me another prescription for those pills—"

"No. I won't."

"—then I have nothing more to say, or to ask of you."

As she opened the door she heard him say something. But when she turned, smiling anxiously, for an instant almost vulnerable— when she turned, he was merely staring at her, blank-faced, assessing. His eye dropped to her hips, to the long stretch of thigh outlined by the tight jeans she wore, then to her legs, her leather boots, to the floor. And that was that.

Yet others told her she was egotistical: she valued herself too much, could never love anyone as she loved herself. Her image of herself was exaggerated, magnified. Jean would never have accused her of such self-love, nor would her mother—who loved Annie best, in that desperate, hopeless, rather exotic way in which mothers love certain children, knowing their love is misplaced; but her father had told her, several times. Her father was an unusual man—the owner of a small but fairly profitable dairy farm who was also a lay-minister and also a part-time music instructor in the county public schools. He was abrupt, outspoken, with a temper as bad as Annie's; she supposed she had inherited it from him, along with his tall athletic frame and his too-bright red hair and pale, creamy-pale complexion. "You love yourself too much," he had said. Twelve years old at the time, Annie had been weeping because she was so tall. Five feet eight and a half. And growing, always growing. Growing! She wept because she was the tallest student in her class and because she was the smartest student, because she had no friends, because she felt superior to the friends she had, and could not resist making wise remarks about them; she wept because her skin had broken out and her fantasies of cold, hard, careless beauty were being mocked. She locked herself in the bathroom and stared at her image, weeping angrily, hopelessly. She hated her body, her small hard breasts!— hated them. She hated her red hair, which drew all eyes to it. Even on the street, even on the Greyhound bus, she felt people look at her—adults, not her classmates, grown men and women who should have ignored her, since she was still a child. Men stared, especially. Men stared. And she hated them, hated their watchfulness—though at times she courted it—at times she hated them for watching her and then, as she drew closer, losing interest in her. *Too young,* they might have thought. *Not pretty enough,* they might have thought. She ran home filled with an inexplicable, senseless rage—locked herself in the bathroom and wept. Her father shouted at her to unlock the door. "You love yourself too much, it's a kind of sickness," he said in distaste. "What does it matter how tall you are?—or if you have pimples? What does it matter to anyone except you? The world exists, you know, apart from you." For several years they had battled—she had hated him, had really hated him; now, an adult, she recalled her hatred with amazement and almost with a kind of pride, that she had been capable of such passion. She had not understood her father, really. She had thought it unjust that he should accuse her of loving herself when she despised herself, wished to be anyone except Annie Quirt, anyone, any other girl; wasn't that proof of her innocence? She had thought that contentment was an indication of self-esteem, not knowing that discontent, of the kind that raged in her, was far more egotistical.

"Who should I love, then?" she said, sneering. "You?—Mother? Jean? Billy? —*God?*"

"You might begin with any of us," he said, mildly, "and work your way up to God."

She had not understood him then when he spoke like that, nor did she understand him now. Her father's faith embarrassed her. It was so calm, so effortless, it so lacked the kind of combative spirit she had witnessed in others—in other "believers"—that she could not relate to it at all. So she never referred to it, and she tried not to think of it. About the self-love, though, she believed he might be right. Someday she must write a letter home, a spare ascetic letter, and tell him he was right after all—that should please him.

"What does it matter, whether we love or hate ourselves," she said, talking to herself as she sometimes did, making dinner one evening a few days after her sister had left. " . . . if the results are identical. . . "

Her thirty-first birthday had come and gone. Now she was into her thirty-second year. She would have liked to feel something—a sense of panic, of loss. Instead she felt only that queer suspension, which she had begun to feel some years earlier, past the highest point of her adolescent spirit, her rather ruthless idealism—a queer numb suspension, as if she were waiting for something to happen without any faith that it would happen. Still, she must wait.

The doorbell rang. When she went to open it, rather timidly, she saw that it was no one she knew—it was Warren Breck.

—◆—◆—

"Of course I didn't forget you. Never. How could I forget you . . . ?" he said, smiling. He shook his head as if with the absurdity of the idea. "And your letter, your lovely marvelous letter . . . your letter came at a crucial time in my life, how did you know? . . . how could you have known what it would mean to me?"

They had been holding hands, almost gripping each other's hands. Annie knew she had gone white, deathly pale. In this man's presence she no longer felt familiar to herself, she felt estranged, unpleasantly excited, she would not help staring and staring at him. She loved him. She *loved* him. He was the Warren Breck of ten years ago, his brown hair cut, still, in the same styleless fashion; the lenses of his glasses thick, so that his pale brown eyes were enlarged, and looked appealing, like a child's eyes; his clothes not quite the same clothes but just as ill-fitting—a dark brown plaid sports coat and dark brown trousers, a white cotton shirt of the kind boys wore, for play, the neck stretched from having been pulled over his head many times. He had a wristwatch that was rather fashionable, however—a thick leather band with more than one buckle, like something a motorcyclist might wear. It gave his long, slender, rather bony hands a look of dramatic strength.

They held hands and talked. They talked for hours. She offered him dinner—he tried to eat but was too excited—she was too excited—so she offered him wine and he drank several glasses, distractedly, all the while staring at her. His voice was high, child-like, absolutely the voice of a decade ago, when he had raised it to question Dr. Hotchkiss or Tony or one of the others, frail in texture and yet quite fearless, in a way superbly confident. She remembered him, she remembered him so clearly! She kept interrupting him to laugh, to kiss him on the cheek, to squeeze his hand and his arm gaily, with an almost frantic triumph. He had come to her—he had actually come to her. To *her*. He must have half-loved her, as she had sensed. But he had been too timid to approach her. Too shy, beside his friend Tony. Still, he must have sensed how she had liked him . . . how very fond she'd been of him . . . perhaps in a way she had loved him, had loved him all along. . . . Hadn't she kissed him once, at a party? Drunk, all of them, and noisy, and completely happy—hadn't she kissed poor Warren Breck goodnight, despite his obvious embarrassment and the alarm and resentment of the poor plain girl he was with? She had loved him all along, she believed. All those years.

"Maybe you really did sense that I'd come to a crisis in my life," Warren said. "I know it's ridiculous, but . . . but why not ? There are mystical connections between people sometimes . . . between people who are, you know, sympathetic with each other. There are these connections, I'm sure. As a scientist and a rationalist I'm opposed to such things, even to entertaining them," he said, grinning, "but as a human being . . . as one who has experienced certain coincidences, certain small miracles. . . . Do you think it might be possible, Annie?"

"Yes? What? That I sensed—?"

"That I communicated with you somehow—"

"Yes, I think it's true," Annie said passionately. "I know it's true."

They kissed. Both were trembling. Annie caught her breath, suddenly frightened, awkward as a young girl; for an instant she seemed not to know how to kiss, where to place her lips. She was so intensely aware of him. He was warm, nervous, giddy from the wine, as she was, tense, extremely self-conscious. *She loved him. And she was kissing him.*

"I know it's true," Annie whispered.

"Nothing much has happened to me," Annie said slowly, as if she were telling the truth; as if the truth rather astonished her. "I'm the same person I was at the age of twenty-one. Really, I'm the same as I was at the age of . . . of fifteen or twelve. Aren't you? Yes? I thought so. Nothing much has happened, it's as if I've been running in place for years," she said dreamily.

"You look exactly the same," Warren said. His voice was not so shrill now; he sounded loving. "You're even more beautiful, maybe. I used to stare at your hair, watch the sunlight in it, it was hypnotic,

so many angles of light . . . hypnotic. *He* didn't appreciate you
enough, didn't value you enough."

Annie chose not to pursue that subject.

They lay together in Annie's narrow bed. Without his glasses
Warren looked even younger. There was something ethereal about
his face: the large solemn eyes, the thin lips which did not quite close
over his front teeth, the slightly receding chin. Strange, that she
should have thought him homely, once—he was sweet-faced, appealing, utterly delightful. She took his face in her hands and kissed
him. She could not resist kissing him, like that; could not resist
touching him. He was grateful for affection, like a puppy. As a lover
he was rather nervous, at times frantic—but Annie did not care, she
understood his anxiety and his excitement—they must become
better acquainted with each other, with each other's bodies—and
hadn't he been almost monastic for years?—so she did not care, it
really did not matter to her. Love forgave such things. Love did not
even notice such things. They lay together, in each other's arms,
delighted as children, giggling, whispering, sharing secrets, reminiscing. Was it a dream?—it was so lovely! It was so perfect. Annie
slept, and woke, and moved into his arms; and slept again; and,
waking, they tried to make love, self-consciously; and then they lay
together like conspirators, in a kind of dream, contained within the
dream, not wishing to wake. Again and again one of them would
exclaim: "It's incredible—seeing you again. I can hardly believe it. A
miracle, isn't it? A miracle?"

He had brought a single large suitcase that contained all his
"meaningful" belongings. Books and notebooks, mainly, but some
clothes as well. He left Lake City, Florida, on the very day that
Annie's letter had arrived: she had looked up his parents' address in
the Rochester, New York telephone book at the main library, had
sent it there, asking them to forward it. Though the letter had been
written in a feverish haste she had, the next morning, calmly put it
into an envelope without rereading it, drove to the library, calmly
and deliberately addressed the envelope, and mailed it within the
hour. And Warren's parents had forwarded it to him in Lake City
. . . and so he had come to her, making the long trip in two days. "I
didn't even want to take time to write back," he said. "I just had to
get here. To you."

"I love you," Annie whispered, starting to cry.

Like newlyweds, they were, those first several days. There was no question of Warren staying elsewhere—she had insisted he move in with her. And he had seemed to expect that. Annie's apartment was on the sixth floor of an undistinguished stucco building on the very border of an excellent residential neighborhood, and not far from one of the city's larger parks. Advertised as a "luxury" apartment, it was really quite ordinary, even shabby; and it was very small. A narrow bedroom looking out upon a wall some fifteen feet away, a living room with a tiny "dining area", a kitchen so small that Annie could make meals standing in one place, merely bending and stretching; a windowless, depressing bathroom that was also used for the cats' litter. When Jean had stayed with her it had been claustrophobic, but with Warren it seemed rather cozy. If they bumped into each other, if they got in each other's way, they merely hugged and kissed and laughed greedily.

The second evening, Warren made dinner: he'd gone out to buy the very best fresh fish available in the city, and some vegetables at an open-air market, and two bottles of French wine, and some crusty rolls at a French bakery. Annie was troubled, that he should spend so much money. But he merely laughed, saying that this was their honeymoon, wasn't it?—and they must celebrate.

The dinner was excellent. Annie believed it was excellent—she said so, repeatedly—but in fact she hardly tasted it. She was watching her lover, studying him; she could not help wondering at the miracle that had come into her life. *He was exactly as she remembered.* Perhaps his hair was a little thinner. She noticed that, now. And his manner was at times highly excitable, almost frantic. He perspired easily. The cats made him nervous, so Annie put them both in the bathroom, where they yowled and scratched against the door. "I've never understood pets, the politics of owning pets," Warren said, smiling self-consciously. "I just can't see it, you know—living intimately with animals—even if it's to combat loneliness. But your cats are beautiful creatures," he said quickly. "The long-haired one especially—beautiful, like you. Like you." The sweet gravity with which he spoke reminded Annie sharply of the Warren of ten years ago, who had discussed philosophical and political subjects with such earnestness, and at such length, refusing to acknowledge his listeners' wandering attention. He had done them all the honor, Annie saw now, of presuming them to be his equals.

Dinner began at 7 and lasted until after 10. They finished both bottles of wine and opened another, a gift bottle someone had brought Annie last fall; they held hands, talked and talked and talked, always circling back to their undergraduate years, to their friends and acquaintances and professors, to the rooms they had rented, the places they had frequented, the old, enormous, drafty library—which had been replaced by a new one, Annie told Warren, all glass and steel; did he know? He didn't know. He hadn't been back, he said, since the day of commencement.

And then there were the ten years to be accounted for.

Well, her life was—it was a fairly ordinary life, she believed. Rich, varied, adventurous—though not too adventurous—not *too* adventurous, like the lives of certain people she had known; young men and a few young women who had cracked up, died of overdoses or by more deliberate means—but—but she hadn't known many such people, of course. Hadn't known them well. "My own life has been rather conventional," she said. Warren stared at her lovingly. He did not blink, did not register any emotion at all, when she said this. Perhaps he was not even listening.

Annie went on to say, haltingly, that she hadn't married—hadn't wanted to marry—had had no interest in marriage at all. Her relationship with Tony had not lasted; Tony was too shallow, didn't know what he wanted to do with his life, they had quarrelled over some trivial subject and parted and lost contact with each other . . . the last she had heard, he was in California. Doing what?—she didn't know.

Warren shook his head slowly. He didn't know either, and didn't care. "That son of a bitch never appreciated you," he said softly.

But Tony no longer mattered, Annie said. She never thought of him. Never. Nine years had passed—a small lifetime—so much had happened to her—so many people had drifted into her life, had become temporarily entangled with her—though not *too* entangled, she said quickly; she had always been, well, rather detached—like Warren himself, she had always kept a certain intellectual distance between herself and the world. . . . After graduation she had gone to England and Europe for a year, had wandered around, with Tony, and then they had quarrelled and there had been other friends—did he remember Janice?—yes, he would remember her, they had been in some of the same classes—one of Annie's closest, dearest friends—and then Annie had returned to the States, had studied for a Master's degree in art history at the University of Michigan—had liked—*loved*—Ann Arbor; had come close to marrying a man there but at the last minute decided against him—decided against marriage itself. She had made a few close friends in Ann Arbor and still kept in touch with them. The girls especially: a very nice girl named Fern Enright to whom she still wrote, though not so often, of course, as she should write. (It was so easy, wasn't it, to lose touch?—all along the way? One stage of life and then another and another, always people attached to each of these stages who are irreplaceable and dear yet somehow flimsy, precarious: so easily lost. Did Warren agree? Yes?)

Well, she had liked Ann Arbor very much. At least at first. Of course there were unhappy, desperate people there, really suicidal people, in the mid-6o's, and she had had to keep herself clear of them. Such fools, Annie said, her mouth twisting as she recalled certain incidents and then dismissed them, hoping Warren would not question her. He merely smiled, to show his interest; he asked no questions.

She was friendly with a few people but kept herself detached from others, as always: all her life she'd been rather alone. Not lonely but *alone*. She had been a serious student in graduate school—quite different from her undergraduate behavior—and had done a lengthy study of the art of Isabel Bishop, a fine painter. Was Warren familiar with Isabel Bishop's work? No? Well, she was a fine American artist, one of the outstanding "urban realists" of the Thirties—not so well known as she should be, Annie believed—of course not a *great* artist, that could not be claimed, but an excellent one. At the same time, Annie said, as if anticipating a query from Warren—who was, in fact, simply smiling at her—her æsthetic principles were really more international, more "modernist"—she sympathized with the American Scene painters and their loving, meticulous work—their noble attempt to create a distinctly American tradition, but imaginatively she was more deeply engaged, perhaps, by—by the others—by Abstract Expressionism, still—though it was now denounced, and though people liked to say they were now bored by Pollock, she still felt a genuine excitement standing before his canvases— And— And, well, she said with a slightly annoyed smile, since Warren was not responding at all, after Ann Arbor she had

tried to paint for awhile without luck and had done a little part-time
teaching—at a small college—and—and that hadn't worked out, the
administration was terribly intolerant—narrow-minded—so she
had quit and come here and had been working at a gallery
downtown—a promising job, it had seemed—the Hunter Gallery
dealt with some fine work—a promising job that had turned sour,
since Annie had been used simply as a receptionist and clerk
and secretary and clean-up girl—bossed around, treated
patronizingly—and paid very little for the surprisingly long hours
she worked. So she had quit. Had quit a few weeks ago. And—

But Warren was not listening. Had not been listening.

He stared at her forearm and touched it lightly with his finger.

"What's this, Annie?" he said. "Did you hurt yourself?"

Annie glanced at the scar and moved her arm away. "It's nothing.
An accident."

"An accident. How?"

"I said an accident," Annie snapped.

Warren blinked. He mumbled an apology—he had not meant to
be rude. Of course it was none of his business.

Annie said nothing and poured more wine into their glasses.
Might as well finish the bottle. Their third. She looked at him and
smiled, forced herself to smile, and he smiled at once, eagerly. He
was drunk: but as a child might be drunk, innocent and disheveled.
She loved him. She had called him to her, and he had come. Out of
the past he had come in obedience to her. In obedience to love. She
loved him, loved him. Certainly. Obviously. Otherwise why was he
here, why were they drinking together, why was she smiling at
him . . . ?

Begin with Warren, then, she thought. *Begin with Warren and
work your way upward to God.*

In the morning they made love again, and again it was not quite
right. Warren was breathless, clumsy, exasperated. He labored
above her with his eyes shut tight as if in terror of their flying apart.
"I love you, love you," he said almost angrily.

"I love *you*," Annie wept.

She rose from the sweaty sheets and went into the bathroom to

shower and he remained there, dozing. In her bed. His head damp
on her pillow.

She would never be alone again.

That day she was oddly exhausted. It tired her to talk to Warren,
as if they had been laboring together to comprehend something for
hours, for days, and had failed, and yet could not stop. He was
sweet—she adored him—and yet why didn't he shave, why didn't
he shower?—why did he stay so close? He showed no inclination to
leave the apartment. He turned on the radio and moved the dial
slowly from side to side, listening to a station for a few minutes, then
moving on. At all times there was a guileless half-smile on his face
like something crudely sketched on a blank sheet of paper.

The telephone rang and Annie spoke hurriedly and apologetically, explaining she was busy. Warren's eyebrows rose; he listened
closely to what she said, but never asked her, afterward, who had
called. When she asked him if he would like to go out—to the Art
Institute, to a movie, to visit friends of hers, he did not seem very
interested.

"I'm content here," he said, smiling. "It's paradise, here."

"But—wouldn't you like some fresh air?"

"I'm perfectly content here, Annie."

She went out to buy groceries. She had to get out of the apartment.

Walking along Annie rehearsed a conversation: *Aren't you a
doctor, Warren? What has happened? Didn't you go to medical
school?—Aren't you a genius? What is happening—? Why are you
here?* Her legs felt long and awkward as stilts. Her head rang with
words. It was raining and she had rushed out with no umbrella or
raincoat, wearing only a thin cotton shirt and blue jeans and sneakers
so worn that her smallest toes peeped through. She began to cry
again and her tears mixed with the rain.

"I love him," she said. "I do love him. . . . I must love him."

She walked a half-mile to the park. Something was wrong, gravely
wrong, but it must be articulated before she could deal with it. From
the few vague things Warren had said about his present life, she
judged that he had no work—hadn't finished medical school—
perhaps he hadn't even gone to medical school?—she didn't dare
ask. She didn't want to hurt his feelings; and she had the idea that he
wasn't quite the Warren she recalled—his thinking processes had

atrophied somewhat. But probably that was her imagination. He had always been shy, clumsy, not very good with conversation, at times almost mute: poor Warren!

"Love, love, love. . . ."

She struck her hands together, half-fisted, prayerlike.

Skirting the playground area, which was deserted this afternoon, Annie happened to see a figure across the way—a man—moving slowly and sluggishly in the direction of the woods. In a streaked trenchcoat, head bowed. He did not turn, did not notice her. She strode by. On an ordinary day the park was filled with young mothers and hordes of children, white and black, and a few couples, and straggling indeterminate figures, mostly male, who walked along the wide gravelled paths in utter isolation, like creatures blundering through a single, singular dream, which could not be shared with anyone else. In poor weather there were no young mothers, no children, but often the solitary people showed up— often, Annie was one of them—head bowed, heart pumping, mind racing with perpetual unanswerable shouts: *What do I do now? What now? Now? I had wanted a life so different*— Nearly six feet tall, slender but not slight, sharp-eyed, quick, her red hair falling straight to her shoulders, Annie must have seemed intimidating to anyone who saw her; at any rate, none of the other solitary wanderers ever approached her.

That day she went to a neighborhood library and, sitting on the floor by the shelves of art books, spent an hour or more looking through books—turning pages quickly, desperately—studying Van Gogh's drawings and Cezanne's landscapes and crude, touching woodcuts by anonymous Germans of the late medieval period— then paging quickly again, as if she were looking for something specific, though she could not have said what it was. Her legs ached; she must leave; Warren was waiting for her; she had not yet done the grocery shopping. . . . Then, by accident, she discovered what she must have been seeking: her breath was drawn sharply inward when she came upon the watercolors of Nolde, beautiful, indefinable, utterly perfect. *Here,* she thought simply.

At six the library closed and she returned to the apartment and saw that there was no one there—no one. "Warren?" she called. Her voice lifted in astonishment. "Warren?"

She set the bag of groceries down. "Warren . . . ?"

The apartment was empty. Even the cats were gone. She called them—called them in a voice that wailed absurdly. The bathroom window was open, and there was no screen; Warren must have opened the window deliberately so that the cats could get out, along the ledge, down the fire escape. They had both been strays, at times she had disliked the nuisance of having them in so small a place, but she had been very fond of them.

Annie was leaning out the window, calling the cats, when she felt a hand on her back.

—◆—◆—

"I thought maybe, you know, they stopped you on the street . . . made you come to the station for questioning. I thought maybe something had gone wrong. Something serious."

"No. No, Warren."

"—because you were gone so long."

"No."

"You were gone for hours," he said accusingly. "You must not love me, you must have been lying."

"I love you, Warren."

"They didn't arrest you? They didn't trace the car and take you to the station and interrogate you and force you to betray me? —Because they can do anything they want, anything. And you're a woman. They could have hurt you and forced you to betray me and then let you come back here—to put me off my guard."

Annie shook her head. "I didn't—there was no one— Nothing happened."

"But you must not love me" he said. "Otherwise you wouldn't have stayed away so long."

He took off his glasses and rubbed his eyes and made a tired, exasperated noise. Annie had to go to him, had to put her arms around him and kiss him. Still he was hurt, sullen; he did not respond.

"You're not much different from *her*," he muttered.

"Who do you mean, Warren?" Annie asked carefully.

He shrugged his shoulders. ". . . leave the house to go shopping, stay away for hours . . . days . . . invent all kinds of insulting excuses . . . any fool could interpret their true meaning. What if I get

hungry? I'm normal, a normal human being, I need to eat like
anyone else . . . what if there's no food in the house and I get
hungry? She stayed away for days. She thought she could hide.
Pathetic bitch," he said softly.

Annie stood beside him, unable to move. She wanted to walk
away but could not. If she embraced him more enthusiastically, if
she brushed the messy strands of hair out of his eyes, and kissed him,
everything might be restored; but she could not move.

"Who are you talking about, Warren?" she said.

"My son would have been three years old," he said suddenly.
"What day is this? Where's a calendar? —Yes, see, it's the 14th
today, he would have been three years old on the 15th, I have an
excellent memory for dates and he was born on the 15th of
August—but— But—"

He began to cry. His glasses fell into his lap, then to the floor. He
cried, his face screwed up like a baby's, and Annie stood above him
staring, blank, frozen.

"—my son—she tried to—they all tried to—sneaking behind my
back, planting evidence against me—eavesdropping—spying—at
the police station she uncovered herself—the slut—they saw her for
what she was—and the burns on the baby—*she* did it—she lied—
her family lied— Is she in touch with you, Annie, was she someone
we both knew?—from college? Were you talking on the telephone
with her, Annie, is that why you were gone so long?"

"No, no."

"Are you telling the truth, Annie, or—"

"I'm telling the truth, Warren."

He looked up at her. Not so young now, and yet curiously
childlike: his skin was grayish, drawn, his brown eyes were blood-
shot and opaque as marbles. Annie wondered if he could see her. He
was nearly blind without his glasses.

"Annie," he whispered, taking her cold hand, "Annie . . . you're
so beautiful, so beautiful. . . . I remember from years ago, how
beautiful you were, you are, I love you so much and I need you, you
won't betray me, will you? . . . So beautiful," he said, blinking up at
her. "Tony didn't appreciate you. The bastard. That one week, you
thought you were pregnant, do you remember? . . . and he was
drunk for three days straight and wouldn't leave my room, said he

was holing up there, wouldn't come to the telephone when you called, the bastard . . . wouldn't let me study in peace . . . none of you let me study in peace . . . but I didn't mind, I liked you all . . . envied you. . . . I loved *you*, Annie Quirt," he said dramatically, gazing up at her with those glistening myopic eyes, "and I will love you the rest of my life."

—◆—◆—

"I'm in trouble. I'm in bad trouble."

"But I can't talk now, Annie. You know that."

"Is anyone in the office with you?"

"I said I can't talk now. —Do you want money?"

"I'm in trouble, I don't know what to do—I don't know what to do—"

There was no reply. Annie wondered, in a panic, if he had already hung up.

"Look," she said, "I haven't bothered you, have I?—I haven't telephoned you—it's been a long time, hasn't it? You told me to call you, practically begged me to call—"

"I didn't *beg* you to call, Annie, you or anyone else."

"—there's someone here with me, he's sleeping now, he sleeps all day, he's been here two weeks now and—and I can't—I'm afraid—I don't know what—"

"Do you want money? I can't hear you very well."

"—I don't want to call the police, I don't want to turn him in— I'm afraid—I can't think what to do— I—"

"Do you want money? I'll send you a money order. All right? All right?"

"—money? I—"

"I'll send you a money order, Annie. Goodbye."

"But John—"

"Last time it was $500 and this time, dear, it's going to be only $250. That should about discharge it, Annie, right? Goodbye."

"Wait— I need—"

"Goodbye."

—◆—◆—

The playground was deserted; since morning rain had fallen steadily and there were puddles beneath the swings, beneath the monkey bars, at the bottom of the slide. Annie crossed the playground, hands in the pockets of her raincoat. She was bare-headed. She thought her plastic scarf was in the pocket of her coat, but it wasn't there. So she was bare-headed in the rain and, after a while, she did not notice.

There was no wind. The rain fell quietly, steadily. From time to time Annie shivered. Her feet were wet; the cheap canvas tennis shoes had soaked through.

I can stay here as long as I want, she thought. *There's no one here.*

Impulsively she climbed the slide, taking the steps two at a time. She was a big powerful handsome girl. Well-loved. Enviable. People glanced at her, and then looked again. Stared. She could handle her life as she wished. She was capable of anything. At the top of the slide she paused, hands on the railings. She surveyed the shabby little playground with its asphalt paving, and as much of the park as she could see—the duck pond riddled with rain, the trash containers filled to the very top, overflowing, the paths in all directions empty. A memory of Warren flashed to her, not the Warren who slept open-mouthed in her bed—at this very moment he was sleeping—but the Warren of a decade ago. He had been walking quickly along Salina Street one day, shoulders hunched slightly, head bowed, a rather ludicrous figure in his khaki jacket, his ill-fitting cheap trousers, his tattered shoes—walking along without watching where he went, so that he bumped into Annie as she came out of a store: bumped into her, mumbled something, and hurried away without seeming to recognize her. She had turned to watch him, sneering. He had half-run away, not looking back.

Now she stood at the top of the slide, gripping the wet railings. She could not recall having climbed the slide, and she did not know why she had climbed it. But it seemed as good a place as any on this rainy afternoon.

walled City

A man's shadow appeared suddenly on the other side of the grimy, opaque window of the door, and a moment later someone knocked on the glass and called her name. A few yards away, only half-dressed, Annie froze; she was too surprised to be frightened.

The man spoke English. She believed she knew who he was; in a few minutes he would go away. He rapped on the window softly at first, then rather impatiently. Then he tried the door knob. "Annie? Annie?"

She did not move. His shadow darkened, as if he were leaning forward to press an ear against the window. Then it lightened again and faded and she heard him walking away. She heard him on the stairs, his footsteps heavy and slow.

It was the first time, in this city, that anyone had come looking for her. She stood for several minutes, in the doorway of the small, dark kitchen, until her heartbeat returned to normal.

Solitude had become a habit. Solitude nourished her.

She did not write home, because she would have felt the compulsion to explain herself; she did not care to drift into personal conversations, since such conversations invariably led to self-explanation. People felt the instinct to defend themselves by way of establishing certain small truths of an intimate nature, as if setting up boundaries. Annie had come to Quebec City to live without boundaries and without the need to erect them. It surprised her, that she was capable of living so solitary a life; at the age of thirty-four she had come to think of herself as morbidly dependent upon other people. But she lived alone now. For weeks she had lived as chastely and minimally as a nun.

She rented a small apartment on the fourth floor, the top floor, of the Château Saint Stanislas, at the very end of Rue St-Louis. It was expensive, but not so expensive as other hotels with elevators and *air climatisé* and *TV-couleur*. The single window, facing the boardwalk and the river, was impractically and unnecessarily small, no more than three feet by two, and for some reason it could be opened only a few inches. So the rooms were usually hot, the air humid and motionless. The bedroom was shabby but it did contain a small desk, and a bureau with a mirror set so that, perversely, it cut off Annie's view of herself at the shoulders; she had to squat in order to see her face. There was also a kind of living room, a very small room with a shabby sofa that faced the door, and a narrow kitchen with a toilet and shower stall opening directly off it, divided from the kitchen by only a crude folding door. From the bathroom Annie could reach easily to the stove.

There were roaches and water bugs. There were odors of mildew, faulty plumbing, cooking. A sense of age and dust. The stairs were steep, especially the flight of stairs leading from the third floor to the fourth. Other tenants, some of whom were visiting Quebec only for a day or two, sometimes ran up and down the stairs, calling out to one another. It was not their noise that disturbed Annie so much as their exuberance, their playfulness. Once, a young couple who had rented the "suite" next to hers returned late at night and Annie clearly heard the young man cry out "Oh God!" as they entered the room, and his wife began to giggle—hysterically, it seemed—and Annie lay awake, wondering what had happened. Roaches, probably. A small army of roaches. Or it might only have been that the room was stifling hot. But Annie resisted the impulse to go into the tiny bathroom, where she could have heard every word of theirs.

But the apartment was not the worst place she had ever lived in. And she believed herself in far from the worst phase of her life. That was over, accomplished, past. She had not triumphed but she had survived. Coming to Quebec City was part of her strategy of survival: both retreat and adventure. Challenge. She would live alone, without loneliness; she would contemplate her life; she would draw, perhaps even paint if things went well, under no pressure whatsoever to produce anything remarkable, or to subject herself to the judgments of other people. She had, without knowing it, always subjected herself to others—eager for their praise, their admiration, their awe, even their jealousy and spite. Now she was in a part of the world where no one knew her. No one cared about her. She would experiment with anonymity, with a kind of freedom that had always frightened her.

The apartment was dark and ugly and comically depressing, but the view from the window was magnificent. Annie stood there for long periods of time, sometimes sipping coffee, staring out at the St. Lawrence River, at the boardwalk directly before the hotel, at the ships, the sea gulls, the docks of the lower city. During the day the boardwalk was usually crowded with tourists; Annie preferred the scene at night. Sometimes unable to sleep, she stood at the window, naked, staring at the infrequent light across the way, at the water reflected in moonlight, at the red neon sign of an all-night tavern in the lower city, right on the waterfront—*La Riviera,* she thought she could read. A place for men, for sailors and dock workers; truck drivers; factory workers on odd shifts. At one time in her life Annie might have tried that place—might have enjoyed the sensation of walking in, alone, at two in the morning—but that time in her life had passed. She thought: I've been hurt too badly. It might take the rest of my life to heal.

Then she thought, angrily: No. I just don't want to do it.

—◆—◆—

She loved the Old City; she had never seen anything quite like it in North America.

Every day she woke early, partly because of the noise in the hotel and on the street. She forced herself to eat a small breakfast, sometimes standing at the window, and by seven-thirty her excitement would be such that she couldn't wait to get outside, to get walking. She took her sketch-book with her and walked. Walked. Except when it was raining very hard, she walked for hours every day. The city fascinated her; she felt she would never tire of it. And it was something of a novelty, to be alone in a foreign city, to be alone as tourist; in the past she had always seen things in the company of

other people, had shared their excitements, their prejudices, their
views; with men, she had often been more concerned with the
relationship between them than with the actual condition of the
exterior world, and in any case, in their company, she had always
verbalized her responses, had never really allowed herself time to
absorb sights and impressions, to feel. Now she had time. She had a
small infinity of time. She walked, sensing herself invisible. Like a
girl, like a child. A stray sentence came to her, from Pascal, from a
book she had owned years ago but must have lost, in her various
movings: *Our nature consists in motion; complete rest is death.*

She walked quickly, a long-legged woman, curiously refreshed by
the many hills of the city, the innumerable stone steps. There was
something yearning in her, something at times almost frantic, like
desire, but so generalized as to be more spiritual than physical; it
seemed concentrated in her eyes and in the muscles of her legs.
What might be awaiting her!—the hilly streets and narrow crooked
sidewalks of the Old City were fascinating, mesmerizing. They
existed securely in a dimension new to her, one she might try to
draw—she was unembarrassed, sketching old buildings and
churches and squares, not caring if passers-by glanced at her work or
even paused to watch her—but one which, despite her most passionate efforts, would always be beyond her, utterly foreign, *other*, a
dimension she could not conquer or assimilate. Or even translate
into language: the usual words struck her now as inadequate. Fascinating, marvelous, colorful, vital, "picturesque"—what comically
inadequate words!

Annie had studied French for four years in college, and French
had been one of the languages she had taken an examination in, for
her Master's Degree, some years ago. She had believed vaguely that
she knew French. But in Quebec City the spoken language bewildered her. She could read well enough, had no trouble with the local
newspapers, certainly no trouble with signs in shops and restaurants. But the language spoken by people in Quebec was not the
French language she knew. The first several days, she had been
almost panicked at her inability to understand. Her own French
sounded so pitiful, so childish, she was sometimes interrupted by
the remark "I can speak English; let us speak English, please"—and
this hurt her absurdly, for she felt foolish as well as rebuffed. Once,
asking directions of a young, pleasant-faced man in the Place

D'Armes, imagining her query quite skillful because it was so well-rehearsed, she had been shocked when the young man interrupted her rudely and said: "For Christ's sake speak English!" She had walked away, trembling with anger.

Now she took lessons with a French tutor, by way of the extension division of Laval University, but the sessions were held only two mornings a week, and she did not feel that she was improving very rapidly. It was possible that she was too old—or that the earlier habit of speaking English was too deeply imprinted in her mind. Out on the street, in a shop or a restaurant or a café, she seemed to lose her confidence, sometimes grew dizzy, even nauseous, and stammered out parts of her requests in English. She knew the Québécois preferred this, she knew they resented English-speaking people attempting their language, but she wanted to speak it—wanted to understand it. At times her desire to understand was almost desperate, as if it were a challenge from some deeper part of herself which she could not control.

But the impact of the city was primarily visual. And sensuous. And in a way private, as if there for Annie alone. She felt invisible; she walked wherever she liked, even at night, and no one seemed to notice her. A city of walls, archways, blank plain facades, shutterless windows . . . gray streaked stone, aged brick, cobblestones . . . narrow streets no more than alleys . . . open markets and traffic-crowded squares and innumerable statues, monuments, plaques, churches and churchyards. . . . In one of the squares she studied a plaque in honor of the French general Montcalm, whom the British had defeated and killed in 1759, and was touched by the total lack of irony or anger in the words, and by a sense of the sanctity of death implicit in them: *Fate in depriving him of victory rewarded him by a glorious death.* Most of the churches were small, scaled to human size, cool and dark and pleasant inside, less exotic than Annie would have supposed. She examined the statues, the woodwork, the floors, the stained glass windows, most of which were crude but beautiful, strong blues and reds and yellows, fascinating. In a small church on the Rue St. Cyrille she knelt for a while, utterly alone, her hands clasped together on the back of the pew in front of her, staring at the rose window above the altar. It was a sunny day. The colors were vivid. She waited, as if for something to happen, some sign to be revealed, and gradually the noises of the street subsided, even the roaring of motorcycles and motorbikes seemed to fade, and she found herself drifting in a wordless, unthinking bliss, aware only of the stained glass and its bright, clear colors. . . . A small shadow appeared behind it, suddenly, and disappeared almost at once: it must have been a bird.

The world is perfect, Annie thought.

It has always been perfect.

During July it rained often. There were thunderstorms, even hailstorms, and harsh slanted winds from the river. Annie had to stand in doorways and beneath arches, shivering; she was never dressed warmly enough for these violent temperature changes. But the torrential rains fascinated her also. She tried to sketch the look of the streets under the impact of the rain—delicate, living waves of rain, raindrops, moving across the pavement as if according to a design. Once she stood in the doorway of the American Consulate, looking out at the river; behind her, someone typed and typed, almost without hesitating, for half an hour. Another time, during a lightning storm, she wandered through the old, rather ugly foyer of the Château Frontenac, the prestige hotel, astonished at the large numbers of middle-aged and elderly women who were being herded to and fro by uniformed guides—widows, were they? The language they spoke was always English and their words were always, always inconsequential. *What time is it? Are you going back up to the room? Is it still raining? Where are we going for dinner?* . . . It would be no loss, Annie thought, to surrender language entirely. Tourists spoke quite openly in her presence, often complaining or making jokes, as if assuming she could not understand them. There must have been something about her sandals and jeans and shirt and her hair tied back with a scarf that made them think she was French-Canadian; she eyed them with a certain disdain.

In good weather she often walked along the river, then up and through the immense park, to the provincial museum, where she took notes on the French Canadian art on exhibit. She envisioned a study of some kind, an essay with photographs. . . . But she did not want to make plans, did not want to be ambitious. In this phase of her life she had no ambition at all.

The provincial museum was a pleasant surprise. It was not formidable, was not even air-conditioned; it seemed to Annie small enough for her to master. She knew very little about Canadian painting, almost nothing. The only name familiar to her was Jean-Paul Riopelle. There were other abstractionists of his type, obviously European in influence, but Annie found herself far more interested in earlier artists—Ozias Leduc, Adrien Hébert, Marc-Aurèle Fortin, Marc-Aurèle de Foy Suzor-Côté. She was much taken by Suzor-Côté, an Impressionist, whom she had never heard of before. Of course the artists were all derivative: she could see that the first instant she entered one of the gallery rooms. Turner, Constable, Monet, Cézanne, Van Gogh. . . . But the paintings had their own vitality, direct, light-filled, piled high with snow, sharply shadowed by bare trees or pines, almost primitive in their shapes and colors. The farmhouses and snowy fields and woodlands of rural Quebec must have exerted a tremendous influence over the artists, quite apart from their European models. Annie stood before each of the paintings in turn, deeply absorbed. She had not felt such an interest in art since she had first entered college, a small lifetime ago, to major in art history. People passed by her, around her, and she did not notice, did not pay them any mind. Even their inconsequential chatter, in English, did not distress her.

Solitude. Silence. Anonymity. . . . The world must have been perfect always, Annie thought. It must have been my perception of it that was sick.

But the nights were long. The bedroom was often hot. Noises from the stairs or from gay, drunken people out on the boardwalk disturbed her, and she paced about the apartment, naked, hoping for a breeze from the small window or for a thundershower to clear the air. It rained often, sometimes twice a day, and yet the temperature rose after each storm, maddeningly. For a while the streets smelled of rain, there was a pungent, lovely taste to the air—then it grew stagnant again, and the apartment became unbearable.

Sometimes she walked out after dinner, joining swarms of tourists along the Rue St. Louis or the Rue St. Jean. People walked in the narrow streets, slowing traffic. There was a festive tone to the night, which grew more lively as the hours passed. By nine o'clock the last of the charter buses with their middle-aged and elderly women passengers were gone, and the streets belonged to young people. They strolled in couples and in small packs. The license plates on the automobiles were from California, New York, Michigan, Massachusetts, Missouri, Ohio, even Arizona, even Texas. Annie resented these people but knew she had no reason to resent them— wasn't she one of them, herself?

Along the Rue St. Jean there were fairly inexpensive restaurants and cafés; sometimes Annie went to them, a little self-conscious at being alone, but curious about what she might observe. Most of the young people were more than a decade younger than she but they did not look much different from her—they wore jeans and shirts and sandals, and the girls wore their hair like Annie's, straight, quite long, sometimes tied back with scarfs. That had been the style of Annie's generation and it had not changed. Over a period of weeks Annie met a number of people, men her own age or older, who came to sit with her or introduced themselves on the street, where she might be standing to listen to a guitar player or a ballad singer. She was shy with them, noncommittal, tense. She did not want to mislead them. It annoyed her that nearly all of the men who approached her were English-speaking, and tourists; apart from salesmen and waiters and the people who ran the Château Saint Stanislas, she had not really met any Québécois at all. Sometimes she replied to opening questions in her schoolgirl French and got in return French of a sort, often with Midwestern or New York City accents.

One night, in August, she stayed later than usual, at the Cave à Vin, not wanting to return to the heat of her apartment. She had been taken up by a noisy good-natured group of eight or ten people, most of them men, all from the States; though several were living in Quebec City as landed immigrants. The Cave à Vin was crowded even on a weekday evening. People were standing and milling around as well as sitting at tables, jammed together in the semi-coolness; there was a constant shrill din, a kind of festive, manic, melodic gabble of voices, some French, some English, underscoring the recorded music—which was rock music Annie had first heard in Ann Arbor many years before.

Annie was brought to one end of the long narrow table by a man named Henry, whom she knew very casually; she was introduced only to the several people near her, who had to cup their hands to their ears to hear her name. Annie? Annie what? Quirt? —That's a strange name! One of the young women wore a black-and-scarlet striped jersey dress and many transparent beads, and her dun-colored hair was cut very short, giving her an abrupt, dramatic appearance; she stared at Annie for a while, without speaking or smiling, and then turned away for the rest of the evening. Annie instructed herself not to care, not to care. Not even to notice. But as the minutes passed and she had one drink after another—an excellent white wine she would never have bought for herself—her own dramatic sense gathered strength, and she found it easy and agreeable and in a way exciting to attract the attention of the young woman's companion, a bearded man of about thirty-five, wearing a beret, and interested in—it developed as he leaned across the cluttered table toward Annie—the French-Canadian Separatist Movement: Did Annie know any of the Québécois involved in it? Could she possibly introduce him to them? Annie laughed, thinking him ridiculous. He must have misinterpreted her laughter; he moved his chair around to her side of the table, in order to talk earnestly with her, and it developed that he was a Maoist in principle though not in practice, intensely interested in the various People's Struggles of North America; he would like to help their cause in any way possible, even if it was only by writing sympathetic articles about them, hopefully to be published with *The Nation* or *The New Republic*.—Did Annie know any of the Separatist leaders? Did she know anyone involved in the movement? He had been in Quebec nearly a week, he said, and so far he hadn't met anyone important at all; in fact, he had been snubbed by the very people he wanted to help.

As he spoke in her ear Annie looked around the little café, which seemed to her now not so desperate and absurd as it had sometimes seemed, when she had strolled by on the sidewalk, on other evenings. There were several tables of young girls, girls alone, girls in their early twenties who must have driven up to Quebec together, looking for—for what? They were young, pretty, costumed in fairly orthodox styles; they reminded Annie of her classmates at the University of Michigan, who tended to wear their hair alike, to dress alike in blue jeans and shirts, to experiment with the same kinds of men and drugs. Brave noisy groups. Children. There were many couples, jammed together at the café's small tables. It interested Annie to see that there were a number of interracial couples—that too had been a kind of gesture, a decade earlier. A white man with an exceptionally thin, and rather morose black girl whose hair billowed out, weightless, about her head; another white man, his shirt open to his belt, with a pretty black girl in an Oriental outfit; and a handsome bearded merry black man at the table next to hers, with a white girl whose face Annie couldn't see. There were many men together, young long-haired boys, and many tables like their own, where people sat together as if they belonged together, though in fact, no doubt, they were strangers. Annie had another drink. She felt quite happy. There was something she had wished to recall—but she could not recall it. At midnight someone ordered sandwiches for the whole table, and more wine, and Annie found herself eating greedily the café's summer specialty—*Le Grand Hot Dog Ameri-can.* There were chunks of gristle in it and the bright-dyed pickle relish tasted acidic; and the roll didn't taste like bread—didn't taste like food of any sort. Annie was fascinated. She took one bite after another, experimentally; her mouth watered. Another man had come to join her, perhaps intrigued by the interest the man in the beret had taken; he and Annie agreed that the gristly meat and the relish and the roll were vile, and yet delicious—they were going to order two more of them.

His name was Philip. She didn't catch his last name. She had assumed he was with one of the other women—a frail blond with a girlish wounded look—but it developed, as he chattered about himself, that he was divorced—almost divorced—would be di-vorced in exactly three weeks' time. A no-contest divorce, it was, and yet—did Annie know about such things?—complicated just the same, and expensive. Annie shook her head mutely. She didn't know. She didn't think she knew. It struck her as funny, that she had never married—and now everyone she knew, old friends and classmates, and stray acquaintances of her generation, were di-vorced: so she had missed the one and was now missing the other. It developed also that Philip was an artist—a sculptor. He had been granted a temporary visa here in Quebec and was living alone, living very happily alone, in an apartment a few miles out, on the Chemin Ste-Foy, near the University. Annie judged him to be in his late thirties, though there was an alert, boyish, almost childish quality about him. He laughed often. He laughed easily. She liked that— she was laughing a great deal herself—and it annoyed her, that a few people in her range of vision looked so ridiculously sombre, even melancholy. What was wrong with them? Did they want to spoil everything? They really annoyed her. Always had. Philip laughed so hard he had to rub his eyes, and once he dropped his hotdog and the bright relish and mustard dribbled down his shirt, and even that was hilarious—his shoulders shook helplessly.

He asked her about herself but she answered only vaguely, in very abstract terms. He did not seem to mind; he was happiest talking about himself, about his work, his plans for the future, his travels, the places he had lived. Annie tried to listen. Tried to concentrate. The Cave à Vin should have been emptying out, but in fact it was livelier than before—a group of at least a dozen long-haired boys and girls had just come in, all very suntanned. Several looked glassy-eyed, their mouths slack and smiling. Annie heard a girl mention the word Aspen: she must have meant Aspen, Colorado. The group had just come from Aspen or were planning to drive there, it wasn't clear. . . . Annie felt dizzy suddenly. Something was wrong, wrong. The café swarmed before her, as if reflected on a curved, distorting surface, she seemed to see all the faces and the gaudy colors of costumes and the busy arms and shoulders and the swinging hair run together. . . . So many, many people. There were so many people in the world. Broken and shimmering and bodiless and faceless. She had known so many people. She pressed her glass against her closed eyes and faces like the silly, slick, frozen faces on playing cards—jack queen king joker—were shuffled together, dealt out, stacked together again and again dealt out, colors swarming messily together, shimmering, all expressions the same expression, all eyes and mouths identical, faces gone, obliterated. Shuffled and reshuffled. Dealt out. She had known so many men—had been so many separate people, herself.

Men she had known: a crowd of them. Known and loved. Loved but perhaps not really known. Or had she loved them. . . . There was Tony with whom she had travelled in Europe: his frank sensuality changing as the weeks passed and the inexpensive hotels and bed-and-breakfast places they stayed in began to upset him, some of them filthy, the mattresses stained, the very air charged with the stale intimacy of strangers; until it was Annie herself, Annie's body, that drew his disgust; and what had been *love* between them fell apart to reveal two irritable, self-centered strangers who did not particularly care to see each other any longer. Her first love. Her first passionate headstrong love. The sort of *love* she had been led to believe was worth any sacrifice, even the sacrifices of friends. And there was . . . there were . . . A man who had told her at once, with a disarming sincerity, that he was married. But not happily. Of course! Not happily married. In fact very lonely in his marriage. Did you know, Annie, that it's possible to be completely alone within a marriage, he had told her, wistfully, or are you too young. . . . Are you too young. . . . It was a question that would no longer be put to her. She smiled quickly and faintly, thinking of that. No longer young. No longer? But so many years . . . ! So many years of being young, enviably young. And beautiful. Strident, bold, brash, reckless, beautiful. Or, if not quite beautiful, at any rate striking. . . . Then there was the man who showed up at her apartment to live with her. To love her fiercely, and to live with her. Forever. His name was . . . His name . . . She had written him a breathless letter, she had written him a letter to call him to her, out of an inexplicable sentimental impulse she had not recognized as maudlin and reckless at the time: no, on the contrary, it had seemed to her an altogether admirable thing to do. Ought one not to follow one's instincts, one's impulses? And so the man had arrived at her apartment. Without warning. He arrived, moved in, loved her and would not leave. Worshipped her, so he said. Beautiful Annie! I will love you forever. A stranger, babbling to himself. What had she to do with him? But she had beckoned him to her and must lie with him, in his arms, telling herself it was love: it was romance: it was daring and impulsive and necessary. . . . He had not wished to leave her. Had hinted, even, that it might be better for them both to die than to lose their love. (*Warren Breck* was his name.) She had not been able to dislodge him from her apartment and so she stayed away for days at a time, with friends, wandering the streets, sitting in the public library, waiting, waiting, talking to herself of the stupidity of her life, arguing with herself, where had she gone wrong, why had she gone wrong, who was the man who claimed to love her and to wish to die for her, with her, in her very arms . . . ? The bizarre truth was that Warren Breck was wanted by the Florida police. For child abuse. For assault against his wife. He gave himself up, evidently telephoned the police one day when she was gone, and they came to get him, to take him away, and afterward had questioned Annie for several hours, eying her with fascination and scorn. But why was he with you?—where did he come from?—had you known him well before?—was he your lover?—were you close friends? Why had he come to *you?*

Philip touched her arm, her shoulder. She awakened. She listened. He was leaning quite close to her, talking about Ann Arbor; evidently she had told him she'd gone to school there, though she couldn't remember; it turned out they had been neighbors without knowing it, what a coincidence—seven years ago—was it that long?—it didn't seem, somehow, that long ago. Philip had been a part-time instructor in the Art School, he'd lived for two years on a street that intersected one of the several streets Annie had lived on, he'd liked Ann Arbor very much but had moved on, for various reasons, heading for the Southwest. . . . What a coincidence, he said, as if strangely moved, and began to name names: did Annie know any of these people? She felt a little sick by now; the hilarity of the evening had begun to wear off. He named names and Annie listened and when he said *Judd Bradley* she must have flinched, because he paused, shrewdly, and spoke of Judd with a fond mock anger: "A reckless character, isn't he . . . doesn't take care of himself, or his talent . . . he's divorced now, I didn't know his wife well, did you? . . . did you know him? I suppose everyone in Ann Arbor knows Judd, eh? . . . I dropped in a few months ago and he was just out of the hospital, looking a little thin, but still drinking as much . . . still as argumentative as ever. They say no one had seen him for a few days and someone ran over to check and looked through the window and saw him there, on the floor; he was in a coma, evidently, and would have died. . . . So you knew him? Know him?"

"Yes," Annie said. Then she said: "But I've known a lot of people."

When the Cave à Vin closed she went with Philip and some of the others to someone's apartment on the Rue Arago, in a building on a very hilly street, and from there, quite early in the morning, to another apartment in another building, which turned out to be on the Chemin Ste-Foy; but the others were gone now and she was alone with Philip, whose last name she still did not know.

—◆—◆—

It turned out to be Lundy.

Philip Lundy.

She had not showered at his place but had walked all the way back to her own. A foggy morning, but warm. Too warm. . . . In the cramped shower stall in her apartment she had spoken his name out loud and felt nothing, nothing, not even surprise or distress; not even disgust.

She liked him well enough. They had dinner together two or three times a week. They went to the Cave à Vin quite often; he was usually there after nine o'clock, and she sometimes joined him. When they were sober they didn't talk much. When they were drunk Philip did most of the talking. He was a quick, nervous person, with dark curly hair, thinning at the temples, and rather weak-looking, watery eyes, which smoke irritated; Annie thought it strange that he should spend so much time in places where people smoked. But she did not criticize him, did not argue with him. Did not care, really. He talked about his work, his plans for future work, his past successes and past disappointments, and she listened, watching him closely, liking him, feeling a genuine attraction for him, though it could not go very deep; that was impossible.

He was a sculptor, he said; did she know what that meant?

It meant that everything was material, potentially: material in the basic sense of the word. It might begin by resisting but eventually it would surrender, if he chose to pursue it; otherwise it would be broken. Did she understand? He laughed, enjoying his own audacity. He might have been joking. Annie laughed, as if she believed he were joking. She had tried at first to talk to him about her own ideas, and about the paintings she liked in the museum, but he had dismissed them contemptuously—and that Suzor-Côté, what a fraud!—the post-Impressionists had failed to come to grips with the structures that underlay everything, with the basic fact of life which was—not life at all, but death. Everything else, Philip said, was fraud.

His sculptures were small, peculiar, quirky things, rather ugly, rather striking. He called them "artifices." They were fashioned out of once-organic material, for the most part, things he found in fields or alleyways or trash heaps or in the gutter: the skulls of mice, rats, squirrels, even cats or dogs; stray bones; mangy bits of fur or hair. In his hands they achieved a quasi-living appearance . . . though,

Annie thought, staring at them, they were really a mockery of life, an ironic, cruel comment on the nature of organic life itself. "How ugly, how really ugly," she said. "How horrible." Yet her tone was admiring, she had to grant Philip his subject, his style, his art. It was the first law of art, which Annie had long ago accepted: one must grant the artist his art. It was only the skill with which he or she executed it that mattered.

"They're meant to be comic, fundamentally," Philip said. He spoke guardedly. She knew he was watching her, watching closely. As she judged his work he was judging her. She knew. His friend Judd Bradley had been like that—Judd, with whom she had been in love, and who had hurt her very badly. But that was years ago. Another Annie had suffered, another Annie had gone through the now-familiar cycles of the ritual; the woman who studied Philip's triumphant little monsters was someone else entirely. "They're fossils, you see?—the design, the pattern in the skull—and all these little things, see?—broken bits of bone and teeth. You shouldn't like them, really; I don't like them myself. I don't feel comfortable, even, sleeping in the same room with them. This one here, this is my "domesticated monster," it still frightens me, I don't think it's finished yet and I've been working on it for weeks . . . dreaming about it . . . struggling with it. Sometimes it wants to become a legitimate, zoologically respectable beast, and at other times it strains toward the human, it seems to want to acquire a soul. I'm afraid I'll wake up some morning to see that the face has turned into my own. . . ."

Annie laughed, out of nervousness. The creature was about three feet high, the largest of the sculpures in the work-room. Its head had been fashioned out of what appeared to be a dog's skull; its face, which was almost human, but slanted, melted, had been fashioned out of clay and paint. Its eyes were slits. Its snout was vaguely smiling. The body was misshapen and bulbous, stomach thrust forward in a parody of good-hearted robustness, and its penis was tiny, thread-like—inadequately hidden behind bony hands.

As if irritated by her silence, Philip said carelessly that these artifices were merely experimental. This phase of his life was merely experimental.

Annie touched the creature's hand with her forefinger, lightly. She had to touch it, to break the spell; to be convinced that it wasn't somehow alive.

She laughed. She said, "It isn't you. It doesn't look like you. . . . No more than it looks like a hundred other people."

But the creature stayed with her. She found herself thinking about it, seeing it in her mind's eye, when she had other things to think about. She did not think about Philip. Not very often. Dinner with him, eaten late, after an hour or two of drinking, a walk along the Chemin Ste-Foy, a few hours spent with him in his apartment, in his bed—that was all; there was no need to think of him in any other context. But she remembered the artifices and felt, at times, inexplicably exhausted, almost depressed.

Now, even when the nights were cool, she found it difficult to sleep. She lay awake, composing letters in her mind—letters of explanation, apology, regret.

Different parts of her body itched. She scratched the back of her knee so hard that it began to bleed. Bedbugs? . . . But there weren't any bites. She got up, went into the kitchen, opened the refrigerator door and stared listlessly inside; then closed it again, and in the instant of allowing the door to swing shut she seemed to see a child, a vexed unhappy child. . . . This must have been something she'd done as a child, prowling the house at night.

At her tiny window she stood, leaning forward on her elbows, gazing out at the river. Tonight there was a drifting wet fog; she couldn't see any lights on the opposite shore. The boardwalk glistened. It was empty. For the first time it struck Annie as rather absurd, that five cannons were set up on the boardwalk, pointing toward the river. They had been used to defend the French settlement against the English invasion, two centuries ago; but when the English had invaded, the French soldiers hadn't fought very passionately, were defeated without much trouble. And the cannons did not look authentic. They looked in good shape, as if fairly new. Boarded up for the night was the shanty with its green and white striped canopy and its signs advertising 7-UP and Coca Cola and Grand Hot Dogs. . . . She remembered having seen, a few days before, another concession stand housed in part of an aged wall, not far from the Plains of Abraham. It had advertised not only 7-UP and Coca Cola and hotdogs, but something called New York & New

England Pizza as well. The long, low building near the old fortress
that had once been used for the storing of ammunition was one of the
city's most expensive restaurants, La Poudre. . . . Annie remembered having been amused by that, weeks ago.

She turned from the window, her eyes filling with tears. She did
not know what was wrong. Her body was uncomfortable, ungainly.
Her skin smarted. Philip sometimes suffered from violent
headaches, which could come upon him at any time, even when he
appeared to be enjoying himself, and Annie felt not a tingling
sensation, not quite pain, in her own head, just behind her eyes. She
thought: I'm not going to sink into this. Not again.

She had tried to kill herself, some years before. The thin scar was
still visible, on the inside of her left arm; but she rarely looked at it. It
was not proof of anything. It did not mean anything. She had tried to
slash her veins not because of love—though she had believed herself
"in love" at the time—but because of her own confused perceptions,
her own sick self. The man had not mattered. She hadn't loved him,
she had really loathed him. His death would have pleased her, in
fact. Just as hearing about Judd had pleased her, in a dim, half-
conscious way—hearing that he'd been sick, in the hospital, had
almost died. Good, let him suffer! Annie gloated. Let them all suffer!

But that was the sickness in her that spoke. The gloating, the
harsh triumphant glee—it was not really Annie, not Annie herself.
Not the woman she recognized. It was a child, a miserable self-
hating child, wanting others to suffer as she suffered. Quirt, Annie.
Quirt. *You haven't met Annie Quirt, have you,* Judd had written, *a
big 6' tall gal with red hair, not so beautiful as she thinks she is, a hell
of a joker, quite something, but prematurely used-up if you know
what I mean. Used & recycled. She's driving me crazy but it's ok. I'm
crazy about her.* . . . She had come across the typed letter, never
completed, in the mess in his room. Had read and reread it and,
stricken, ashamed, frightened, had slipped it back into his pile of
papers. *It's ok, I'm crazy about her.*

For a year and a half he had actually seemed to love her, and she
had certainly loved him. Now she could not remember him—not
clearly. She didn't care to remember him. Or the others. Faces,
names, bodies: like cards, playing cards, shuffled and dealt out and
reshuffled. It was important to know, Annie thought desperately,
how little any of it mattered.

She sat at the little desk and tried to write a letter to her parents. Page after page, her neat clear penmanship, handwriting that was almost like printing: . . . *I know I've disappointed you all along . . . that knowledge has hurt me despite the things I've said . . . but no longer, now I feel different . . . I feel stronger . . . I really do, I can't explain, I feel a new strength, living here by myself . . . free of the past . . . free of degrading and warping entanglements. . . .*

She began to reread it and was disgusted. She ripped it up.

That strident tone, that defensiveness!

She started a letter to a friend, a woman her own age, living now in Oregon. But there was nothing to say. A recitation of facts, a brief rhapsodic description of Quebec City, a listing of the artists she had discovered. . . . She had nothing to say to her friend, nothing personal, nothing engaging. Old friends, old lovers. Former friends. Former lovers. Nothing to say, nothing to say. . . . *I know as little at the age of thirty-four as I did when I was a child. Can you help me? Can anyone help me?* But she wasn't going to write that.

When she saw Philip she tried to tell him about her sleeplessness, her restlessness, her misery, but he countered by saying that he too suffered from insomnia; he always had, even as a boy. His migraine headaches had begun at the age of fifteen.

"There's no solution, then?" Annie asked.

"To what? To migraine headaches? —No. Evidently not. No one knows what causes them."

—◆—◆—

Once, hurrying to the Cave à Vin shortly before nine o'clock, she believed she saw Philip on the street before her, in a small group, with his arm around the shoulder of a dark-haired girl. She wasn't certain it had been him. She turned away at once.

Another time she did see him with a girl, a quite young-looking girl in a denim outfit. They were sitting in a sidewalk café, just the two of them, and this time Annie made no effort to escape. She walked past, not hurrying. Philip called to her, asked her to join them, but she merely smiled and waved and walked by. It pleased her, afterward, that she had been so unmoved, so indifferent. She had really not cared at all.

Unmoved, indifferent: free.

The tiny bathroom and the shower stall in her apartment sickened her. She tried to use them as little as possible. Two, three, four, even five hot days might pass before she showered; six, seven. . . . Her hair was long and thick and should have been washed every four days, at least, but she sometimes let it go, it was so much fuss, what did it matter? Philip and his friends were not very clean. Their fingernails were ridged with dirt, their clothing was usually soiled, they obviously didn't bathe or shower very often. What did it matter? It was absurd, to imagine that such things mattered in the slightest.

A sensation of lassitude spread itself in her, like a hand slowly filling a loose, limp glove.

"You were with someone else last night, weren't you," Philip said one night. "I know. I have ways of knowing."

"Don't be ridiculous," Annie said angrily.

They were both slightly drunk.

"My friends keep me informed. They have my best interests at heart," Philip said, blinking rapidly. " . . . I thought you were my friend too."

"I am your friend, for Christ's sake. What are you talking about?"

"But you lie to me. You're lying right now."

"I'm not lying, but what would it matter? I have the right to lie if I want to," Annie said.

She waved her hands about and laughed, at the absurdity of their conversation.

"You're just a slut, aren't you," he said. "You can't even lie convincingly. . . . I can smell other men on you, can't I, isn't that what I smell?"

Annie slapped him, hard. He shoved her. She struck at him with both fists and he stumbled backward, against his work-table. He tried to grab her wrists.

"You're crazy! You're drunk!" Annie cried.

"For Christ's sake—"

"You're drunk! You don't make sense! I hate you!"

They were both panting. Philip wiped his face on his shirt. When he looked at her he was smiling, a queer thin pinched smile. Annie caught that look and began to laugh, helplessly. It reminded her of something, of someone. . . . They laughed together.

What does it matter? Annie thought.

"You know I was only joking," said Philip, afterward.

They made love in his messy bed, which was shoved into a corner of the room. Annie grasped at him, her eyes shut tight, her entire body clenched, yearning, straining; there was a bitter, willful tension in her that, too, was familiar, reminded her of something she had experienced in the past, many times, many times . . . many times.

Annie slept for a while. Then woke. Out on the street someone roared by on a motorcycle, and when the noise died away it was taken up by someone else, another cyclist.

Philip woke abruptly. For a moment he seemed disoriented. Then he moved to embrace her and Annie embraced him in return, mechanically. They lay for a while, unspeaking. The bed wasn't very comfortable; its mattress sagged in the middle. Annie was ashamed that her hair was so greasy. She should get up, shower here in Philip's place, shampoo her hair, wash herself, wash herself harshly and thoroughly. But it was too much effort. It was even too much effort to shift her body away from the wet places in the bedclothes.

Philip yawned. He began talking idly. Without much passion he complained of his wife, and of a certain Detroit gallery that had treated him poorly, and of one of his friends here in Quebec, who owed him $50. Then he went on to speak of Judd Bradley; Judd also owed him money. ". . . With someone like Judd, though, it's hopeless . . . it's his character . . . nothing mean about him, nothing stingy, but he's forgetful; he just forgets. You said you'd met him, Annie? . . . Well, he and I have a very interesting relationship. I wouldn't call it a friendship, exactly. In fact I don't think he really likes me . . . I think he humors me, the way he humors a lot of people. I don't mind. It's fascinating. . . . I first met Judd about eleven years ago, at a friend's place in Provincetown, and there was something between us at once . . . a kind of understanding that excluded other people. We didn't especially *like* each other, even then. It used to madden me, that superior smile of his, the way he'd lift his eyebrows when someone spoke and he didn't agree with what was being said. You might not have known him well enough, I think he just revealed certain facets of his personality to close friends. Helen and I—Helen's my wife—*was* my wife—got to know him fairly well, one summer on the Cape, in an odd way he seemed to like Helen, at least he didn't mock her as he did other women. The strange thing was, Judd and I discovered we had many things in common. Our backgrounds were the same—we'd grown up in the same kind of neighborhood, our fathers were both small businessmen, very small businessmen, in fact both our fathers had gone bankrupt. It's a terrible thing for a child, it's so shameful, and the process of going bankrupt is a very slow one . . . no one knows who hasn't been through it. And there were other things we had in common, that don't sound like much, probably wouldn't strike you as significant . . . we'd both been obsessed with sports in high school, football especially, and then in college we lost interest completely, and now we both think sports of that kind are ridiculous. And we both went through periods of infatuation with the work of a sculptor no one knows, I won't even bother telling you his name, you wouldn't recognize it; he's dead now, had only a few exhibits, never got anywhere. But the most remarkable thing of all," Philip said, speaking with more interest now, "is that Judd and I discovered we had been in love with the same woman. . . . Not only that, but we'd been involved with one or two others, at different times in our lives, and it only gradually developed how our lives had run parallel, as if we'd been threaded together by other people, by strangers. Judd is four years older than I am. He looks a decade older. When I last saw him I felt almost frightened, he'd aged so, and at the same time I felt a thrill of satisfaction . . . that maybe I would outlive him, anyway, I'd outdo him, though he seems to have gotten to everything ahead of me. . . . That's nonsense, of course. I really like him. I like him without having to trust him. There are men like that, a very few men like that, whom you respond to, instinctively, without feeling the need or even the desire to trust them: can you understand? . . . Then there was always the curious fact of these women between us, how we had shared several women, without knowing it. . . ."

He was asleep when Annie left; she moved quietly in order not to wake him.

—◆—◆—

A few days later he came looking for her, and when he rapped on the door and called her name she remained silent, in hiding; her blood pulsed violently, she was afraid she might faint. But nothing happened. He did not know she was in the apartment, he went away, and she did not faint.

She kept to herself after that. No more prowling along the Rue St-Jean. No walks along the Chemin Ste-Foy. There were days when she spoke with no one except shop-keepers, in her hesitant French; but she did not mind. She liked silence well enough. Perhaps she would learn to inhabit it easily and instinctively, as she had always inhabited a world of language, of other people.

In the complex of shops near the Hilton Hotel, a man and his wife approached Annie one afternoon in late August, asking her querulously if she spoke English—if she could please give them directions to the Frontenac Hotel. Annie listened politely, smiling as if she did not understand what was being asked of her. In French she told them she was sorry, very sorry: *Je ne parle pas anglais.*

The man turned abruptly away, shrugging his shoulders.

That night she woke to hear Philip at the door again, trying the knob. "Annie? Annie?" he was whispering. "Are you in there?" She lay without moving. "Annie . . . ?" Half-asleep she made plans for the morning. She would drive out of the city for a change, out to Montmorency Falls. She would make sketches for possible paintings. She would get up early, as she had during the first weeks here. She would. . . . Waking completely she sat up, startled, listening to the silence. No one. Nothing. The hotel doors were locked at one o'clock and no one could get in without a key.

She wondered how long, for how many years, she had been perfectly safe, perfectly alone, without knowing it.

All
The Good People
I've Left Behind

I. ANN ARBOR, MICHIGAN. NOVEMBER 1960

"Should we leave?"

"But—"

"I think we should leave. It's too crowded."

"So soon? We just arrived—"

"Maxine? Ted? Should we leave or stay a few minutes or—"

"To be polite I think we should—"

"We can stay a *few* minutes, can't we?"

"What did you say? It's so noisy I can't—"

"I think we should stay a few minutes, Alex. To be polite."

"All right: half an hour. But no more."

Alex and Fern Enright and their friends the Mandels are in the Hechts' apartment one rainy Saturday night, at a party that is much larger and noisier than they had anticipated. So many people!—a good number of whom they don't know—and the stereo is turned up high—and Fern sees with dismay that some of the guests are already drunk. (Or high on marijuana—*are* they smoking marijuana, that couple in the doorway?) Deanna and Jerry Hecht rent a fairly large apartment on the top floor of one of the old, handsome Victorian mansions on Erie Street, but the rooms are too small for so many guests, and there is an atmosphere of frenzied gaiety that Fern—in her delicate, somewhat hypochondriacal condition—finds repulsive. Alex, of course, is startled and a little chagrined and perhaps even offended, since he had been led to believe that Deanna and Jerry were inviting only a few privileged couples over: seeing this crowd, noting so many strangers, he wants to leave at once. (Since childhood he has been unable to tolerate the thought of being one individual among many—one cell lost in a vast indecipherable tissue—though he is not really aware of his feelings, and believes he is angry at the Hechts simply for having misrepresented the gathering.) Ted Mandel, wiping his tortoise-shell glasses on his shirt sleeve, blinking nervously and irritably at the profusion of lights and faces and music too amorphous to be registered, dislikes all parties anyway, and would have preferred to spend a quiet evening with the Enrights; but the Enrights and his wife Maxine dragged him here (and of course he, as usual, had to drive; and the Datsun has been stalling this past week) and so, perversely, he ignores Alex's reasonable suggestion that they leave before anyone notices them. No matter that he will be forced to spend most of the next day grading papers and will have only a few desperate hours to work on his dissertation—no matter that he will probably get into an argument with some fool here (he has always been doubtful of Jerry Hecht's taste in friends) and will probably have a sinus attack because of the smoke: he is here and he'll stay for a while at least, and pretend to be enjoying himself. (If he doesn't Maxine will notice and be disappointed in him and perhaps even pity him, as she did before their marriage: Poor brilliant tongue-tied Ted Mandel! Doesn't he know how *easy* it is to talk with people, and how *enjoyable* life is when one makes an effort to communicate?)

Maxine, of course, doesn't mind the crowd at all. Not at all. She sees a half-dozen people she knows, another half-dozen she will soon get to know; she likes Jerry Hecht quite a bit (though his crude flirtatiousness seems rather out-dated), and doesn't mind Deanna, and there is that shy, sweet, ungainly friend of theirs, Darrell Ednie, a bachelor with marvelous manners who has always seemed rather impressed with *her;* and there is Merrill Pritchard; and Ron Hammersly; and Cynthia Swanson whom she halfway likes (Cynthia perched on the arm of a chair and laughing wildly at something being said by Dean Reneker, a broad-shouldered, handsome young man who once went out with—and was deeply involved with—a friend of Maxine's no longer in Ann Arbor); and Bob Eliot; and the Rinzlers; and that gorgeous red-headed girl Fern knows from somewhere, Annie, what is her last name?—Annie at least five feet eleven and therefore the tallest girl at the party so that Maxine at five feet nine needn't feel enormous—needn't feel awkward at all. (Of course it has been years since Maxine has really felt *awkward*. She is a full-bodied, exuberant, beautiful young woman of twenty-four with shining black hair that falls loose about her face, and long dark subtly painted eyes, and a complexion that seems to glow, to shimmer, with health. Her manner is playful and audacious. Her fingernails are a bright scarlet. She is wearing a silk acetate dress from Jacobson's that fits her snugly about her wide, generous hips, and flares out in a profusion of tiny tucks above her shapely legs; its V-neck is cut low to show the tops of her breasts; its bold, bright colors—aqua blue threaded with green and orange—are exactly right for her. Even later that night, when she's a little drunk and Fern Enright tells her, in the Enrights' kitchen, that she and Alex are expecting a baby—and how typically quaint *that* is, Fern's choice of words: she *and* Alex are expecting a baby—Maxine will not really feel awkward. She is supremely in control of herself and has been since the age of nineteen, when it somehow happened—wonderfully, improbably—that three young men pursued her at the same time with a desperation she could not comprehend, though she learned to cherish it.)

What is that music? Fern, her eyes watering from the smoke, examines record albums; she doesn't know if she is merely hiding from the party or whether she is genuinely interested in what she has been hearing. When they first arrived some very bizarre music was playing—sitar music, evidently: someone named Kartick Kumar, from India—and now it's ballads, folk songs, lovely melancholy haunting sounds. "False-Hearted Lover," "We Are Crossing Jordan River," "All the Good People I've Left Behind," Woody Guthrie's "Ranger's Command." Odetta. Pete Seeger. (Only a few months later Fern will hear Joan Baez singing "Silver Dagger" and "House of the Rising Sun" and "Wildwood Flower," and she will realize that she first heard Joan Baez at the Hechts' that evening: and her eyes will fill with sentimental tears: and for the next decade she will associate Joan Baez's clear, deceptively "fragile" voice with the complex of emotions surrounding her first pregnancy at the age of twenty-three.)

Jerry Hecht barges forward to welcome Maxine; he kisses her on

the cheek, then again on the ear. She laughs and pushes him away.
Ted, watching, manages to smile since he knows it is all meant in
jest, it is merely a gesture of affection. (Perhaps an affectation.) He
lights a cigarette, having misplaced the one he was smoking—has
someone else taken it?—or did he drop it?—and wonders if anyone
notices his strained unconvincing smile. Or hears his forced laughter.

He can't help it—he experiences pain when he sees Maxine so
obviously enjoying herself with another person—with another man.
The pain is not metaphorical, it is physically and spiritually real: a
kind of spasm in his chest, as if the muscles about his heart contracted suddenly.

He turns away and joins Alex, who is standing next to that tall
red-head in the floor-length dress (it is made of some rough preten-
tious fabric and appears to have been hand-painted: peacocks and
tendrils and simple, stylized, cream-colored blossoms); the two of
them are listening, or trying to listen, to a rangy, nervous young man
with a somewhat blemished skin—Hammersly—Ted can't remember his first name though Maxine introduced them only a few
days ago, at the Pretzel Bell—Robert?—Ron?—Rod?—a drop-out
from the graduate program in English who is rumored to be (or who
presents himself as being) a genius of some sort. He is telling Alex
and the red-head about his plans for an "enormous encyclopedia" of
a novel. Engagingly ugly, wearing glasses with frames that resemble
Ted's, he gestures broadly with both hands and speaks in a high-
pitched, rather combative voice of the need for literature to become
less and less human—more and more stylized—designed to mock
the merely emotional, the merely personal. He will retreat from
active life, he declares, and spend the next ten years on an immense
"clockwork" novel: he will take with him dozens of books, history
and science and philosophy, and the wilder sort of mysticism, and
perhaps comic books as well, and he will work slowly, very slowly,
with grim cold infinite patience, and thread together fragments from
all these books along a continuum of his own creation (but it will be a
mockery, of course: a mock-narration), and when the novel is completed it will be—ah, they're smiling, are they?—they doubt
him?—when it's completed it will be proclaimed as a masterpiece,
an epic, a work comparable to *Ulysses*.

"Comparable to what?" the red-headed girl says, cupping her
hand to her ear.

"To *Ulysses! Ulysses!*" Hammersly shouts.

"Why not *Finnegans Wake*, while you're at it?" Alex says.

Hammersly waves them aside, dismissing them.

(Ted, whose area of specialization is David Hume—whose dissertation topic is Hume's "positivism" and his refutation of Spinoza—has not read *Ulysses* or *Finnegans Wake* and he suspects that Alex, a biochemist, has not read them either; but he is impressed with his friend's remark. He feels, in fact, a small thrill of something close to childish glee—a sense of triumph at Hammersly's apparent anger. Hours later, safely home and in bed with Maxine, he will confess to her that the reason he dislikes parties is because they seem to bring out in him perplexingly infantile emotions: he loathes himself at such times. If he cannot be mature and civilized and intelligent, if he cannot be equal to his own high intelligence, he truly loathes himself. It is no one's fault but his own, however—no one's fault but his own. And he will ask her in a soft, guilty voice if she still loves him, and she will answer, sleepily, that of course she loves him: loves him very much.)

"Isn't he a pompous bastard?" Alex asks, flushed with victory.

Ted agrees but the red-headed girl holds herself apart, her gaze moving across the room. She is a strikingly beautiful girl of about twenty-one or twenty-two who reminds Ted of his own wife, though she is much thinner than Maxine. He is about to say something to her when she sights a friend and bounds away, calling out happily, and Alex and Ted are left together, side by side. (Oddly, they often find themselves in this position at parties, as if they are observers, witnesses, not really participants. When they first met, a few years ago, it was at a party no less foolish and hectic than this one; they found themselves on the periphery of a group loudly discussing the University of Michigan's football team and its prospects for the coming season, and turned to each other, at the same moment, with the same expression of mild contempt.)

"Should we—"

"Maybe we should—"

"—want to hunt up Maxine, and I'll get Fern—?"

Darrell Ednie is passing a dip made of cream cheese and chives, and Maxine scoops up some of it, a lavish amount, on a cracker which is in the shape of a clover-leaf. She is in a veritable glow of pleasure; she knows herself unusually pretty tonight. It annoys her that her friend Fern hangs back, unable (or is she unwilling?) to enjoy herself. She is looking through Jerry Hecht's record collection and before long Alex will join her and they will both want to leave—naturally, since they make no effort to meet people—and Ted of course will want to leave—and they'll be back home by midnight. A late-night supper at the Enrights', a few drinks, and then bed. And tomorrow Ted will be frantic to work, as usual; and Maxine can expect her mother to telephone anywhere between noon and six o'clock. She hates Sundays. Hates Sundays. . . . Annie Quirt drifts by and sticks her finger in the dip and tastes it and pronounces it "delicious" and Maxine sees, annoyed, how Darrell Ednie and Dean Reneker look at her: she's striking, yes, but rather obvious; her hair is strawlike, a garish orange-red, not very convincing. But then she sits on the carpet at Maxine's feet and asks Maxine about a mutual acquaintance, and they talk a while, and Maxine decides that she likes her, really—there is something vulnerable, almost child-like about Annie. (Though there is nothing child-like about the rumors that surround her—the most recent being that Annie is involved with one of the instructors in the Art Department, Judd Bradley, a married man, of course, and considerably older than Annie. You're going to be hurt, Maxine thinks, not without a tinge of satisfaction; that bastard will really hurt you.)

But she is saying, "What a lovely dress," and fingering the material enviously, and Annie is saying at the same time, "Your earrings are beautiful—are your ears pierced?" And then Ron Hammersly squats beside Annie, toad-like, and asks her if she'd like to leave, if she's had enough, rather rudely ignoring Maxine. (She is hurt though she takes care not to show it: she can't know that Ron has taken a violent dislike to both her husband and Alex Enright.) Maxine finishes her drink. She notices Alex picking his way through the crowd to get to Fern, which means they will want to leave in a few minutes. And Ted, where is Ted?—ah yes: gazing wistfully in her direction but reluctant to come over, for fear of interrupting her if she's enjoying her conversation with Annie and Ron. (If only Ted were not so—not so painfully timid; not so uncertain of himself.)

Now Alex is beside Fern, towering over her. They are very much in love, Maxine can see. Anyone could see. Fern is prettier than she thinks but she carries herself poorly, as if she were embarrassed by her body. Slight, slender, with short brown hair cut in no distinctive

style, her brown eyes set wide in her oval face, she is dear to Maxine,
a wonderful friend, but sometimes rather exasperating. (She drinks
only 7-UP or Coke, for instance, or at the very most Mogan David
diluted with a soft drink.) Tonight she is wearing the green jersey
dress and the pale green stockings Maxine helped her choose, in one
of the nice clothing stores on State Street, but her posture is so
poor—can it be possible she isn't aware of how she looks to others?
Maxine, who has grown to be justifiably proud of her body, who has
put aside forever the neurotic shame of her early teens, will speak to
Fern one day soon about this: must speak. (But so bluntly that Fern
will never really forgive her and, many years later, it is the not-
quite-conscious memory of Maxine's unaccountable rudeness that
will finally determine Fern's rejection of her.)

"So soon? You're leaving so soon?" Jerry Hecht cries, not quite
smiling. "You just got here—"
"Yes, you just got here," his wife Deanna says accusingly.
They mumble excuses and apologies and then another guest
appears in the doorway—a young Negro who must be nearly seven
feet tall, an amiable grinning giant in a slick bright red raincoat; his
arm is tight around the shoulders of a very pretty blond girl, who
appears to be drunk or high. Both Hechts rush forward to meet him.
"Duane Jackson," they cry, "we didn't know you were back in
town—"

Ted has trouble starting the Datsun. He turns the ignition on
impatiently and the motor stalls. He turns it off and tries again and
waits, holding his breath, for Maxine to say something—but fortunately she does not. ("Ted, for Christ's sake," she often says, "why
are you in such a hurry? You always want to break things.") In the
back seat Alex is hugging Fern. They are laughing about something.
Ted can see, in the rear view mirror, his friend's wife's small pale
face—she has a habit of narrowing her eyes when she laughs, as if she
were doing something forbidden, something naughty.
Maxine stretches and yawns and gives off an odor of perfume and
liquor and smoke—she seems to be in a very good mood, not at all
annoyed about leaving the party early. "Hi," she says, squeezing
Ted's hand. "How are you, honey?—was the party boring for you?"
"It was all right," Ted says.

"No one for you to talk with, I suppose," she says matter-of-factly, "except Alex. A waste of time for people like you."

"It was all right," Ted says magnanimously.

Both Ted and Alex are brilliant young men. They have heard the word "brilliant" applied to them throughout their lives. Innumerable teachers and professors have praised them, and given them extravagantly high grades, and they see no reason to doubt their elders' judgment. Alex was valedictorian of his high school class in Highland Park, Illinois, and a full-tuition scholarship student at Michigan for four years, and he is now completing his doctoral program in biochemistry with a NEA grant; he is fairly tall, and wears his hair in a stiff-looking crew cut that exaggerates the thinness of his face. Ted graduated from the Bronx High School of Science, won a New York State Regents' scholarship to Cornell, switched from science to philosophy in his senior year and came to Michigan for his M.A. and Ph.D. degrees, a swarthy-skinned, habitually worried-looking young man of twenty-six, shorter than Alex by two or three inches, and perhaps even more "brilliant" than Alex. (His I.Q. is said to be about 160: so his high school teachers hinted.) He has an unfortunate habit of pinching at his lips and nose when he is particularly agitated, a habit which has already begun to annoy his wife. He too wears his hair short, and his clothes are, like Alex's, rather ordinary and nondescript—to his parents' annoyance. When he thinks of himself he thinks of—of nothing at all: his face in his mind's eye is dim, blank, empty. Not a face. An essence. It is easy for him to think of Maxine's strong, beautiful face, or Alex's face, or Fern's, or the faces of his several professors, and it is certainly easy for him to think of his parents' faces; but his own seems not yet formed. In a way he is still a child, ten or eleven years old.

But he isn't a child. In a few years he will be thirty.

Round and round his thoughts go pursuing the tricky David Hume, drawn off at times—too often, really—by cloudy thoughts of his wife and his marriage and his future (where *will* he get a teaching position?—will it be at a university equal to his and his professors' expectations?—better yet, will he ever complete his dissertation, which grows more complex and muddled with every painful week?) and the possibility—no, the probability—that he and Maxine will begin having children in another few years.

(When Maxine tells him in the morning that Fern is pregnant—yes: pregnant—the baby is due in June—he will react very strangely indeed, with an explosive sound halfway between a giggle and a cough.)

The Datsun starts, thank God, and he drives up Erie Street and across to Hill and out along Brandon, past the fraternity houses, past the faculty homes, feeling quite pleased with himself. He doesn't know why. (Maxine's touch?—Maxine's perfumy warm loving presence?—Fern and Alex in the back seat, chattering about the party?)

"You know—I wish this could go on forever," he says. He means the night, the drive through the rain, the nearness of the four of them, their rather snobbish rejection of the Hechts' party; their affection for one another. "I wish—"

"Watch out for this intersection," Maxine says sharply. "Did you see that car?—it isn't a four-way stop, dear."

Married students' housing is east of the University, in a series of dormitory-like buildings covered in brown siding. From the outside the buildings look almost attractive, but they are thin-walled, and the lack of privacy is disturbing to Fern. An only child, a chronically "high-strung" girl, she finds it difficult to adjust to the proximity of her neighbors. Quarrels and boisterous laughter and the shouts of children and the sounds of televisions and phonographs and even, occasionally, the sounds of love-making; noisy plumbing, doors slamming, car motors being started early in the morning—it is all disturbing and sometimes depressing.

"I can't live here," she told Alex when they first moved in. She wept in his arms often, that first year. "I can't stand it here."

"Honey, please, what are you saying?" Alex asked, in anguish. "Don't you love me? Don't you love me? Don't you love me?"

Newly married, very much in love, they often misunderstood each other. They tripped over each other's words, half-deliberately; it was not uncommon for them both to burst into tears. (Maxine and Ted discussed this charming peculiarity in their friends' marriage, at length. Ted thought it silly and demeaning, and Maxine pretended to think it unnecessary, though in fact she regarded the Enrights with compassionate envy. "You're so *fortunate*, you don't know how *fortunate*, really," she told Fern a half-dozen times.)

Over the months, however, both Fern and Alex have become adjusted to life in the married students' quarters. Like the other tenants they publicly denounce it, of course, and want to leave as soon as possible, but Alex is able to sleep here as well as he's ever slept anywhere, and Fern has become halfway fond of their cramped apartment. It is their first home, after all. She believes—correctly, as it turns out—that she and Alex will never be quite so happy again.

Now Maxine is admiring the way she has decorated the kitchen: autumn colors of green and gold and dark orange. Those copper pans?—a wedding gift, yes. From Alex's sister. The Corning Ware casserole dish—a gift from her grandmother. Fern is pleased with Maxine's admiration though they have had this conversation before, and Maxine's enthusiasm, her cheerful busyness, are a little distracting in such close quarters. (In the living room Alex and Ted are talking animatedly; Fern wishes Maxine would join them. She doesn't like to be helped putting food on the table, Maxine's presence makes her nervous, but she has somehow slipped into the custom of allowing Maxine to help since it seems in a way important to Maxine. Important, too, are their exchanges of confidence at such times. It was in the Enrights' kitchen some months ago that Maxine told Fern how much she loathed—her word, loathed—Ted's parents, and it was while Fern was helping Maxine make dinner for a gathering of couples, last spring, that Maxine told Fern how envious certain other people were of them: not only of Alex and Ted, but of the Enrights and the Mandels as friends. *Friends.* "Around here where people are always stabbing one another in the back," Maxine said passionately, "it's something of an oddity, I suppose." Fern had been rather surprised: did people stab one another in the back often?—had she been missing a great deal? Tonight she tells Maxine about the outcome of the pregnancy test and finds herself trembling with the audacity of what she is saying. Maxine's pupils seem to darken. She immediately embraces Fern. "How wonderful! Oh how wonderful for you! For you and Alex!" Maxine whispers.)

Spaghetti with meat sauce, and Italian sausage, and mushrooms. Toasted garlic bread. Green salad with oil and vinegar and chickpeas. Chianti. Grated romano cheese. From the other room the urgent, well-rehearsed voices of the "Kingston Trio"—"Woke up this mornin' feelin' mighty mean, Thinkin' 'bout my good gal in

New Orleans"—a record from Fern's undergraduate days at Western Michigan. Alex's and Ted's on-going argument, which their wives have come to fondly mock, about immortality—free will and determinism—the function of reason—the meaning of "instinct." And life: what *is* life?—consciousness?—reality itself?

They finish two bottles of red wine and open another. Everyone is talkative tonight, even Fern. Easily and effortlessly they move from solemn philosophical topics to a discussion of movies (both Alex and Ted agree that the greatest living actor is Marlon Brando: they vie with each other, doing imitations of Brando in "On the Waterfront" and in "Viva Zapata!" Maxine has earned their grudging regard by being the only one of the four to have seen Brando's first movie, "The Men," many years before.) After movies they discuss music, and books, and suddenly they are exchanging bits of gossip about their friends in graduate school—someone is about to quit in disgrace, someone else has already received an offer from an excellent university in the East, still another is having serious difficulties with his dissertation. Ted and Alex swing back onto the topic of philosophy again. What *is* the truth? There must be an absolute truth, of course, a final, imperishable standard against which finite truths are measured. Otherwise—

Otherwise what? Chaos?

"But we may have to learn to live with chaos," Ted says cheerfully.

"You!" Maxine mocks. "Why, you get upset if I hang your shirts on the wrong side of the closet! And you should see him fly into a rage," she says to Fern, "if I happen to use his towel—just drying my hands, you know, not even thinking about what I'm doing. Chaos indeed!"

Alex laughs politely, but it's clear that he is primarily interested in talking with Ted. And Ted loves to talk, of course. Whenever possible he leads the discussion back to his area of specialization— David Hume's refutation of someone and someone's subsequent refutation of him. (The history of philosophy seems, to Fern and Maxine, a ceaseless drama involving innumerable small triumphs and small defeats, one great man supplanting another, reigning for a time, and being in turn supplanted by someone else. Such a lot of fuss over so little!) Ted speaks brilliantly and passionately of the need to relentlessly examine one's intellectual assumptions. What *is* reason, after all? Is it possible to be truly rational, or is it possible that all thoughts are conditioned by emotions, however hidden? Can there be anything approaching an impersonal thought? A "thought" not determined by its human subject? . . . Maxine enters the discussion, stating, not for the first time, that one must be a "complete" human being and that Ted's philosophical heroes seem to have left the human element entirely out of account, even when they were pretending to include it; Fern, cleverly repeating something her philosophy professor said a few years back, points out that most philosophical systems can't really be refuted but at the same time are totally unconvincing. Alex disagrees. He disagrees heatedly. There are certain things that are incontestable, like the evidence of one's senses, one's own intrapsychic experience, if that experience is accepted as an end in itself and not referred to the so-called "objective" world. "My own experience is incontestable," Alex says. "And whatever operates within the dimension of my experience is real enough: it's as much of truth as we're required to know."

If Alex believes fiercely, Ted disbelieves; if Ted believes, Alex disbelieves. They love to talk—to hammer things out. Occasionally all four of them burst into laughter. The Kingston Trio is replaced by a mournful singer of Portuguese ballads, the third bottle of chianti is emptied, Fern's eyelids begin to droop. Free will and determinism? Are the terms merely words, without meaning? Sometimes Ted insists they are, sometimes he is willing to listen—politely, patiently—to his friends' opinions on the subject. There have been nights when free will has won out; other nights when determinism, fatality, the dreaded "block universe" has won. Of course they are all free—within limits. Of course they are all conditioned—aren't they? Economically, biologically? In terms of the environment? But they *feel* free. And if they feel free what else matters? Even Ted is forced to agree reluctantly with Alex on the issue of intrapsychic experience. ("However deluded that experience really is," Ted cannot resist adding.)

The garlic bread has grown cold and rather stale but they continue to eat it, breaking off bits of crust. Fern eyes the spaghetti plates and would like to take them to the sink, to rinse them, since the spaghetti sauce is hardening, but she doesn't move . . . is too tired, too lazy, and moreover doesn't want to disturb the others. Dessert? No one wants any. Even Maxine, who loves to eat, and whose appetite has, upon occasion, rather astonished Fern, declares she wants nothing more—maybe another glass of wine, that's all. Ted doesn't care for any dessert; he *cares* that they listen to him and not, as usual, distort his meaning. It is very important that— The causal relationship between one event and another— The possibility of free *wills* rather than a single overarching *will*— (Fern, suppressing a yawn, pretends to be listening but in fact hears only patches of words. Maxine is chewing the last bit of garlic bread, nodding enthusiastically. Alex is simply waiting to restate his position.)

"It's of the utmost importance that people understand their philosophical assumptions," Ted says. "If they don't—they're liable to be blown hither and yon, taken up by one idea after another, and tossed aside, and run over by history. But the diabolical problem is that philosophical assumptions are so bound up with emotions, with semi-conscious feelings, that it's next to impossible—for the average person, I mean—to drag them into the open and clarify them. And so—"

"That's right," Maxine says heatedly. "The average person doesn't have a clue about his—his prejudices, his quirks—that sort of thing. How else do you account for—well, prejudice against Negroes? And anti-Semitism?"

She glares around the table, knowing herself melodramatic and impressive; she shakes her gleaming hair out of her eyes. Of the four of them only Ted is what might be called *different:* that is, he is Jewish. His grandparents are from Russia by way of Poland. But Maxine has brought this issue up before, and they've all agreed that prejudice is simply stupid, and anti-Semitism the stupidest prejudice of all, and moreover Ted had not really been talking about prejudice—not really—so in a moment Alex swings the conversation back to first principles.

Consciousness— Life— Reality—

The "mysterious equation" that constitutes the difference between living matter and inanimate matter—

The possibility that death is somehow locked into life: into life on the cellular level. In which case—

Fern watches her husband fondly, but with some apprehension. She knows—as Maxine and Ted do not—that Alex's father is dying of cancer, a rare form having to do with the lymph glands; she knows that Alex loves his father very much, more than he is willing to admit. His love is angry, childish; but it is love all the same. It will not be denied even by Alex himself. . . . So, now, rather drunk, he is talking about "death" as if it were an antagonist, a personal enemy, an insult. Ted listens closely, nodding, pushing his tortoiseshell glasses up more firmly into place, obviously waiting to restate *his* position. But Alex speaks vehemently. He would like to devote his life—his "career"—to breaking the code of the cell's relationship to death; there must be some very simple explanation for the phenomenon. ("What phenomenon?" Maxine asks blankly, and Ted mutters, *"Death."*) Is death merely a virus . . .? An accident . . .? Could it be—not *cured,* of course, but circumnavigated? Aging, after all, is a process only dimly understood by science. We don't "grow" old at all. Some forms of life, and not solely the most elemental forms, don't age—don't even mature in the usual sense of the word. And it's well known that human cells can be kept alive for extended periods of time by means of cell culture in vitro: well known, yes, but not understood. What does it *mean?* Surely it has some very profound, very immediate *meaning?*

(Alex looks at them, blinking. Fern can see that his lips are trembling.)

In any case, he continues, though he isn't making himself clear—he's had too much to drink, for one thing—he believes that certain discoveries will be made within the next decade, discoveries having to do with cancer, which may very well alter the history of mankind. "What is cancer except insanity on the cellular level," he says, "and why shouldn't it be stopped? It *isn't* inevitable. From a certain point of view not even death is inevitable. . . ."

Maxine stares at him. ". . . not even death is inevitable . . .?" she says softly.

"These discoveries are going to be made," Alex says flatly, "They . . . are . . . going to be *made.* The government is going to finance. . . . Private industries are. . . . The future will be changed, our very way of looking at life and death will be changed, don't you believe me?—eh? And I plan to be part of it. I am going to be part of it. . . . Unless," he says slowly, pausing, aware suddenly of how he must sound to the Mandels, "unless . . . I never finish my Ph.D. and never get into a position where I'll be doing research of my own. Which is entirely likely, after all."

They protest, they laugh away his worries: of course it isn't likely that Alex Enright will fail. Absurd, the very thought.

Absurd.

By one-thirty both couples are in bed. Fern's mind is swamped with images of the party and the poor drab figure she presented in its midst . . . mousy, self-conscious, all but mute: how is it possible that Alex Enright loved her well enough to marry her? And appears to love her still? . . . She sees again Maxine's glorious laughing face, she sees again Annie Quirt's lovely long hair and her slightly snubbed nose (she *must* become acquainted with that girl: there is something very appealing about her), she sees pretty Cynthia Swanson making a playful move to sit in someone's lap. And there is Fern, practically hiding; as self-conscious as if she believed everyone knew how unworthy she was of her husband, and how frightened she is of having a baby.

Beside her Alex slips into a heavy, child-like sleep, fairly trembling with the intensity of sleep. He is not dreaming: he sees, or experiences, a small galaxy of images. Flashes of scenes, faces, snatches of words, an indecipherable multitude of impressions. In the morning his head will ache and he'll drag himself about, ashamed of having drunk so much, trying to recall exactly what he said to the Mandels. ("Did I say I'd be in on the discovery?—the 'cure for cancer'? Oh God! Why didn't you shut me up, honey?") Now he sleeps half-turned toward Fern, his rasping breath against her ear. Fern lies close beside him, on her back, both hands pressed lightly against her abdomen. Her lips move but she is not praying. She says Love, love, love. Love.

In their bedroom across the wide barren courtyard from the Enrights, the Mandels fall upon each other, greedy and playful. Maxine is alternately girlish and voluptuous; Ted is sometimes tender, almost timid, and at other times (so Maxine has taught him) almost brutal. Maxine is the first woman he has made love to, and it is a source of anguish to him—rarely admitted—that he isn't the first man to have made love to *her*. (She was, in her own disdainful words, "a little wild" as an undergraduate; she knows now that most of her behavior was simply to spite her mother—it had nothing to do with real affection and certainly not with love.)

Afterward, exhausted, they drift into sleep: Ted unaccountably sees himself reaching after a girl's retreating back, a girl with long untidy red hair; Maxine, her body queerly alert, her loins slightly sore, folds her arms tight across her breasts for some reason, and thinks of . . . of the spaghetti sauce at Fern's . . . Maxine's own recipe, basically, but Fern must have added . . . must have added rosemary, and a bay leaf . . . and bits of bacon; it turned out very well indeed. She thinks also of her friend's husband, who is capable of such odd, gawky, unpredictable charm . . . and of her own appearance (glimpsed in windows: lovely surprising reflections in night windows!) . . . her large breasts, her fairly narrow waist . . . her attractive legs. There is something disturbing she doesn't want to think about; what is it? Not Ted muttering about the car. Not Ted speaking so lengthily at the Enrights'. (What the hell *is* he getting at, much of the time? Why must he be so pedantic?—is he imitating one of his beloved professors?) . . . Something to do with the future, possibly; with change. The evening was so perfect: why must things change? *Why must things change?* . . . But she is drifting into sleep now and her words mean nothing, mean nothing disturbing; instead they have become hypnotic and meaningless and pleasant. *Why . . . must things. . . . Why must things change. . . .*

By two o'clock they are all asleep.

II. CLEVELAND, OHIO. AUGUST 1963

"Please—we've been planning on it all along—"

"But you haven't enough room—"

"Yes, Alex, where would you and Fern sleep? It's really out of the question—"

"The sofa in the living room opens out—it's no trouble, really—"

"But we don't mind staying at a motel—"

"Why, we've even stayed at a motel visiting Maxine's parents—"

"Look: *we've* slept on the sofa when Fern's parents came to visit—"

"It's no trouble, really. It's no trouble."

"But—"

"We'll be hurt if you—"

"Now wait," Ted says suddenly laughing, pulling at his hair in mock distress, "*wait*. Maxine and I realize it wouldn't be any trouble for you—I mean in theory—but we also realize that the sane, pragmatic, *kind* thing to do is take a motel for the night: which I'll do

just by telephoning: I noticed a Holiday Inn out by the expressway.
No, no—don't interrupt!—I'll just use your phone here, all right?"
"But—"
"All right?"
Fern sighs and smiles and leads him to the telephone. She is of
course much relieved—not only does the baby cry at unpredictable
hours during the night, but Christine is in the habit of crawling in
bed with them, especially on weekend mornings when Alex sleeps
until 8:30 or 9. And she has not failed to notice—in fact it worries
her, that she must have inherited her mother's keen eye for such
details—that her friend Maxine's smile seemed almost—what?—
alarmed, distressed?—and it was obvious that she did not want,
absolutely did not *want*, to spend the night at the Enrights' after all,
though she had accepted their offer warmly enough in her most
recent letter.

For one thing it turns out that Ted suffers from insomnia.
"The thought of suicide can get one through many a long night,"
he says cheerfully. Then, seeing Alex's reaction—the raised eyebrows, the parted lips—he goes on to explain, hastily, that the
remark is of course not his: it is Nietzsche's. A famous remark, of
course, which he is using in a light manner. Unseriously.
"Insomnia," Alex says slowly. "Poor Fern too, once in a while,
though not so much lately—is that right, honey? About two years
ago—"
"Christine was such a restless baby," Fern says.
Christine, a slight, rather beautiful two-year-old with her
mother's soft brown hair and eyes, and skin that looks so lovely—so
soft!—that Maxine stares in wonderment, comes to stand beside her
mother's chair, pressing and rocking against it. Fern embraces her,
she pretends to resist, she giggles and whines and looks put-upon,
all the while glancing at Maxine and Ted; she has said only a few
words so far, as if she finds—or pretends to find—the Mandels
threatening.
"Aren't all children restless?" Ted says, sipping at his drink. "It's
normal, isn't it? A good sign? You wouldn't want a—you know, a
child who merely acquiesced to adults' expectations—"
"Of course not, Ted, why would Fern and Alex—? Of course not,"
Maxine says.

The four adults gaze fondly at Christine, who is now plucking at her mother's fingers, pouting. Ted feels his face darken and wonders if his irritation shows—Alex was always so quick to notice changes of mood, in the old days at Ann Arbor; he knows himself crudely and unjustifiably treated, since in fact his good-natured remark about children and restlessness was meant to indicate his lack of irritation at having the conversation taken (once again: for perhaps the fifth time since he and Maxine arrived) away from adult concerns and directed toward one or the other of the Enrights' children.

(Later tonight at the motel he will walk about the room, still exasperated, not so drunk as he pretends to be. "Isn't the sky a lovely shade of blue!"—"Yes, *isn't* it!—the exact color of the new baby bonnet Mother Enright bought for Linda." "What in Christ's name are we supposed to think about the Bay of Pigs?"—"Pigs! The most darling pigs—piglets, I mean—on the Romper Room—Christine's favorite television show. Do you and Maxine watch it—?")

"Is it really serious?" Fern asks, widening her eyes.

"Serious? What?" Ted asks.

"Your insomnia."

"Oh—that." He blushes, laughs, finishes his drink. It is a very strong drink: Alex's ineptness, or deliberate? "Not worth mentioning."

"Ted's family loves to talk about health," Maxine says with a broad, fond smile. "I should say *unhealth*. Don't they, honey?—everything from gall stones to terminal cancer, a nerve twitching in Ted's mother's right eye to—what was it last time?—one of Ted's great-uncles operated on, half his stomach removed—"

"Oh no: really?" Fern says, blinking. She is distracted, of course, by Christine's presence; she is also edgy about the fact that Christine is listening so closely to the conversation and may very well remember parts of it. She is such a bright, inquisitive child. . . . *Half his stomach removed, Mommy? Who was it? Who did it to him? They won't do that to me, will they? Will they? Mommy?*

"That's unfortunate," Alex says nervously.

Ted adroitly changes the subject.

They talk about the Enrights' new house. Ted and Maxine think it is very attractive; Alex says it is nothing exceptional but will do for a few years—anything is better than renting an apartment or a duplex

and tolerating a landlord's whims; Fern agrees vehemently. "Yes,"
says Maxine, getting to her feet, "to own your own home—to be
paying on a mortgage instead of—" She goes to the plate glass patio
door, drink in hand, and looks out into the back yard. Rain falls
lightly, grayly, at a slant on a concrete terrace with a small portable
barbecue and several lawn chairs. Beyond the terrace is a long
narrow rectangle of grass, bounded on each side by a chain-link
fence. Past an unruly hedge of forsythia shrubs there is a house that
resembles the Enrights', another small "ranch" of buff-colored
brick. "It's just so frustrating," Maxine says, "to keep paying rent
year after year. At the end you simply move out and have nothing to
show for it. . . . Do you remember that terrible place in Ann Arbor
where we all lived? Well, our place in Springfield was almost as
bad—in some ways worse. Wasn't it, Ted? Jesus, I'm so relieved to
get out of there, it wasn't just the way the adminstration was treating
Ted, or even the ridiculous weather—a kind of tornado belt, did you
know?—but our neighbors were impossible. So inconsiderate. Letting their kids run loose—television on so high— Yes, you're very
lucky. This house and the children and Alex's job—"

"We don't intend to stay here forever," Alex says. "The job is all
right; it's fine. For now. But in two or three years we're planning. . . .
I might apply for a post-doctoral fellowship at that research center in
Galesburg, and maybe go into university teaching after that. Fairbanks Laboratories is fine for now, but. . . . The people there are
quite nice."

"Yes, they're quite nice," Fern says happily. "Alex's supervisor,
and some of the wives. . . . There are nice people in this neighborhood, too, A very nice woman who reminds me of—did you know
Laney Cole, Maxine?—at Ann Arbor?"

"No. I mean I knew her but not very well."

" . . . someone who reminds me of her. Two doors down."

"Oh."

Maxine continues to stare out the window, her lips set in a wide
appreciative smile. She wears a checked pants-suit that fits her
snugly about the hips; her hair has been cut into a sophisticated
bouffant style that is quite flattering; for some reason she seems
self-conscious. Fern keeps telling herself that her friend hasn't
changed at all—is exactly the same. (She knows that she hasn't
changed much except for the fact that she's a mother now and that

her mind drifts back onto her children at the oddest times. And onto the fact, the idea, of children. Here she has been anticipating the Mandels' visit for weeks, planning the dinner she will serve, listing in her mind the things she wants to ask Maxine, and now, while Maxine is talking animatedly of the incredible treatment Ted received at the small college in Illinois he taught at—"I should have known better than to accept a position there," Ted murmurs, laughing humorlessly, "they *were* blacklisted by the AAUP in 1959"— Fern discovers her mind drifting onto the possibility of another pregnancy, another baby, another miraculous incredible child. Both births were difficult, and after Linda's Fern was left quite exhausted, but for some reason she is fascinated with the idea of having babies: *having babies.* Astonishing. She really wonders whether anyone else has ever thought about it. The fact that a baby is conceived in a woman's body, that it somehow absorbs life from her, grows, grows wonderfully, not-to-be-stopped, takes on a life distinct from hers— how is *that* possible, she wonders, have philosophers or theologians ever attempted to contemplate *that?*—the fact that it is born, enters time and history, enters a particular family, is either a boy or girl—a human being—Really astonishing! Her eyes fill with tears as she thinks of it. A kind of birth-daze is upon her, more powerful and more seductive than the frequent erotic spells she felt in the early days of her marriage. She must tell Maxine about this overwhelming sensation, this conviction that—that she somehow knows or is in contact with the secret of—but of course Maxine might not understand, Maxine hasn't yet had a baby, she even hinted sadly in a letter that she and Ted might not be in a position to have children (odd: *children:* why not just say a *baby* to start with?) for some time, until he's reasonably settled at another college. So perhaps she ought to be careful about speaking too reverently of the "secret" of life, of life's happiness; she has the idea that certain of her neighbors here mock her fondly behind her back because of her enthusiasm for her children. Even Alex has teased her once or twice. Has been lightly sarcastic, even. So. . . .)

Fern makes an effort to follow the conversation, which is now about President Kennedy's administration and certain "ideals of culture" which Ted finds very attractive; and Alex seems to agree; and Maxine is of course much more enthusiastic. (She became "active" in politics on a small scale in Springfield; helped the Democrats elect a state senator and a congressman in last year's election.)

Ted has a few doubts, of course—he's too skeptical by nature not to doubt even those beliefs he most cherishes—but in general he feels good about the political climate and wishes only that he could force himself to take an active interest, to *do* something. Alex agrees vaguely. In his case he's so swamped with work, spends sometimes nine and ten hours at the laboratory, and back home here there's the lawn to cut, and innumerable household chores, had Fern mentioned in a letter how the damn basement flooded last spring?—one thing after another! But he's curious—Ted isn't dissatisfied with his work, is he? (Alex knows very well from Maxine's letters that Ted *is* dissatisfied but can't resist inquiring.) Ted shrugs his shoulders. Makes a droll face. Finishes his drink. (So that Fern rises automatically to refill it—grateful for something to do.) "It's the teaching, mainly. Just not the sort of thing I was trained for. Jesus, they know so *little*—! It's absurd to be teaching those farm kids Plato and Descartes when they can barely write . . . can barely think, in fact. Poor befuddled bastards. The sort of high school instruction they get in those small towns, my God, it must be really something. Teachers who are halfway illiterate themselves. . . ."

"Ted, you're exaggerating," Maxine says brightly.

"All right, I'm exaggerating," he says. "I know. What really hurts is how little they care about what *I* care about. I admit it—I admit it. Everything is so different from the way it was at Ann Arbor. I guess I took things for granted there, and at Cornell. And at home. Jesus, sitting around and talking about Wittgenstein . . .! Free will and determinism, David Hume, life and death and language, logic. . . . I can't even force myself to reread what I've written on that goddam dissertation. Maxine mention it . . .? Three hundred pages of a first draft and I'm so sick of it my head reels, just the thought of it . . . I'm not exaggerating: there's really a kind of sickish dizzying sensation in my stomach right now. So I'm going to dismantle it and begin again and maybe relate Hume's methodology to Bertrand Russell and Wittgenstein, that sort of thing, semi-historical but mainly analytical; more challenging. Unless they work me too hard at this new college . . . or I fall all over myself, tripped up on my own grandiose ideas. Jesus, isn't it something? You finished the whole works years ago, Alex, and pushed off, you're a Ph.D., a *doctor* of philosophy, and I'm still struggling. . . . Manfully and stoically, but struggling. Poor Maxine: she hears this all the time."

Maxine says nothing. She is examining the pretty chintz covering of an easy chair—such gay, clear colors—just the sort of thing she's always liked. Someday, she thinks, she'd like material of this sort for a bedroom or guest room. Wouldn't that be lovely?—and pale green wallpaper, maybe. (And when she has children she won't sacrifice her home to them. The Enrights' colonial furniture is practical, of course, but dreadfully ugly; and that braided rug, machine-"braided", is impossible; and the formica-topped tables—! The only nice thing about the Enrights' house is the big plate glass windows, though it must be boring to look out, day after day, into that graceless back yard or, what's worse, across the front yard and the pot-holed street to that ranch house across the way, treeless and ugly.)

". . . shouldn't really be discouraged," Alex is saying slowly. "The academic world, at least. . . . Different structure, different approach to work. . . . Attitude toward money . . ."

"Yes, certainly," Ted laughs. "The attitude toward money is certainly different." And he mentions, rather unnecessarily, the salary he will receive at Rockport College in Scranton, Pennsylvania—a sum so low that Fern, returning with his drink, half-wonders if he is joking. But of course he is not. "Still," he says, shrugging his shoulders again, "it's just a temporary position until I finish the Ph.D. Then I hope. . . . Well, maybe the dissertation will be published; there's a distinct possibility, my adviser said. So. . . . We'll see."

"Have you had any news from people at Ann Arbor?" Fern asks suddenly.

Fern and Maxine have been writing, of course. Since both couples left Ann Arbor two years ago. Much of what they say consequently, isn't really new: Ron Hammersly disappeared, is said to have gone to live on a Greek island—or in a cabin in Utah, or maybe Alaska; Cynthia Swanson and Dean Reneker finally got married and are living in Boston; Annie Quirt finished her M.A. and some of her work was included in a traveling exhibit in Michigan and Ohio; Darrell Ednie went to New York City where he's working in a public relations firm, Maxine heard, though Fern heard it was a school of some kind. Deanna and Jerry Hecht?—well, the Mandels had a falling-out with them—Maxine is a little mysterious about the nature of their disagreement and Fern is never to learn anything more about it though in fact it was quite trivial: the Hechts "forgot" a dinner engagement with the Mandels at an Ann Arbor restaurant— and so far as anyone knows the Hechts are doing "well enough" somewhere in Michigan, possibly Detroit. (Jerry did get his Ph.D. and must be teaching at a university and could Fern imagine anyone less suited for university teaching than that abrasive, self-righteous bastard—?) Merrill Pritchard?—still at Ann Arbor, maybe. Maxine doesn't know, Fern doesn't know. He was always so private, so quirky. (Ted says he always expected Pritchard to kill himself—or at any rate wouldn't have been surprised to hear he had killed himself.) There was that big blond, Schiller, what was her first name?— Barbara?—awfully nice girl—woman, rather, since she was at least thirty when they knew her—a genius, everyone said—received some sort of fellowship from Stanford—exploring new means of teaching advanced math to high school students. But Maxine didn't know her well and Fern didn't either and they have nothing to say about her except she was "nice"—and wasn't it a pity she never got married?

"Well, she *was* so intelligent," Fern says doubtfully.

Maxine and Alex and Ted laugh at once, as if she has said something unusually witty. She looks at them, blinking and smiling. What is so funny . . .? She doesn't quite understand.

"God, I envy you. She's darling. Just darling."

Maxine takes the infant from Fern carefully, her face flushed. Both women are very moved. Fern smiles, smiles, perhaps to hide the emotion she truly feels. (She wants to say, impulsively, how beautiful Maxine looks holding Linda in her arms—how right it seems, that she should be holding a baby, standing by a crib, in a semi-darkened bedroom.)

"She *is* awfully nice," Fern admits. "Not so cranky as Christine. . . . Christine had colic, did I tell you? Yes? But Linda is so sweet, just a dream. She looks like Alex, doesn't she? Around the mouth?"

Maxine seems not to hear; she is crooning at the baby, rocking her gently in her arms.

" . . . so lucky, you and Alex. You just don't *know*."

"Well, I suppose . . . I suppose so," Fern says, embarrassed. "I mean, I think I know. I'm grateful for . . ."

"Isn't she just a darling? And so pretty! Babies her age are sometimes so homely. . . ."

"She *is* pretty, isn't she?" Fern says. "Alex's mother goes on and
on about her, wants us to take more pictures, you know, professional
photographs of her and Christine, and it's expensive . . . and the
lights are so bright I can't think it's good for children, can you? . . ."

"What? No. I suppose not."

"But Alex's mother just insists."

Maxine kisses the baby lightly on the forehead. The baby's small
pudgy hand darts out, her fingers snatching at Maxine's nose. "Oh
what a little darling!" Maxine cries, laughing in delight. But her
laughter is somewhat loud and the baby is frightened and begins to
whimper. Reluctant, a little chagrined, she surrenders the baby to
Fern, who busies herself at once changing a diaper. "Yes," Fern
mutters, bent over the baby, "Alex's mother is always fussing. . . .
You wouldn't believe it."

"Really?" Maxine says.

They talk for a while, disjointedly, about their husbands' families.
Maxine notes Fern's limp, styleless hair, which looks as if she tried
to cut it herself; and is it thinning?—at Fern's age? Her friend's
posture is still rather poor though she's filled out somewhat, must be
ten pounds heavier than she was the last time they saw each other,
and apart from a certain strained look about the eyes she *is* a
good-looking young woman; Ted is cruel to speak of her as "ferret-
faced." (Not that Ted dislikes Fern: he is very fond of her, in fact. He
is always comparing Maxine's new friends to Fern Enright, unfavor-
ably.) Her breasts are fuller, her hips . . . legs a little thin, still . . .
but she's an attractive woman and Maxine must fight the impulse to
take hold of her shoulders and shake her and tell her to be proud of
herself, not always so subservient to her husband. Alex is good-
looking, a fine man, an enviable husband, of course—and no doubt
many people wonder why he married little Fern, sweet as she
is—but it's annoying, Maxine finds it annoying, that Fern should so
automatically and unconsciously defer to her husband. (Years later
Maxine will experience a discomforting sense of *déjà vu* when Fern
tells *her* not to be so deferential to Ted—but Maxine won't remember this moment while Fern is changing little Linda's soaked
diaper.)

Possibly to compensate for her critical feeling toward Fern,

Maxine tells her friend about certain of Ted's problems. She is "offering" some bad news—not bad, exactly—but not particularly good. Not only does he really suffer from insomnia but for the past six or eight months his stomach has been acting up and they were afraid he might be getting an ulcer . . . though evidently he isn't: at least the doctor in Springfield didn't think so. ("Of course, what do doctors know . . . ?" Maxine says wearily, imitating her mother-in-law unconsciously.) And the trouble at the college wasn't, in Maxine's opinion, always the fault of other people. Not always. The admistration was shifty and narrow-minded, yes, and Ted's department head was a chronic liar, but more disturbing was the fact that Ted simply couldn't get along with most of his colleagues. At departmental meetings, at committee meetings, even in the corridor: something prickly in his manner, an inability to resist making sarcastic quips, a penchant, even, for giving his remarks a Yiddish flavor, which was entirely new; a bad habit of laughing soundlessly at the wrong time; an even worse habit of interrupting and contradicting his seniors. Maxine has lit a cigarette while talking and wonders, now, if she should have done so;—mightn't the smoke bother the baby? She waves it away with her hands and seems, as a consequence, rather more frantic than she feels; at least Fern interprets her agitation that way. (After the Mandels leave Fern will repeat Maxine's remarks faithfully, occasionally adding a few words, exaggerating a bit. "It sounds as if the poor guy is self-destructive," Alex will say slowly. "I always knew there was *something* in him working its way to the surface . . .") She says falteringly that Alex is sometimes impatient with fellow-workers at Fairbanks, the young men his own age, primarily, but it's mainly because of their limited intelligence and not because of anything in their personalities. They are all very nice. . . . And their wives are very nice. . . .

"A spiritual crisis, one of Ted's brothers calls it," Maxine says with mild contempt, "something he went through himself around his thirtieth birthday, and evidently the old man did too. . . . I wanted to ask if it was, you know, a kind of family tradition?—or maybe something in the genes? 'Spiritual crisis'—shit. Self-centered and cranky and egotistical and adolescent. Oh I know Ted is brilliant; I love him and I admire him at the same time, anybody would—in spite of his sarcasm I halfway think most of his girl students fall in love with him—I mean, you know—get crushes on him: he's so appealing, like a little boy in many ways. I couldn't help loving him if I *wanted* to. And he's brilliant, yes, it's supposed to be some kind of open secret in his family that he's got an I.Q. of 185 or something, and genius begins around 145, I think—doesn't it?—anyway he's the real thing, his adviser at Ann Arbor is always writing him these long letters, really involved, you know, not just perfunctory stuff, but really involved with—with philosophical problems, or logic or linguistics or whatever it is—you can tell the old boy takes Ted seriously and has high expectations for him. Not to mention Ted's father and mother! God! —Anyway, what was I saying?—I love him and admire him as a genius but at the same time I don't overlook his faults. I tell him he's conceited, he's got to grow up, he's got to learn to live with other people. This college in Scranton—he's fantasizing about it already—always referring back to Ann Arbor, you know, where he had such great times in classes—and with people like Alex, more or less his equals, you know—well, it was a kind of kindergarten, wasn't it?—a kind of paradise. Everybody worked like hell and quite a few flunked out but it was worth it, it was really great, just the companionship of those people; I guess we sort of all took it for granted. So already he's fantasizing about this new college and looking forward to meeting his colleagues and I tell him, I'm trying to be patient with him, you know, just repeating some perfectly obvious truth over and over *ad infinitium:* he can't expect too much of his colleagues or his students, right? He's got to adjust his standards. He's got to remember he's not at the University of Michigan still. . . . Christ, did I mention in my last letter about the mess he got in, giving half his students D's and F's the spring semester? And all the rest C's! And one lonely meager B-! Did I mention it?—yes? And he's so damned stubborn, so self-righteous, there are times I could tear my hair out, I'm so frustrated—"

Fern is listening intently, her eyes wide, her lips pursed in an expression of sympathy. At the same time she is very much aware of Linda—rather hypnotized by the baby's smooth flawless skin, her round eyes, her tiny lashes. Even the urine-soaked diaper is not offensive. It seems in a way proof of—of what?—proof of the baby's physical existence, her healthy, robust functioning. (*Half his stomach removed,* Fern thinks involuntarily, without knowing the source of the odd ugly phrase. *So sad.* . . .)

" . . . and then he's a little depressed from time to time, too. I suppose it's only natural. Something about turning thirty. And that damn dissertation doesn't get *done*. His desk is piled with papers, note-cards, a real mess, I don't dare approach it or he flares up, then again he can be so sweet, so sad and melancholy and, you know, helpless, and he loves me to hold him, just hold him, like in the very early morning before we get up; just hold him in my arms. It's as if there were this terrible abyss of sorrow he comes near to slipping into and I have to, well, keep him from it," Maxine says, her cheeks heating as she wonders—trying to interpret that pained look of Fern's—if perhaps she has said too much; it it's an error to attempt to slip back into the easy intimacy she enjoyed with her friend in the past. But she wants so much to talk to Fern—to somebody. To another woman who will listen sympathetically and not judge.

"It's strange," Fern says slowly, "but sometimes— Well, Alex isn't always— He's learned from his family to be so responsible, you know, to keep up being so responsible, but in fact—sometimes—it's the strangest thing, but—"

It is at the moment that Christine runs into the bedroom, exclaiming something about a big dog going "potty"; and Fern allows herself to be half-dragged into the other room, carrying the baby, explaining with an embarrassed laugh that it's the Dalmatian belonging to a neighbor up the street—Alex is just furious, of course, that the dog is allowed to run loose, and defecate on their lawn, and they've been over and over it innumerable times: should Alex go to speak to the dog's owner, or should they try to chase the dog away, or simply put up with it? Maxine follows along, nodding sympathetically. She hears someone shouting—Alex, it is—and sees through the Enrights' big picture window her friend's husband chasing a skinny spotted dog across the lawn and out of sight.

"Bad dog! Bad dog!" Christine screams,

"Yes, it's a *very* bad dog," Fern says.

"Bad bad dog! Daddy's gonna kill!"

The little girl seems to be positively demented, jumping up and down before the picture window, though her father has already turned back. Maxine and Ted exchange a quick look, their faces impassive. But Maxine can hear her husband's clever mock-Yiddish voice: *So what's this we got ourselves into? What?*

"So you have two daughters," Ted says to Alex. "Well."

"Yes," Alex says, smiling, biting at his lower lip. "I don't mind at all. I'm crazy about them, I guess. . . . Still, I hope the next one is a boy."

"Yes, I imagine you would," Ted says.

A candlelit dinner: white tablecloth, yellow and red roses in a slender vase, linen napkins. Adults only. (Thank God—Maxine worried all through cocktails that dear little Christine would be eating with them.) Fern has outdone herself with the dinner; indeed, she is looking rather tired. An excellent roast, really delicious—whipped potatoes—a curious vegetable dish of green beans, mushrooms, almonds, and cheese sauce—home-baked wheat bread—green salad with the dressing Fern and Maxine always used in Ann Arbor, since both their husbands loved it (vinegar and oil with a dash of sweet basil)—and for dessert a very light, exquisite chiffon cake. Maxine helped a little, but very little, since everything was ready beforehand; even the table was set. She is grateful the meal turned out so well. Somehow, without Fern's having said a word, she sensed her friend's concern—almost her panic. (What if something goes wrong? What if the beef is tough?) The only thing missing from the dinner is, incredibly, wine. Wine. Maxine hopes Ted won't notice but of course he has noticed; driving out to the Holiday Inn afterward he will say, "Do you think they just forgot?" and Maxine will say, matter-of-factly, "Of course not: there were no wine glasses on the table, were there?" The Mandels will discuss the curious omission for several days and then conclude, correctly, that the Enrights simply forgot—they never have wine with dinner now, don't even have it when they eat out.

Fern merely tastes her food, to see if it's all right; and it is all right; and she's profoundly relieved. For the rest of the meal she watches the Mandels' plates, and Alex's plate, and tries to follow the conversation while gauging if she has enough food for everyone, should they want seconds or thirds. She bought too large a roast but, unaccountably, didn't make enough potatoes. And Maxine has served herself such an enormous scoop. . . . The butter? It's icy-hard, since Alex put the dish in the regular part of the refrigerator after lunch, not in the special compartment marked "butter." (If he scolds her because the butter is hard as a rock she will simply tell him whose fault it was. And it's not the first time, either, he put the butter in the wrong place.)

But in general the meal is an unqualified success. Everyone compliments her. Maxine is generous with her praise—and quite sincere, Fern can see, since she's eaten so much; she wants to know the recipe for the chiffon cake. Ted reminisces for a while about their dinners at Ann Arbor. What great spaghetti sauce the girls concocted—and do they remember the time the four of them drove out to Grass Lake and had a picnic, grilling steaks, cooking corn on the cob?—one of those heartbreaking beautiful summer evenings. And do they remember the night Maxine rashly invited a dozen people over, and threw together a delicious casserole, some kind of turkey and cheese and noodle dish? ("Not quite a dozen people," Maxine says. "You're exaggerating.") And they had a kind of gourmet dinner that one night, each of the girls bringing a special dish, and someone—was it Deanna Hecht, of all people?—served lobster thermidor, a god-awful expensive dish?—but really great. ("Yes, it was Deanna all right," Maxine says, showing that she can be generous where Deanna is concerned.) And then again. . . . Another time. . . .

Fern listens, nodding, her eyes bright. She is very tired. From time to time she believes she can hear Christine; then again the baby; but evidently it is only her imagination. Beyond her friends' and her husband's genial conversation there is the profound, enchanting silence of the babies . . . her babies . . . a kind of tremolo . . . soundless music that calls to her, wells up inside her. The others are talking about a new singer, Bob Dylan, whom Maxine professes to "adore" and Ted "has to admit" is really powerful, in a sort of primitive Midwestern way . . . and Alex is more qualified, not knowing what Dylan's music means, if it is "music" at all; in any case, he argues, isn't it rather derivative? Woody Guthrie, for instance. . . . Fern half-nods, not knowing if she has heard the singer or not. She and Alex haven't bought any records for years except those that come by way of a record club, so she tells herself that on Monday she'll go to the record store at the mall and see if they have something by Dylan and then in her next letter to Maxine she can mention. . . . Then they are talking about Kennedy again, and then about Rockport College, then the impending visit of Alex's mother, a widow; then Darrell Ednie—he was, of course, a homosexual—that much was obvious—but did he *know* he was?—and was he a practicing homosexual? (Maxine is quite lively on the subject, repeating several times that she liked Darrell very much and felt so *comfortable* around him, it was a relief to be near a man who wasn't, you know, always judging you sexually, assessing you—like most of the others.)

Fern serves more coffee and asks them to come into the living room where it's nicer, and, fairly reeling with exhaustion, she begins to clear the table, rinsing most of the plates, but quietly, quietly, so that Maxine won't know what she's doing and come out to help. (In fact Maxine does know what Fern is doing but prefers to sit in the living room, in a monstrously ugly but very comfortable wing-back chair, her shapely legs crossed, her head back so that she can gaze along the curve of her cheeks at both Ted and Alex. In the plump, warm confines of her body her heart beats hard; she is a little drunk with both food and liquor and the excitement of the past several hours, and certain erotic thoughts push their way into her consciousness. Such as—what would Alex be like as a lover? He has sometimes gazed at her in such a contemplative way. . . . And once at a New Year's Eve party in Ann Arbor he kissed her quite seriously; not at all playfully as the other men did. She narrows her eyes now, watching him. Imagining him taking hold of her shoulders as he did then and bringing his mouth down to hers and pressing it against hers hard. . . . She is stirred by the vision; she sighs and reaches for her pack of cigarettes. Ted, without glancing at her, tosses a matchbook. He and Alex are swerving into one of their fond, foolish discussions about life and death and whatever, a great deal of serious, high-sounding words that leave Maxine behind. . . . What *is* Fern doing out in the kitchen? She can't possibly intend to wash the dishes, can she, while her guests are in the living room?)

Fern goes quietly into the bedroom, where Linda's cradle is pushed against one of the walls. She checks the sleeping infant and stands there for several minutes, simply staring; she is not thinking of anything at all. Unconsciously she times her breathing with the baby's. She is very tired but she could stand here, like this, for half the night. "What a darling baby! A darling!" Maxine whispered. And of course it is true. Both Linda and Christine are darling children, unusually attractive. Christine is really beautiful; that's no exaggeration. And bright. Almost too bright. She takes after Alex, as Alex's mother has said more than once. ("Except her eyes and her coloring are yours, Fern," Mrs. Enright said generously. "And she's going to be pretty just like you.") It was unfortunate that she became so excited over that ridiculous dog, and while the Mandels were here; but possibly they didn't notice. But Linda has been perfect: hardly a whimper out of her all evening.

Poor Maxine, Fern thinks.

Alex makes his guests a night-cap. He is ambivalent about drinking again this evening; if he gets carried away he'll be miserable in the morning and sleep late and Christine will come bouncing on the bed and before he knows it, half the morning will be gone. He tries to read *The New York Times* on Sundays, and makes an effort to keep up with several professional journals, including the *American Biochemist,* where a brief piece of his appeared when he was still a graduate student; but he is falling farther and farther behind every week. Other magazines accumulate as well—*Newsweek, The Saturday Review, U. S. News and World Report.* And of course there are innumerable chores to perform on Sunday, left over from Saturday. (Most of today has been wasted because of the Mandels' visit.)

Alex and Ted have Scotch, Maxine requests a gin-and-tonic, and Fern consents to a glass of sherry. Now that it's clear out they stand for a while on the terrace, gazing at the stars and the moon, talking in a desultory way about their plans for the future. Maxine, it turns out, has not only been active in politicking; she has been trying to write poetry, and has been working with ceramics. ("I'm just a gifted amateur but I try very hard," she says, giggling. Ted disagrees: "Maxine is really quite talented," he says.) Alex and Fern hope to play tennis next year; there's a tennis club some of Alex's colleagues belong to in Cleveland and they hope to join, if they have time. ("Well, we've got to *make* time," Fern says sleepily.) If everything goes well, Ted and Maxine hope to buy a house in another year, in Scranton; more precisely, in a suburb of Scranton. They won't be too far from Cleveland, really. The Enrights will have to come visit. . . .

"Yes, and you'll have to come visit us again," Alex says. "It's really been a long time. Hard to believe."

"It *is* hard to believe," Maxine says. "How time passes."

Ted slaps at his neck. "What—? A mosquito, I guess."

"Oh those damn mosquitoes," Alex mutters.

"They're all *around* here," Fern says, her voice rising suddenly.

"There's some marsh or swamp or something across the way, the
man who owns the land hasn't drained it properly, aren't they going
to sue him or something, Alex?—and in the meantime these damn
mosquitoes! Be careful they don't come back inside with us. On our
clothes."

"It's too bad," Ted says, this time slapping at his arm.

Alex makes them all another drink. Even Fern has another glass of
sherry though she is now almost giddy. (Ted, watching her, thinks of
how attractive Fern really is, even with her hair mussed and her
bright red lipstick partly eaten away and her legs so thin and
pale. . . He remembers dancing with her once, years ago and
being agreeably surprised by her child-like docility. She is considerably shorter than he, probably no more than five feet one or two, and
must weigh no more than one hundred pounds. Amazing, that she
should have had two children already—such a narrow-hipped young
woman. She appears to be so *innocent*. One would suspect her of not
really knowing how children are conceived and born—and here she
is, a mother, a wonderfully devoted and competent mother of
twenty-six. By contrast, Maxine is flamboyant and womanly, an
overtly sexual being; not at all maternal. (In appearance at least. In
reality—when she cradles him in her arms, and kisses and laughs
away his neurotic apprehensions, she is very motherly indeed.)
Maxine is a dramatic, exciting presence, especially when she is a
little high, as she is now, and flirts with everyone—even with Fern;
her make-up has become smudged as the evening wore on but she is
still very striking. A fine voluptuous figure of a woman in slacks, and
that ruffled blouse with the V-neck: yes, Ted finds her very attractive. But his attention shifts to Fern . . . who sits back on the sofa,
giggling, her eyes narrowed to slits. She almost spills her sherry;
Alex takes the glass from her adroitly and sets it on the coffee table.)

It is time for the Mandels to leave but no one makes the first move.
Alex is *very* ambivalent about this part of the evening: he wants his
friends to leave, has been hoping they will leave for the past hour
and a half, but at the same time he doesn't want them to leave, he is
actually keeping them in his living room by introducing new topics
of conversation and offering to fresh up their drinks. Oddly, he is
eager to resume reminiscing about Ann Arbor and their acquaintances there; he even asks Ted about certain professors, men whose

names figured in Ted's conversation at one point years ago but who have now dropped away. He gets Ted to talk at some length about his difficulties at Springfield, though the subject obviously makes Maxine uneasy; or bored; he finds himself talking rather loosely about his plans for a post-doctoral research fellowship, and about something he had read the other evening in *Scientific American* (God, he can't even remember who wrote it) about the controversy in neurophysiology: does the brain contain the mind or only generate the mind? Ted seems eager to talk on this subject but his remarks are muddled. ("The mind-body controversy," he mutters. "Dualism. Cartesian schizophrenia. Returning now in a new form.") Fern yawns, Maxine interjects a comic query, Ted appears offended but cannot think of a reply. Alex sips at his drink. He wants the Mandels to leave and yet he doesn't want them to leave. He is even a little on edge, waiting for one of them to make the first move. ("Well," Ted will say slowly and sleepily, "I guess it's that time. . . .") There is so much for them to talk about—! Yet the silences grow more frequent; they are like miniature abysses, like pot-holes.

Maxine feels uncomfortable; she has eaten and drunk too much, and it had been her intention to lose at least ten pounds before she and Ted moved to Scranton. Her hips are broadening, there are fatty bunches of flesh in her thighs, and her breasts are really too heavy: stylish women now are terribly thin, almost flat-chested. Androgynous creatures whom Maxine affects to pity but does, in fact, rather envy. (One of the compulsive fears of Maxine's life is breast cancer; she has the erroneous idea that large-breasted women are more susceptible, and attractive large-breasted women are most susceptible of all, as if they are to be punished for their attractiveness.) If she were Fern, for instance. . . . If she were Fern she would, first of all, do something about her hair. Perhaps even bleach it a little. She would certainly wear high heels; she would wear smart, stylish clothes that emphasized her slight body. She would wear eye make-up, and pluck her eyebrows into a more graceful, becoming arch, and. . . . Ted too is staring at Fern. While Alex talks haphazardly and drunkenly about something connected with Fairbanks Laboratories Ted is staring at Fern, with awareness; merely staring. Maxine watched him calmly. She is not jealous: she tells herself that he is drunk, he is very tired, he doesn't know what he's doing. No doubt he is thinking about David Hume or Wittgenstein.

No doubt he is plotting one of his exquisitely clever, convoluted arguments which will be unintelligible to the rest of the world—even to his long-suffering adviser at Ann Arbor.

". . . forefront of the pharmaceutical revolution," Alex is saying.

"Yes?" says Ted.

"Really very promising . . . but not what I intended. Not what I intended."

"That's right," Ted says groggily.

". . . in my position? What would you do, Ted? If . . . ?"

Ted shakes his head slowly. He takes off his glasses and rubs his eyes like a weary old man—a habit Maxine detests. "Jesus, I don't know," he says giggling. "I don't even know what I'd do if I were in my *own* position."

Saying goodnight at last Fern and Maxine kiss each other's cheek. "It was a marvelous evening," Maxine whispers. "It means so much to us, seeing you and Alex again . . . and seeing you both so happy." Alex kisses Maxine a bit clumsily, bumping her nose with his own. Then, still clumsily or with the pretense of clumsiness, he kisses her full on the lips: and she feels the effect of that kiss in her loins at once, a mild electric shock.

Ted shakes hands with Fern, rather formally, almost shyly. (It disturbs him to realize this young woman is a mother: is no longer really a girl.) Fern, standing on tip-toe , with the inspired grace of a very innocent, daring child, pecks at Ted's lips.

Everyone is smiling broadly. Everyone is happy.

Nearly two o'clock. The Enrights walk to the curb with the Mandels, breathing in the clear night air. What a fine time they had together, and how quickly the evening passed—! They must visit each other again soon. And they must get into the habit of telephoning. Not just at Christmas but at any time—any time at all.

"Yes, let's do that," Fern says passionately.

III. CHICAGO, ILLINOIS. OCTOBER 1968

Jacqueline Dunwich's birth-date is 1949; to Ted, born in 1934, this is the most extraordinary thing about her.

No, not quite. (He can hear Maxine's cynical laughter.) There are other attractions: her small lovely heartshaped face, her warm brown eyes, her waist-long brown hair, always freshly-shampooed and gleaming with frank good health. Her charming, artless manner: she manages to be eager and shy at the same time, rather forward and yet hesitant, maidenly. Her smile; her slightly crooked front teeth; her smell of soap and mint (toothpaste?); her very short skirts of denim, or felt, or coarse wool; her knee-high white boots (imitation leather); her bright sweaters that are so small, so snug, they might very well be bought in children's stores. (She must be no more than a size 5 or 6, Ted thinks vaguely, excitedly. And what is Maxine now?—14?) And there is, of course, her undeniable intelligence. She is a straight-A student at Franklin Heights Community College, she has a full-tuition scholarship, she was the only student to receive a grade of A+ from Professor Mandel last semester. So quick-witted, and yet so modest! So devoted to her studies. So attentive to Professor Mandel. During his big lecture class every Monday, Wednesday, and Friday at eleven o'clock she takes fastidious notes, looking up only when he is obviously joking—looking up at him with that fluid brown gaze that makes his heartbeat accelerate.

(There are so many girls who resemble her these days—pretty, long-haired, intelligent, almost reverential. And young: heartbreakingly young. Ted broods upon their mystery . . . lies awake at night beside his sleeping wife, brooding, puzzling, contemplating.)

("Dr. Mandel, I was wondering—"

"*Mr.* Mandel, for Christ's sake! *Mister.* You know I detest formality."

"Yes—"

"I've asked you to call me Ted anyway, haven't I?"

"Yes, but— But—"

"Is that so very difficult, Jacqueline, to call me *Ted?* To imagine me not as Dr. Mandel, not as Mr. Mandel, but *Ted—?*

"No, but I— It's just that I—"

"I understand: formalities are protective devices, like personae or masks shielding one's deepest self. But the time for such devices is past."

"—time for such devices—? Past—?"

"The past itself is past. Fading. Dead. We who live now—in 1968—must make a heroic attempt to free ourselves of the deadness of the past. You understand, don't you?— the point I was trying to make in my lecture this morning on Blake and Swami Yoga-nanda—?"

"Yes, Dr. Mandel, I think I—"

"Look: call me Ted. Will you, please?"

"—Ted.")

"But doesn't it upset you?" Fern asks nervously.

"Not at all!" Maxine says. She smiles widely; she has never seemed so relaxed. Lying back against the half-dozen brightly colored pillows, her beringed hands clasped loosely about her knee, she is something of a surprise to Fern, who hasn't seen her in person for several years. Maxine in the flesh, Maxine so powerfully and dramatically *real*—it will be difficult for Fern to explain, when she telephones Alex in the evening, the impact Maxine made upon her. Of course they have talked on the telephone—during one period, when Fern was pregnant with Terry, and not altogether well, and lonely on the weekends when Alex had to be out of town, she and Maxine called each other often, and Fern found Maxine's interest and affection quite supportive; during another period, when Ted was once again dissatisfied with his job, and evidently hard to live with, Maxine telephoned Fern once or twice a week just to air her problems. And of course they wrote. Fern was conscious of the circumscribed nature of her life when she tried to set it down for her friend's benefit—what news was there?—Alex's good fortune with his job, mainly; the various illnesses and small adventures of the children—but she forced herself to write, half-doubting Maxine's sincerity when she mentioned, as she often did, that she "loved" receiving letters from Fern. Maxine's letters by contrast were breezy, spirited, filled with names—writers, poets, visiting lecturers, television and film personalities—and deft, clever remarks attributed to Ted or herself, and marvelous comic descriptions of neighbors, in-laws, college people. They seemed written in haste, and yet gracefully enough—and it was quite true that Fern looked forward to receiving them. ("A letter came from Maxine today," she would tell Alex excitedly, as soon as he stepped in the door. "Should I read it to you?—parts of it?") Though she was acquainted now with a fair number of women her own age, and really quite good "friends" with one or two, whose children played with hers, Fern always thought of Maxine as her closest friend. They kept nothing from each other; they were sisters, really.

And so it is unsettling, and puzzling, to see Maxine in the flesh, and to feel—to feel somehow—disoriented, perhaps excluded: uneasy. For one thing Maxine looks different. She is a few pounds heavier, her hair is short and curly and seems to have been dyed a red-black-plum color, her eyes have been carefully made up with inky-black mascara and a sort of orange or russet eye-shadow that is peculiar, but finally attractive; she wears large, gypsyish pierced earrings and skin-tight blue jeans studded with fake jewels and a near-transparent black blouse, evidently Indian in origin. Her feet are bare and not very clean. (Fern hates herself for noting such details but she can't help it—in recent months she's been struggling with Christine over certain matters of personal cleanliness.) She laughs often, as if punctuating her remarks; she nods emphatically as Fern speaks, a habit that makes Fern a little nervous. (In trying to explain her self-consciousness to Alex later she will hit upon the notion—a quite correct one—that Maxine was humoring her, drawing her out, as one might "draw out" a child or a mildly retarded adult, expecting very little and consequently surprised and pleased by whatever is said, however modest.) And the Mandels' apartment is something of a surprise: so very different from what Fern expected. On the tenth floor of a high-rise building near Oak Park, it is rather small, but lavishly furnished with odd items—free-form chairs, gleaming plastic tables, a shaggy "Siberian" rug, bits of chrome and leather and raw unfinished wood, and large "abstract expressionist" canvases that are evidently Maxine's own work. An Indian raga is playing endlessly; Fern can't tell if the phonograph is defective, and continues to play and replay the same record, or if the record is really as long as it seems. ("I find Indian music so relaxing and so meditative, don't you?" Maxine asked, and Fern said, of course, that she did as well: not certain that she had ever heard Indian music before.) Most disorienting of all, however, is their conversation.

"Eat filth?" Fern asks blankly.

"The *idea* of it. The idea of, oh, gobbling up the world," Maxine says, gesturing broadly. She laughs; her earrings swing against her cheeks. "Doing unnameable things—allowing unnameable passions to arise—refusing to deny one's deepest instincts. That sort of thing.

You know. Emotions have been legislated out of existence in our
society: intense joy, rage, anger, terror. They've been banished,
denied, because people are afraid of them. Our society is a linear
one, a rationalist one, it's dominated by what are known as 'left-
brain' people—men who have developed the left hemisphere of the
brain and who have suppressed the right hemisphere. The left
hemisphere," Maxine says, touching her head, "controls rationalist
functions. The right hemisphere is the seat of emotions and
creativity—you know: spontaneity, warmth, passion. I don't quite
understand the process or the details . . . it's all very technical . . .
even Ted, despite his reading, isn't very clear on the subject; I
suppose Alex would understand. The crucial thing is, Fern, that we
must not deny the many possible selves that exist within us—we
must not allow society to dictate to us the sort of personality we will
have. You understand, don't you? There are so many, many
selves—lives—adventures," she says warmly. Fern, sipping at her
Bloody Mary (which is far too strong for her: and she never drinks at
this hour of the day, at 1 PM), finds herself agreeing blankly and
timidly. She wants to concentrate on Maxine's words, she wants so
very much to *like* Maxine, especially now that she and Alex and the
children are going to move to the Chicago area and will be living
within fifty or sixty miles of the Mandels, but her mind keeps
shifting onto other things: the appointment with the realtor at 3:45 in
Lake Forest; the frighteningly high prices of the homes she has seen;
the distracting, cartoonish nature of the red plastic sofa Maxine is
sitting on. And what is Maxine talking about . . .? A weekend
workshop somewhere in Wisconsin, "body awareness," screaming
and kicking and laughing without restraint; the hunger for "unlegis-
lated" passions; the need to return to the clarity and lucidity of the
child's world. (Fern, thinking of her oldest child's increasingly dis-
ruptive behavior, her willfulness, spite, bad temper, *ugliness*—and
most of all her inexplicable acts of cruelty against other children her
own age or younger—would like to question Maxine on this point
but doesn't dare interrupt.) A workshop in body awareness, Maxine
says, involves courage of the sort usually associated with great
explorers—the Antarctic, the bottom of the ocean, the moon. To
become aware of the universe within! To confront one's own
shadow-selves! To have the courage to—to follow through—not to
flee in terror— "To be born is the most difficult task of all," Maxine

says enigmatically, rising to pour herself another drink.

She has noted all along poor little Fern's alarm, but she has decided, compassionately, not to challenge her. After all, Fern is Mrs. Alex Enright, she is now the mother of three children (incredible: Christine must be seven, Linda at least five, and the youngest, the baby, already two or three), she has been living a narrow, colorless suburban life in Cleveland, and all she can think of to say when Maxine asks her how things are is to stammer shyly (but with unmistakable pride) that Alex has been promoted to an excellent "managerial position" and will be transferred to a division of Fairbanks in Chicago: a step upward, needless to say. She is only Mrs. Enright, merely Mrs. Enright, and it would be cruel to upset her; and Maxine must admit that she rather likes the idea of Fern—a kind of fixed point, a sweet and congenial and rather silly norm against which Maxine can measure her own development. ("But don't you like Fern?" Ted will ask. "Of course I like Fern," Maxine will say passionately. "I suppose I love her—I feel very close to her. But— you know—she's hopeless: her hair style and her clothes and her mannerisms and her entire world-view belong to the Fifties! She's going to drift into middle-age without ever having been *young*.") Still, Maxine can't resist talking about the "body awareness workshop" she attended last fall at the Green Bay Institute in Wisconsin, and hinting rather broadly about certain experiments with drugs, and of course marijuana, and the relaxed, liberalized relationship between herself and Ted—much of which seems to have gone over Fern's head. Strange, that Fern should seem so beaten-down, so dowdy, so prematurely aged: a pretty face, yes, but an absurd beauty salon hair-do, and a nondescript blue suit, and utterly conventional shoes. And that Midwestern drawl—! Nasal, little-girl, ludicrous. Poor Fern. . . . It takes an effort for Maxine to realize that Fern does, after all, have three children; she has accomplished motherhood, which has so far eluded Maxine. (Of the abortion she had back in Ann Arbor, when she and Ted had been married only a year, she has never spoken—not with Fern, not with anyone; hardly even with Ted. Of course the abortion was necessary at the time since the Mandels were penniless, of course Maxine does not blame her husband, or herself, and she realizes it is merely superstitious to half-believe, as she does, that her inability to conceive again is in any way related to that operation. Still, she cannot help envying Fern her children and the brainless ease with which she evidently had them; she cannot help resenting Fern just a little.)

She returns with another drink and makes herself comfortable on the lipstick-red sofa, settling pillows behind her. Fern is impressed with the apartment, she can see; staring big-eyed in awe at the psychedelic canvases, probably without comprehending them, though eager to show her appreciation. She is sweet, Fern; sweet and simple and darling and irreplaceable. Maxine leads the conversation onto the subject of house-hunting ("I'm just shocked at how expensive houses are north of the city," Fern says, frowning), from there to the subject of Alex ("He works so hard but it seems to be worthwhile—everyone likes him very much—this new managerial position is such a break for us!"), and to the children ("Little Terry is just darling—just darling. Wait till you see him, Maxine! I can't help loving him the best, I know it's ridiculous, and selfish, but there's just something about a baby—about the youngest child. Christine is a dear, of course, and Linda is just beautiful—and so bright!—but there's just something about Terry, he just mesmerizes me, his birthday was in June and he's three years and four months old now and growing like mad—our doctor said he's never seen a baby so lively and *healthy.*"), listening and nodding as Fern speaks, trying to maintain interest in her words. All along she is thinking of Ted and Jacqueline, of last Saturday's party at the apartment of some new friends of theirs, and of the party planned for this Saturday—at the home of one of Ted's colleagues at Franklin Heights Community College; she is wondering—*What is friendship? What does it mean? To have a friend, to be a friend?* She was looking forward to this visit of Fern's for weeks, and consoling herself for the indifference and flippancy of certain acquaintances of hers here in Chicago by summoning Fern's image to mind, and recalling Fern's generosity; but now that Fern is here in the living room, uneasily sipping at a drink, and glancing every now and then at her hand-bag (as if she half-feared it might be taken from her!), Maxine wonders if there hasn't been some mistake. What on earth do they have in common? As usual they have run rapidly through the diminished list of friends and acquaintances with whom they keep in contact, from Ann Arbor, and Maxine has made a few abortive attempts to talk about cultural matters (she adores the films of Altman and Truffaut and Fellini, but Fern just looks blank at the mention of their names; she adores the "inspired zaniness" of Donald Barthelme, whose stories speak, she believes, to her own vision of the cosmos, but of course Fern has never heard of Barthelme; she has been very impressed with the poetry of Gary Snyder, and has even tried to learn from him, in certain ways, but naturally Fern knows nothing of Snyder—her favorite poet is still Robert Frost, whom she read in college years ago but hasn't glanced at since), and then again about changing life-styles, new and revolutionary views of love, marriage, sex. Slyly and almost fearfully she brought up the subject of Ted and Jacqueline Dunwich, and it rather gratified her—the reaction of shock and disbelief on Fern's part.

"But doesn't it upset you?" Fern asks timidly.

"Not at all. Why should it? I think it's profoundly interesting—and illuminating—and expansive. Husbands and wives don't *own* one another, after all. That's a ridiculous bourgeois conception bound up with property rights—that sort of thing. It can't possibly apply to human beings."

Fern stares at her, uncertain. Should she smile as Maxine is smiling—? Or should she be sympathetic, moved, troubled? (Afterward, remembering the scene, she will exaggerate her own distress; she will resent the fact that her friend deliberately tried to upset her. In her memory Maxine will grow more melodramatic, more florid and grandiose, like an actress in a cramped, overdone set: her beauty marred by too much make-up and those deliberately gay, cheerful mannerisms.) The thought that Alex might someday be interested in another woman is literally terrifying to her—she cannot bear to think of it, she will *not* think of it. Separation—divorce—the state of being husbandless: unthinkable. Yet Maxine chats about her husband's girl friend casually, as if this subject were merely another subject of conversation, no more important than third-hand gossip about the Hechts and Annie Quirt and Merrill Pritchard. Fern is so surprised she forgets to glance at her watch, forgets to worry about the children back home—where Alex's mother is watching them; forgets even about the drink in her hand.

"Of course I'm not upset, Fern," Maxine says expansively. "His infatuation with the girl is bound up with his memories of high school, you see—when he worked so very hard, and despaired of ever having a girl friend, even of being noticed by girls. He was very, very shy, you know; and rather homely; you wouldn't believe his snapshots—! Poor Ted, his face was broken out horribly, he suffered such misery because of it—it's no wonder he wants to relive those years when the other boys and girls were discovering one another. My experience was quite different, of course—I was never shy, not me! I started dating when I was barely thirteen. Ted, by contrast, never really took a girl out until he was a sophomore in college—isn't that pathetic? Nineteen years old. And even then it was horribly awkward, he says; he just didn't know how to relate to a girl. Much of it has to do with his dedication to his studies, of course, and pleasing his parents. They believed he was a genius and expected high grades and praise from his professors—of course he *is* a genius, his I.Q. is—I don't know—around 195, I think—really fantastic; but the poor boy had no natural, emotional life, no spontaneous life, and it was only when he met me that—well, that he began to come alive. He's said many times that he'd probably be dead by now, would probably have committed suicide long ago, back in Ann Arbor, if we hadn't met when we did. . . . And so this relationship with one of his students is very natural, isn't it? I was going to bring it up a few times when we talked on the phone, Fern, but you seemed so—so vague: as if you purposefully misunderstood."

"I did? When—? I think the connection was poor last time—"

"The point is, Fern, that the girl herself doesn't matter. Not in the slightest. She could be anyone—any pretty, bright girl—any *inexperienced* girl. Their relationship is a platonic one, there's nothing physical or sensual about it—Ted is adamant on that. As if I would mind—! Of course I wouldn't mind. We're adults, after all. . . . Ted has always been rather intimidated by me, you know, he exaggerates the number of men I was involved with before our marriage, and I suppose he feels, well, inadequate in certain ways, as a lover, as a man. . . . Essentially he's timid; he's unsure of his body. So of course a girl like Jacqueline Dunwich appeals to him. —Fern, for God's sake don't look so sad—so *pitying*. I wouldn't have brought the topic up if I'd thought it would have this effect on you."

"I'm sorry, Maxine. But I— It's just such a surprise—"

"The important point about the girl," Maxine continues irritably, "is that she's the antithesis of me. Ted admits it. He was the first to admit it. We've discussed the situation many times, Fern, we've stayed up half the night sometimes, sifting through his motives and my feelings and what he knows of the girl's feelings—how deeply she's involved and whether there's much danger of her being hurt. (He says not: it's strictly a platonic, high-schoolish affair, holding hands in his office, a few kisses, occasionally a drink, occasionally a late-afternoon movie—all very self-consciously adolescent, you see.) I've seen her a few times on campus but we've never talked. Ted says I would frighten the girl; so far as she knows, I'm completely unaware of her existence. She's only nineteen and very inexperienced and Ted assures me that it's only infatuation on both sides—nothing serious. 'I can handle emotions, my own or anyone else's,' Ted is fond of saying. I think that's a quote from—Kurt Vonnegut? Alan Watts? Someone like that."

"Ted seems to have changed in the past few years," Fern says hesitantly. "The picture you sent at Christmas—his new hair-style, and his clothes—"

"Very handsome, isn't he?" Maxine says, smiling. "I think it's generally true that men grow more attractive in their thirties and forties. But Ted still has this image of himself, you see, as a skinny teenager with glasses and acne—he has to prove himself, yet. After his disappointment with his Ph.D. work, the way that son of a bitch practically betrayed him—his adviser at U of M, I mean, insisting that Ted finish his dissertation by the end of the year—as if such intricate, difficult work could be rushed!—and the situation at that wretched, ridiculous college in Pennsylvania when Ted was being overworked and exploited—well, it's time he's begun to enjoy life. At first he was very depressed at the thought of teaching in a community college—I really worried about him, Fern, *really* worried for a few months. Giving up his dissertation, abandoning his Ph.D. work, moving here to Chicago and starting again as an instructor—at a school where there isn't even any Philosophy Department: it was very hard on him psychologically. The summer before he started teaching, he sometimes didn't get up before noon, and he got into the habit of drinking . . . and. . . . Well, I mentioned a few quarrels we had; nothing serious, of course, but indicative of his state of mind. Because he never, never quarrels with me . . . we love each other very much, there just isn't anything worth quarreling about. Anyway. . . . And so. . . . Somehow the miracle happened: once he began teaching at Franklin Heights he got to like the students, the big noisy classes, the kinds of subjects that are offered, even his colleagues. For the first time he *liked* teaching. He has a full-load of four courses, and one of them is his own invention, 'The Philosophy of Popular Culture,' which was written up in a local newspaper, it's such a success—over three hundred students, can you imagine? He lectures in a small amphitheatre with a microphone around his neck—I've visited a few of his classes—and he's so very, *very* effective—witty and ironic and zestful—lecturing on the philosophical background of the Beatles' music, and the subversive films of Godard, and—what else?—astrology, vegetarianism, LSD, comic books, Zen— Isn't it a surprise, Fern, that Ted of all people should turn out to be a popular teacher?"

(When Fern tells Alex about this development in Ted's career he will agree that it's surprising, and probably a good thing; Ted wasn't getting anywhere with David Hume and Wittgenstein and Bertrand Russell, after all. And teaching students things they are genuinely interested in must be enjoyable. . . . Alex will sound rather wistful: *he* had always wanted, of course . . . had always planned, vaguely, to return to the university. . . .)

". . . and so it's true, yes, that he's changed. I could see it coming. A little experimenting with drugs, nothing extensive, and the example of some new friends of ours . . . all to the good, of course; all natural, necessary. This is 1968, after all. We can't hide our heads in the sand. And Ted developed so slowly, you know . . . simply had no adolescence at all. So he feels strongly about this stage in his development and I wouldn't dare try to argue him out of it even if I wanted to. You see, Fern, he's always been rather jealous of me. I mean he's been jealous of other men and their occasional interest in me. This business with Jacqueline, it's to prove something to *me*. It's perfectly clear, isn't it? Sometimes he's melancholy over her, and at other times he admits the whole thing is absurd, and we laugh about it together. (He repeats some of his conversations with the girl and the two of us roar with laughter—at three in the morning, when you're a little high, *everything* is hilarious. I swear that everything—everything human is hilarious!) So there's nothing profound about it, Fern. Really. You needn't look so aggrieved. The relationship between Ted and me is a strong one, like yours and Alex's—our marriage is healthy enough to withstand any number of Jacquelines. You understand now, Fern, don't you?"

Fern's eyes are smarting. She is very moved and at the same time annoyed: what will she tell Alex?

"I think so, yes," she says.

IV. CHICAGO, ILLINOIS. MAY 1973

Alex in a freshly-laundered white smock stands not at, but near, a window. Twentieth floor. A gusty sunny day filled with surprises. A week ago he was thirty-eight years old; a curious drumming ran through his head—*No matter, never mind. You won't get any older. No matter, never*— He cannot identify the words, the refrain, but he knows they do not belong to him. (*No matter, never mind:* has it something to do with Ted Mandel? One of his clever indecipherable remarks? A philosophical joke or pun of some kind?) He stands near a high, narrow window on the twentieth floor of an immense building, gazing out, down, into, through.

A pretty young woman in a starched white uniform, wearing a foolish, charming little white cap, gives him a glass of something white to drink. So white!—hideous. Chalky, liquid that is somehow dry, parching, horrible to taste: yet he must taste it.

Must drink.

But no: he starts to gag.

"Mr. Enright—?"

Nauseated. Gagging. Choking for breath.

"Take it more slowly, please. Let me— Are you all right?"

A wan smile. (He is courteous, always; he fully recognizes himself as one of the responsible adults of the world—husband, father, executive, citizen. Choking on the loathesome barium mixture he nevertheless manages to be polite, and even rather friendly, to the young nurse. "Your manner is quite satisfactory," one of his employers said back in Cleveland. "More than satisfactory.")

He tries again, draining the glass. His hand trembles. But he forces the liquid down, swallowing carefully, resisting the impulse to vomit. How horrible the stuff tastes—! It is a child's nightmare, being forced to drink something this loathesome.

("Do I have to eat this?" Terry used to ask habitually. "I *hate* this. I *hate* this." Fern says no, Alex says yes. Or: Fern says yes, irritably; and Alex says no. They glance at each other, surprised rather than angry. Babyhood and much of childhood are a matter of eating, digesting, and excreting: should be simple. But is it? He sees again

Fern's small pale contemplative face, the mildly shadowed eyes, the delicate mouth. She too is dying, he thinks, and then rejects the thought—rejects it furiously.)

"—half-an-hour, forty-five minutes," the young woman in the starched white cap is saying, "before we take the X-rays—"

Yes, Alex agrees; yes. He has brought along some work to do.

He has brought along some work to do.

Work.

High above the streets of downtown Chicago, in a much-laundered white smock, his insides now coated with a loathesome white slime. Even now the middle section of his body hurts. Small needle-like jabs of pain. Onetwothreefour. Waking at night: they are there, faithful as the dial tone of a telephone. Pain. Aching. Throbbing. For months he ignored them, of course. No time. Traveling for Fairbanks, to Los Angeles, to New York City, to London. Even to Barcelona. ("Your manner is very satisfactory," his elders decided. Which meant they *liked* him. And is that an easy accomplishment, to be *liked* by such men? It is not.)

Never a word to Fern, who would have been frightened.

Resourceful as always he has brought his work with him in a small trim leather briefcase. In appearance he resembles an attorney—a young clean-cut unradical trustworthy attorney. Light brown hair, an angular, handsome face, something firm about the mouth and jaw—he is certainly responsible, he is certainly trustworthy. From time to time he squints but the habit seems to arise from within; it is not related to the outside world.

"Mr. Enright, wouldn't you be more comfortable sitting over here—?"

"What? No. I'd rather stand, thank you."

Thinking of his father in the wheelchair, those last months of his life; thinking of his father, wasted to 97 pounds, drained of all wit and vitality and spirit and personality; he prefers to stand near the window.

No matter, never mind.

No matter: nothing matters. Or, rather, there *is* no matter—no material substance. Slowly it comes back to him. . . . Ted Mandel a little drunk on cheap red wine, years ago, a small lifetime ago, in Ann Arbor: explaining something about his dissertation. ("There *is* no matter, no material substance. As a scientist you'd have to agree, wouldn't you? The universe is sheer energy, process, the passing of 'matter' into 'energy' and 'energy' into 'matter.' Unstoppable. Ceaseless. What we commonly consider 'matter' doesn't exist, then, as we would like it to exist— You agree with me, don't you? As a scientist?") Yes, he agreed. Agrees. Vaguely. For the past five or six years Alex has had less and less to do with what might be called "science" at Fairbanks. He still takes an interest in it, of course, still subscribes to the important professional magazines, and makes it a point to take the younger men to lunch occasionally—querying them about their research, their backgrounds, whom they studied with in college. He likes them, wants to like them. He does like them. He isn't jealous of their youth and their relative irresponsibility, he isn't trying to intimidate them, certainly isn't spying on them for the company. How easily a friendly gesture can be misinterpreted, at Fairbanks—!

"How can you work for people like that?" Ted Mandel asked quizzically, the last time they met.

Alex and Fern don't see the Mandels very often now.

The Mandels live near Oak Park, the Enrights live north of the city in Lake Forest. A handsome costly home, neo-Georgian, with an acre of sloping front lawn. That lawn—its fresh lovely innocent green—restores Alex's spirit when he sees it. The physical world is real enough. Isn't it? Real enough. Expensive enough.

Fern loves Lake Forest. "The school system is excellent," she tells everyone. "Last year there were more scholarships awarded to students graduating from Lake Forest High than any other high school in the state, or was it the country?—the world?" Fern loves her friends in Lake Forest; she has come to resemble the other women. Prettier than ever, in her mid-thirties now, with only Terry really young enough for her to fuss over, she is very content in Lake Forest—it is a kind of paradise to her. Once Alex overheard her on the telephone, talking, evidently, to Maxine Mandel. The women must have been arguing about something: in their quiet, elliptical way. (Alex has never *quite* understood his wife, he admits it freely, wistfully. She is so indirect, so faint-voiced—for more than a decade of married life she objected to certain habits of his—humming energetically to himself around the house, for one; making love to her in a certain boyish way—and it was only by accident that he discovered her true feelings.) He had no idea what she and Maxine were talking about but he remembers Fern saying emphatically, "I'm *very* happy here. I can't imagine living anywhere else. Lake Forest is—it's—it's really a kind of *paradise*—"

Alex and Fern rarely see the Mandels now. The women talk from time to time on the phone—Fern says she goes for weeks without returning a call of Maxine's. Talk, talk. He and Ted talked so passionately, at such great length, in Ann Arbor. What is friendship . . .? Is it talk, merely talk? Conversation? Words, yes: but emotions beneath words. Indescribable emotions. Fern and Maxine; Alex and Ted. Emotions. Words. Emotions. He and Ted had been very fond of each other, rather like brothers—ideal brothers; loving each other, really. Loving the quarrels, the contradictions, the late-night disputes. Loving even the irritation, the anger. (In the mid-Sixties, however, when the two of them disagreed about the Vietnam War, they never argued directly at all—shied away from a confrontation.)

The Enrights rarely see the Mandels now. . . .

Alex blinks tears from his eyes. He is staring at the confused Chicago skyline, at the mottled sky. Is it still winter? No. It must be May, well into spring. Somehow Alex has lost track of the seasons. The pain in his stomach began, when was it, a year ago? . . . a year ago. Hard to believe. *Fern, I don't want to upset you, but . . .*

The windows of other buildings catch the sunlight. Like blank, blind eyes: squinting and blinking. A church steeple off to the left, its gold cross unnaturally bright as if lit from within. Elsewhere water-tanks, warehouses, smokestacks. Rather ugly. His city, his world? Whose world? Unrecognizable. He knows no one here. No one knows him. (Could not bring himself the night before to tell Fern he'd made an appointment for X-rays—could not bring himself even to tell her he hadn't been feeling well for months. She would have been alarmed. So easily upset these days. She would have thought immediately—as he did—of his father, of cancer: that slow laborious graceless ugly death.)

Alex stands near the window, staring out. He has seen nothing for quite a while. For a brief, merciful moment he cannot remember why he is here, gazing into the clotted immensity of a great American city. Then something stirs whitely in his bowels.

At 1:20 PM Maxine is still in her bathrobe; hasn't yet washed her face or combed her hair. She dials Fern Enright's number. Listens to it ring. Ring and ring and ring. *Answer it, damn you, why don't*

*you answer it . . . I know you're home . . . I know you're there
listening to the phone ring. . . .* Yet in a way she's relieved that Fern
doesn't answer. Because she doesn't know what she will say.

*I was thinking of driving downtown for the afternoon, to shop.
Would you like to join me? Maybe we could meet for lunch. . . .*

(But Fern has gently declined other, similar offers; she does all her
shopping up in Lake Forest and never comes into Chicago; and it's
already afternoon, it's already past lunch.)

*Fern? Haven't heard from you for a while. How is Linda, how is
Terry? Are they over the flu?*

(And that brat Christine: how is she? And that prig of a husband of
yours?)

*Fern? How are you? . . . Did you see that write-up about Ron
Hammersly, winning that award? I didn't even know he was a
published author, let alone notorious! What do you think about him
staying out of sight like that, refusing to be photographed or
interviewed?—not even meeting in person with his publishers? I'm
going to write a letter to him—I'll buy his book and read it and—Do
you think he'll remember me? Us? Any of us?*

(But Fern probably doesn't remember Hammersly. And probably
hasn't seen the news item either.)

Fern . . .?

The phone continues to ring at the other end and Maxine hangs up
angrily, as if insulted.

Bitch. Selfish bitch.

She lights a cigarette. Runs her fingers through her stiff, rather
greasy hair. What time is it . . . ? 1:30. She should shower, dress,
get out of the apartment, clear her head. Should do something. The
apartment is so empty; so lonely. But the crowded streets are lonely
too. . . . An idea: she might telephone Rhoda. (Rhoda is Ted's new
girl. Maxine is convinced that Rhoda is the new girl, and not Darlene: otherwise why would Darlene have looked at her and Ted so
wistfully the other night?) But Rhoda has a job and won't be home
and anyway her telephone is unlisted, someone mentioned that fact,
was it Ted himself . . . ? Someone.

She dials Fern's number again.

*Fern? Yes, it's Maxine. Have you got a minute? It's nothing much
. . . I'm not really upset. . . . Last night Ted and I had a terrible
scene, pathetic really, he tried to make love to me and failed again*

. . . yes, again . . . and of course he blames me for his impotence . . . as men do . . . as men do. . . . Fern? You won't hang up? Please, Fern. I have no one to talk with now. I'm so lonely, Fern. Aren't you lonely too? You certainly can't talk to that zombie of a husband, can you? . . . I don't know what is wrong with Ted: sometimes I think he's another person entirely, a stranger, not the man I married at all. Do you remember how hard he worked in graduate school, how absurdly serious he was?—how we teased him, even?—it was always such a struggle for me to get him to relax, to enjoy himself. And now he's so different. So flippant, so cruel. . . . So selfish.

At the other end the telephone rings in its dull monotone and Maxine listens to it, her expression hardening. She can't really remember Fern: the woman's insipid face has blurred into the faces of other women, all of them selfish, unfriendly, stupid.

Why does she bother? She hates them all, really.

She will write a poem. Yes: a poem. She will write an angry, passionate poem denouncing women—women who fail to support other women in times of crisis, who fail to be true sisters to them; she might even name certain names. Why not? She will draw Ted into it too. He is a failure as a husband, a failure as a man, which accounts for his desperate attempt to be a success as a lover—a lover of ignorant, unattractive girls. She will expose him. She will ridicule him, destroy him.

She paces about the cluttered apartment, her mind flooding with ideas. What is a poem? How can she begin? . . . Is a poem merely words, is it words strung together by passion? But how can she begin? Years ago she wrote a number of poems, and one of them was published in a small mimeographed magazine, but it was such hard work to write and revise, she gradually lost interest, and Ted hadn't praised her much, and her other poems were returned with rejection slips, it wasn't her fault, somehow the years passed and she accomplished nothing, Ted was to blame, Ted and his cruelty and ignorance. . . .

"You bastard," Maxine says aloud, beginning to cry. "I'll make you pay."

Ted is trying to concentrate on the Assistant Dean's words. He is talking about the budget, about the possibility that next fall's first-year enrollment will be down ("an estimated 25%," the man says sternly), about the probability that certain divisions of the college will have to be reduced. Ted lights one cigarette after another. He is bored, he is nervous, he is frightened. Around the long table sit thirty or more of his colleagues, most of them men, most of them about Ted's age, and dressed like him—casually, sportily, as if they were still in their early twenties. The meeting has been unpleasant so far and Ted supposes it will grow more unpleasant still.

A coil of music moves through his mind. Something tricky, jarring. A new rock group: The Apaches. Though he had not really been listening to the album, the night before at Andre's apartment, somehow the music snaked its way into his brain. At least it is wordless, it makes no demands. ("But do you love me? Do you think of me when we're not together? Are you in love with *her?*") The Assistant Dean is still talking. Can it be possible, he's talked for nearly forty-five minutes? Pages of statistics, graphs, charts. Ted leans forward, sighing. From a distance he gives the appearance of being a reasonably concerned member of the Humanities Division faculty, though there is, as always, that glimmer of a smirk about his mouth.

Music. Discordant and simple and rather sinister. Like a child's toy weapons. Playful and yet—and yet not quite entirely playful. The young people who are Ted's friends are children in his eyes; and yet they are dangerous, prematurely wise. And very exciting.

One of Ted's colleagues has asked the Dean a question and now the Dean is answering him, gravely, at great length.

Ted does not listen, Ted does not give a damn. He is one of the college's most popular teachers; his position is unassailable. He thinks of the music of the night before, he thinks of his young friends' faces, their harsh delighted laughter, their innocence which is soiled and fascinating. He thinks of Darlene. No: not of Darlene. Not any longer, since she spoiled everything for him. He does not dislike her, of course, he feels a certain sympathy, and even tenderness for her, but it gives him no pleasure now to think of her—consequently he will not think of her. Nor will he think of that terrible, foolish scene with Maxine the night before—very early this morning, to be exact. Better to give himself up to the memory of that hard, brutal rock music, which has no words, no soul.

("But do you love me? Have you ever loved me?")

He fights a yawn. He is nervous, yet there is the impulse to yawn;

perhaps to show the others that he isn't really involved as they are. It
is degrading, this exaggerated concern with financial matters. . . .
The spirit yearns for other, deeper things, after all. The dark gods.
The passions. Unarticulated desires. ("Do you love me? Do you
even know who I am?") From time to time he remembers that
sweet, dark-haired girl of years ago—what was her name?—
Jacqueline Dunwich—Dunwich—a comic name, as Maxine pointed
out—and he feels a surge of emotion that is disturbing, yet not
unpleasant. His colleagues suspected, wrongly, that he was having
an affair with her; some were envious, some amused, a few were
apparently quite angry. But nothing happened. He did not lose his
job, he went on to other, more serious affairs, though none of them
were to be as romantic as the one with Jacqueline which was uncon-
summated. (Now he finds that touching: why had he feared the girl
so? Was it her innocence, her virginity, her love for him? Her love
for him which might have bloomed as terrifying in its passion as
Maxine's?)

Of course Maxine doesn't love him any longer. Nor does he love
her. He's certain of that—he's told her many times. Their marriage
is a convenience, a habit, a gesture. Once, high on an opium-and-
tobacco mixture a friend had given him, he had stormed about the
apartment breaking things, ranting, preaching at her about the
ungovernable impulses of the spirit. ("When you're in love with
someone you are fiercely and murderously *jealous!* You don't want
to share that person! Not with anyone! Never! And when you're
willing to share—even when you tolerate the *idea* of sharing—
you're no longer in love and that's that! Do you understand? You
must—you're not that stupid!") Maxine and her tumultuous breast-
heaving sobs, Maxine and her threats, her moods, her accusations:
did he know this woman, at all? He did not. Not really. She was his
wife and yet, in a sense, he had no wife; he acknowledged no wife.
There were a half-dozen women he felt closer to than Maxine—even
women like Fern Enright whom he rarely saw—but he loved none of
them, he did not particularly like anyone, why pretend, why lie?

He is drumming his fingers on the table, in time with the interior
music. Several of his colleagues glance over at him but he doesn't
notice; he is staring into space, into nothing.

Chilling, this sudden sense of freedom, of isolation. He doesn't
love anyone and never did. Nothing follows from anything: there is

no causality. (And he doesn't require David Hume to substantiate his conviction; he *knows* it is true.) A befudddled, lust-maddened young man got married many years ago, violently in love with a striking young woman whose body—let us admit it—intimidated him; he fell in love, and married, and lost himself for a period of years, in that marriage, which was over-heated, overly-passionate, rather melodramatic. But he lost himself in it for a certain space of time. And then, slowly, he found himself again—came to the surface of himself, and was awakened. Once awakened he cannot drift into sleep again. He loves no one, he cannot truly acknowledge that woman who claims to be his wife, alternately screaming at him and embracing him in desperation; he is close to no one—or to everyone, to anyone. Why not anyone? His students, his colleagues, the Assistant Dean, the entire world—why not? Surely it isn't just the revelation of a drug experience that all men and women are related?—are equal?—cancel one another out?

He stares into space, the muscles of his cheeks twitching. Unconsciously he drums on the table, his fingertips hard and impatient.

In the Statler-Hilton, in Room 1108, Fern lies beside her lover, who is telling her about a conversation he had with a Republican congressman from southern Illinois at a fund-raising banquet the week before. Conspiracies, assassinations, bribes, world-wide plots: it is all rather dizzying. Fern half-listens, imagining she has heard it before. (In fact she has heard something similar before, though not from this particular man.) She makes soft, ironic sounds from time to time that are meant to be the sounds of humor. Is it amusing, is it dreadful?—she cannot know, she has little emotion left for large public events, however catastrophic. In 1963 Kennedy was assassinated, and then his brother was assassinated, and then—Martin Luther King?—and others, perhaps?—others whose names she has lost track of. She cannot know, she cannot remember, these details have faded. (A year or two later, reading of two attempts in California against President Ford's life, Fern will be alarmed at her own response: at first a sense of fear, that they came so close to succeeding; and finally a sense of *déjà vu* and disinterest.)

"Well—what do you think of that?" her lover asks with triumphant irony.

"I don't know quite what to think," Fern says.

Her lover is a friend's husband; they have known each other for

years, not well. He is separated from his wife and probably going to
be divorced. Fern is not separated from her husband and has no
intentions of being divorced—she hardly feels herself married, as
she puts it, so divorce isn't necessary. And she loves Alex, really. He
is the father of her children and she loves him very much.

With her lover she is breathless, charming, girlish, a little
scatter-brained. He seems to be delighted with her, with this version of Fern. (His own wife, an alcoholic, is heavy of spirit and no
longer very attractive.) Oddly, she feels no guilt about their relationship. Her lack of conscience interests them both and provides them
with one of their five or six topics of conversation. Obsessively, they
talk about certain subjects . . . sifting through their feelings, and
through the probable feelings of others, trying to assess, to judge.
Since he is going to be divorced, is he therefore "unfaithful" to his
wife? Is it likely that his wife has been unfaithful to him? (Fern knows
the woman and rather doubts it, but, in order to stimulate her lover's
interest in his marriage—and consequently in the drama surrounding his affair—she hints that the wife may very well be seeing other
men; one can't blame her, after all.) Is it possible that Alex
knows?—or can sense? He isn't entirely unaware of his wife's emotional life, surely? (Indeed he is unaware, as Fern knows; but once
again she hints that he may "sense" her love for another man.
Certainly he can sense her sexual revulsion for him.) They talk of
their children: he has two, both boys. She has, of course, three.
Christine and Linda and Terry. Names. The recitation of names. In
all they have five children about whom they talk lazily, naming their
names, listing their accomplishments, their defeats, their hobbies,
their illnesses, their puzzling little mannerisms. (Not that Christine's anti-social behavior is a puzzling little mannerism: it is quite
serious, and Fern knows her daughter should be seeing an analyst,
but she prefers not to think about it and she knows better, certainly,
than to mention it to her lover.) At times they branch out to speak of
in-laws, of friends, of neighbors, of debts, of mortgages, of repairs
needed on their houses or their cars; they often speak of their
distant, improbable childhoods which, recounted now, have taken
on a legendary air. (Are they, perhaps, legendary themselves? Fern
an unknown, unguessed-at heroine, a minor deity? Her lover an
unrecognized god?)

He is considerably older than she—fifty-two; she is still in her thirties. Still! (She feels much older. When she stares at herself in the mirror she is mildly astonished at how young she looks—young and almost-beautiful.) It is easy enough for her to flatter him sexually; he wants to believe, he *will* believe, in his prowess as a lover. Really he wants someone to talk with, someone to talk to. He wants an attractive young woman who will listen to him and flatter him and excite him and allow him to forget—to forget whatever it is he wishes to forget (which he doesn't mention to Fern). Fern has grown accustomed to the idea of being unfaithful to Alex. It is an activity, a way of life. An aspect of personality. For years she was faithful without, of course, thinking of herself as *faithful;* then it happened, not quite two years ago, that she was no longer faithful, and it didn't matter—it didn't matter in the slightest. No one knew, no one observed, no one cared. Alex certainly did not care. The years of faithfulness were revealed as no less provisional than the term of unfaithfulness, which might very well stretch into years: might constitute her future.

Fern strokes her lover's hair as she once stroked Alex's. She talks softly with him, laughing from time to time. She is a petite woman, there is something delightful about her when she isn't frowning, when she is child-like and gay; she can understand why this man seems to be infatuated with her. (It rather amazed her when Alex fell in love with her, long ago. She had always thought of herself as ugly.) She strokes his hair, kisses him, forgets him. She is thinking of—she is thinking of Ted Mandel, with whom she danced back in Ann Arbor at someone's party. Both of them awkward. Warm. Trying to make conversation, trying to joke . . . acutely self-conscious, and conscious of the other. Ted Mandel. Ted. Hadn't she always been attracted to him, in a way . . . ? Slyly she had kissed him once; had pretended to be drunk in order to kiss him on the lips. She had done it—she had done it! Little Fern. Shy awkward self-conscious Fern. She had done it, she had kissed her friend's husband, and now she lies quite contentedly with another friend's husband, and feels no guilt at all.

Had she stroked Ted's hair once? Had they squeezed hands once?—at a New Year's Eve party? She isn't sure. Perhaps not—perhaps she only fantasized it. But certainly she wanted to. (What pleasure it would have given her simply to touch Maxine's husband—Maxine whom she half-adored, and envied, and resented.) Now Ted Mandel is a strikingly handsome man whom she rarely sees since the Mandels' world is so very different from the Enrights': rather self-consciously Bohemian, a little shabby, desperate. (Fern knows in great detail about Ted's "experimental life-style" since Maxine telephones often, keeping her on the phone as long as an hour at a time.) If she encountered Ted in the lobby of this hotel, for instance, or in a downtown restaurant—would she dare approach him simply as a woman, as a woman desiring a man?—or would she find herself acting out the part of little Fern again, a kind of younger sister of Maxine's, sweet but innocuous? Suddenly it seems to her that she wants Ted Mandel; it is Ted she has always wanted; she remembers overhearing Ted and Alex talking, years ago, in the living room of their apartment in Ann Arbor—she remembers the thrill of hearing her husband engage that brilliant, quirky young man in an argument. In a way she was proud of Alex, that he could hold Ted's interest. (What a pity it is that Ted never finished his degree!—and yet symptomatic of the injustice of the world. Ted is a genius, everyone acknowledges his brilliance, yet he is stuck at a small community college where he's poorly paid while Alex Enright is an executive with the Chicago branch of Fairbanks Chemicals and very handsomely paid. . . . It is unjust, yet part of Ted's attractiveness. He is destined to unhappiness; he is doomed.)

Of course it is Ted Mandel she wants.

Two years ago, near dawn of a winter morning, Fern lay paralyzed in a dream in which a swarthy-faced man embraced her. She tried to resist, tried to protest, but it had no effect; the dream overpowered her. She woke in distress, quite upset. The man had had no face. At least she could remember no face. The experience had been a violent, unpleasant one, and she had been haunted by it for an entire day. Not long afterward it happened again: and again the man was faceless. He seemed to know her well, however. He gripped her tight, penetrated her body, possessed her. She woke in alarm, her heart pounding, and for hours she was able to think of nothing else—a dream image, after all, and seemingly insubstantial, and yet so haunting! It was not an exaggeration to say that the dream was more real to her than her children or Alex or the events of that day.

In an erotic daze she fulfilled the various tasks of her life. Her mind was always elsewhere, however; always with *him*. She disliked him, loathed him, feared him—and yet she could not resist thinking of him. He was faceless. Yet he knew her well and she appeared to know him well. (Was he her true husband?—her true lover? Perhaps it had always been a mistake, with Alex.) She felt him in her loins, the aftermath of sheer sensation, violent and without sentiment. A lover. A dream-lover. He came to her a third time, and thereafter Alex was supplanted; for how could be compete with so powerful, so magical a lover?

And so she began to day-dream of her anonymous faceless lover. She willed him to return: but he stayed away. For weeks he stayed away. And then, inexplicably, he returned again. (His loving of her had nothing to do with Alex's: it could not have been said to compensate Alex's. For sometimes the dream-lover appeared not long after Alex had made love to her, and sometimes he appeared when Alex had not made love to her for a considerable period of time.) She was melancholy with love for him . . . and restless, and nervous, and frightened; at the same time she freely acknowledged the absurdity of the situation. (Though she mentioned it to no one, of course—it was too sacred to share.) While dreaming of him she resented the children's interruptions. She resented being forced back into her trivial daylight self—mother, wife. The telephone's ringing was an interruption; the necessity of going out to dinner parties was an interruption; at times, merely talking with Alex annoyed her. (He knew so little, for one thing. He was so profoundly and smugly ignorant.) When her lover stayed away she began to look for him—in her friends' husbands, in strangers on the street. She stared at their faces, tried to calculate and judge. Was it possible that . . . ? Was he someone she might approach, after all . . . ?

Eight months after the dream-lover first came to her she became involved with a man, her first "lover." The term was archaic, quaint, rather courtly and charming. (Was she a "mistress"? The term wasn't adequate but she could think of no other.) The man was exciting at first and then disappointing; he was not *the* lover. And so she drifted from him, and drifted into an involvement with someone else. . . . She was able now to think quite dispassionately about sexual matters. As a young girl she had been overwhelmed with embarrassment at the mere mention of sexual behavior, and had not cared, even, to think about it in private; now, in her mid-thirties, she thought of sex almost constantly, but without emotion. What was it, after all? What was meant by "sex"? Had it primarily to do with an

individual's body, with bodily sensation?—or must it be in relationship with another person? The former seemed a mere physiological
phenomenon; the latter a social phenomenon; must they necessarily
and inevitably be related? She could not see why.

Just as marriage is a social event, so adultery is a social event: Fern
is dependent upon a man in either case. Consequently the marriage
and the adultery strike her as being nearly identical . . . far less
mesmerizing, less compelling, than her relationship with the
dream-lover. His visits are unpredictable, the effect of his love is
intangible, other-worldly. In a way he is not sexual at all. He is a
creation of the imagination, a god of the unconscious; he is far more
than merely physical. He has no "existence" and yet he means more
to her, in a way, than husband and lover and children. . . . She can
think about him for hours, entirely absorbed in his mystery, adrift in
a half-pleasant, half-apprehensive reverie, not "unfaithful" to Alex
or to her present lover so much as unrelated to them entirely. They
are, after all, only human men. When she thinks of her dream-lover
she is not Fern Enright, she is no one's wife and no one's mistress:
she is no one at all: utterly free.

And yet she cannot resist searching for him, in the human world.

At times she is fiercely convinced that he does exist, he *must* exist.
When her lover disappoints her (as he is disappointing her this
afternoon with his stale, self-promoting gossip—she must make
excuses and leave early, must escape) she has the idea that another
lover would not disappoint her. Another lover might reveal himself
as *the* lover. She is young yet, she is only thirty-six though she feels
far older, she is more attractive than ever before, it isn't too late. . . .

Ted Mandel. Ted. The memory of her standing on tiptoe, cutely,
to kiss him full on the lips. Perhaps, all along, it has been Ted of
whom she dreams . . . ? Ted whom she truly loves . . . ?

Her lover falls silent and then, after a long moment, accuses her of
not listening to him and not caring for him; of thinking instead of her
husband. At once Fern begins to apologize. She hears her soft,
breathless voice and does not recognize it—how perverse, really—
how hilarious the deception—but since it is the voice her personality
has perfected, since it is the voice men have admired, she will not
reject it now.

"I'm sorry," she says gently. "I was thinking only that it's getting
late—it's after three—I should be leaving soon."

"I suppose you can't help yourself," the man says with a cynical, elderly sigh.

V. JUNE 1976

"Mother, Mrs. Mandel is on the phone again—"
"Tell her I've just left, Linda. I'll call her back tomorrow."
"How can I tell her *that*, for God's sake?"
"Tell her you'll take a message."
"She sounds sort of funny—"
"What do you mean, funny?"
"Sort of weird, like she's angry or something."
"Angry? But why? She isn't angry at you, is she? —Look: just tell her I've left, I'm not home."
"Can't you tell her yourself?"
"Linda, please!"
"Tell her yourself ! I'm not going to lie for you."

Ted, unpacking books in Green River, Vermont, comes across his old Penguin copy of *The Republic*. He leafs through it idly. Who has written all these comments in the margins, in green ball-point ink? *Dramatic irony . . . paradox . . . 'first cause'*. The marginal notations interest him more than the dialogue itself. How young he was then, how impressionable, and yet how keen-witted! Fascinated, Ted remains squatting so long that his legs and thighs ache murderously. He can barely stand—can barely straighten.
"Hey, what are you reading?" Lisabeth asks.
"I'm not sure," Ted says.

The man in the madras vest, James J. Gilmore, has begun to cry.
Alex is embarrassed. He cannot think where to turn his gaze. The photographs of Fern and the children on his desk, outdated, handsomely framed in dark leather—the heavy coral paperweight from last winter's vacation in the Keys—the scattered papers, letters, pamphlets, photostated newspaper items—the file on James J. Gilmore: Alex looks from place to place, pulling nervously at his nose. (This is a new mannerism he has picked up from somewhere—it

annoys Fern very much but she supposes it would be pointless to mention it to him.)

"Mr. Enright," Gilmore says, "I wonder if— I wonder— Is the decision irrevocable?"

The time for weeping is past, long past. Gilmore has a history of small damning blunders since he came to Fairbanks (with all those inflated recommendations); has he really believed no one was taking account?

"I'm afraid it is," Alex says, frowning. He knows from experience that he does not dare smile; he does not dare even look at his man sympathetically. At this point it would be an error. Tears would flow all the more. "As I said. . . ." Leafing through the file he quotes again various warnings, various suggestions, and again the quite generous terms of dismissal—six months' salary; he sums the session up by closing the file and pushing it a few inches away.

"I wonder if— Could I— Possibly an extension—"

"I'm afraid not," Alex says impassively.

Maxine brews a pot of Celestial Seasonings tea; she studies the message attached to the tea-bag. *Wisdom comes through suffering—Aeschylus.*

She makes an attempt to listen closely to the record she has borrowed from the local branch library, following the advice of a corpulent but very intelligent man she has become acquainted with in her night-school class; the record is the choir of St. John's College, Cambridge, singing Tudor Church music. But something is wrong. The voices are guttural and sluggish. For months the phonograph has been playing slow, but it is too much trouble to arrange for it to be repaired. Or did Maxine check out the wrong record? She sips at the tea without tasting it and listens to the low grunting ugly voices as tears stream down her cheeks.

Christine, alarmingly pretty, her long straight brown hair falling nearly to her waist, stands in the doorway telling Fern about the sister of a friend of hers who was badly beaten by her roommate. In Boston, it was. Both girls are art students at Boston University. One of the girls became convinced that their next-door neighbors were spying on them with electronic equipment, and that was weird enough, but eventually she came to think that her own friend was involved—and one night she began to beat her with a curtain rod, and when that broke she went after her with a hammer.

"And we were going to go visit them!" Christine says, giggling.

"You were?" Fern asks.

"Yeah, we were making plans—Lou and me. Really crazy, isn't it? I hope nobody around here gets that bad."

Christine has a full, lazy body that has grown a great deal in the past year. She is sixteen years old but might be eighteen or nineteen; her face too is mature, especially her eyes. That quizzical expression of hers—always rather skeptical, insolent—unnerves her mother.

"Yeah, we were making plans to go to Boston, this friend of Lou's, Rich, did I tell you about Rich?—no?—he's got some girl friend or something in Boston, or maybe it's his girl friend's friend, or something, and he's going around July 1 and we can get a ride with him if we want. We might go anyway."

"You might . . . ?" Ferns asks.

"I said we might, yes."

Christine smiles at her mother, leaning against the door-frame. She is wearing a pair of very tight blue jeans and a pull-over jersey blouse that strains against her breasts. Fern tries to smile in return; it is her first reaction, always. (At the same time she is wondering who this attractive but rather sluttish-looking girl is—what have they to do with each other? In Christine's room, on Christine's creamy-white walls, there are four-foot-high posters of straggly-haired, leering, lipsticked creatures in costumes that range from ordinary blue jeans and denim vests to rhinestone-studded silks and brocade; the creatures are evidently masculine though they wear make-up and even their eyelids are painted. Fern wonders—does her daughter dream of them jumping down from the walls, does she dream of embracing them, inviting them into her bed? Perhaps, already, in the over-heated secrecy of night, they have penetrated her plump, beautiful body.)

"Why, is anything wrong?" Christine says, still smiling.

Fern knows that in another moment the girl's smile will vanish; her face will swell with a child's direct unreasonable anger.

"Nothing is wrong," Fern says slowly.

"Nothing is wrong," Fern says, alone.

Ted and Lisabeth have set aside Wednesday for a day of fast. They drink tea, bouillon, fruit juice, V-8 juice, and a great deal of water.

Once their systems are cleansed they are optimistic about their ability to deal with the primitive conditions of the house they have rented in Green River. "There's a certain sense in which all likes and dislikes, and even pain itself, are functions of the ego," Lisabeth says. "To have a single thought—'positive' or 'negative', even—isn't it maybe an intrusion upon nature?"

"I've thought of that many times," Ted says.

Far away is a land of assassinations, bombings, betrayals, demonstrations, a woman's malicious nagging, a woman's drunken accusations. Somewhere a fetus flushed down a drain: or do they keep them in bottles? Does Ted have a fetus-child somewhere in Ann Arbor, bobbing in a formaldahyde mixture, quivering whenever a jet passes overhead . . . ? It is something to contemplate.

Lisabeth scrambles to her feet. In the kitchen she turns on a gas jet, strikes a match. Tea? Bouillon? Soup? Both are quite weak with hunger.

"Hey, I love you," Ted says.

Lisabeth cut most of her hair off some weeks ago and it hasn't grown back evenly. She is sunburned, a big-breasted, handsome, healthy girl with dark brown eyes, a quick, broad, unreflective smile, and strong, muscular legs. She dropped out of a Master's degree program in psychiatric social work because the sorrows of the world had threatened to overwhelm her. "One must save oneself first, before attempting to save others," she says often.

"Indeed one must," Ted sighs.

At lunch in Dell's Chop House Alex is careful to order an egg dish. Shirred eggs with whole wheat toast. No drink—not for him. He listens attentively to what is being said, and speaks when it is his turn. Graying, austere, kindly, he has become a man whose reflection troubles him occasionally when he sees it unprepared—in the mirrors of cigarette machines, in darkened windows, in automobile hubcaps. He is attractive, still, and his hair is quite thick. He dresses well. He carries himself well. He does not dislike the man he has become; he simply doesn't recognize him.

(Only forty-one!—he thinks in amazement. Is it possible? He feels so much older. His father was in his early sixties when he died and Alex feels at least that old. In a sense, he feels that he has lived beyond his father's age—has overtaken his father at last. He knows more, he knows everything there is to know.)

His associates are talking about the unusually cold June weather,
poor sailing conditions on the lake, the disappointing economy, the
rumor that someone will die soon—no, that someone will be promoted
soon: or transferred. To the West Coast, perhaps, or to England. Or
Ireland, where a new Fairbanks subsidiary is being built near Shan-
non. There is a rumor that one company will merge with another.
That several will be bought up by a famous conglomerate. Alex
listens closely, with one part of his mind. He knows the facts, he
knows what is in store for at least one of the men lunching with him,
but his expression is impassive. From time to time he smiles and his
companions are rather warmed by that smile—it is so sincere,
almost boyish, almost hopeful. (It is the one thing about himself Alex
never sees. His image in mirrors is always so grave when he studies
it.) Talk shifts to city politics, to state politics, to a Republican
fund-raising banquet to be held at the end of the month. Alex listens
with part of his mind and with another part of his mind he thinks of
the single adventure he has had in years: working late with one of his
secretaries, a pretty divorced mother; ordering food sent up from a
nearby Chinese restaurant; around eight o'clock, by accident,
brushing her arm; an awkward breathy kiss; and even more awkward
embrace; and then—nothing. They returned to work red-faced and
embarrassed.

In the restroom a graying gentleman accosts him, smiling at him
in the tinted mirror. Yes? You are—? Ah yes: we know you.

Everywhere he has begun seeing men like himself. Well-
groomed, well-dressed, always with neckties. (The *others* have not
worn neckties in years.) There is something mournful about their
eyes; something too alert about their smiles. "A kind of genius," it is
said. High-level management. The ability to work with people or
to—the expression is ugly but accurate—manipulate them is not an
ability that can be developed; one must be born with it. It is
especially tricky to work with intelligent, clever men, or with men
who are by nature suspicious. However, it can be done. It must be
done. "A kind of genius though never applauded," it is said. His
salary is not astonishing but it is quite satisfactory. Everywhere he
sees men like himself and he assumes that their genius is as handsomely rewarded as his own; he assumes that these men, like
himself, are often overtaken by small navigable fits of melancholy.
They are never at the very top—the very top is made up of presi-

dents, chairmen of boards, directors, senators, governors. Still, they occupy positions near the top; they are the men who make the others possible.

"Genius," he thinks, tasting the shirred eggs. He has brought along a special salt-substitute to shake onto his food. "Sacrifice," he thinks. He watches the graying gentleman eat, he admires his manners, his gracious measured smile.

In the chilly green silence of Vermont Ted and Lisabeth spend a great deal of time talking about the past. Their pasts. Ted has sifted through his childhood, his teenage years, his years at Cornell and at Ann Arbor; he has analyzed his "heavy, neurotic" relationship with his former wife. And there is Jacqueline—Jacqueline with the peculiar last name. And other girls. (One or two of them Lisabeth knew.) Most of the time, of course, he has talked about Maxine. "We loved each other very much," he says, wiping tears from his eyes. Then again: "I don't think we loved each other at all. I think it was a tragic mistake." Wistfully he dwells upon their friendship with the Enrights, though for some reason he slights his own intermittent attraction for Fern. He doesn't want Lisabeth to be jealous—he wants to present her with love affairs that are finished, dead, nearly forgotten.

In turn Lisabeth talks freely about her life. A tumultous childhood, parents who quarreled, separated, came together again and quarreled, and finally divorced; a miserable girlhood ("I had no friends, Ted. No one. No one to talk to.") and a sudden, stupid marriage at the age of eighteen to a man in his early thirties who claimed to be a manufacturer's representative but was, in fact, a kind of salesman for Kinney Shoes. And then separation, divorce. . . . And then. . . . A series of lovers, not all of them entirely kind or entirely sane. One beat her and locked her out of the house in a freezing rain. (She weeps in Ted's arms, recounting the incident. He strokes her hair, her smooth shoulders, he kisses her eagerly: what won't he do, at this point in his life, to make someone less unhappy!) Another, a Jamaican, threatened her with a knife because she refused to have his children. And. . . .

In the chilly green emptiness of Vermont they retell their life stories. The dark of the old farmhouse rings richly with fairy tales, with legends of blessed, blighted children. Ted, hearing his own trembling voice, marvels that he was a kind of hero all along: a wounded prince.

They make love tenderly. Ted must be careful with her; she has been so abused. ("Am I hurting you? Are you all right? Are you certain?") They lie in each other's arms and listen to the frequent rainstorms. One morning there are snow fluries; Lisabeth laughs with a kind of shocked delight.

How strange it is, this world they've come to. . . .

She makes spaghetti with tomato and mushroom sauce; the house is filled with the odors of cooking. Ted is trying to sandpaper the steep, narrow stairs. Often, during the day, they consciously avoid each other. They observe a sacred space around each other. Ted reads through his old books one by one and has been, over the weeks, regaining his interest in certain philosophers. Plato seems rather sly, but Spinoza is profound in a way Ted had not realized previously; Hume is amusing, a master of paradoxical surfaces, but Schopenhauer is disturbing, Nietzsche fascinating, and Ortega— whom he had not read in much depth before—very stimulating indeed. And there is Whitehead. And William James, whom he had always slighted, like most of his colleagues.

In an old ledger he takes notes, writing late at night when Lisabeth is asleep. His eyes sometimes ache; he has difficulty read- ing; is it possible that he needs bifocal lenses?—he doesn't like to think of himself as that old. (He will be forty-two in September.) But it doesn't matter. He is newly inspired, he is beginning to plan, vaguely, a book of some kind—not on Hume and the positivists, after all, but on William James; James who has been so neglected. (It is James's Americanism that interests Ted now. The idea of truth *happening to* an idea, not inherent in it: the idea of the ever- changing, ever-evolving pluralistic universe, which will not be con- tained by one's conceptions of it.)

A book of intellectual curiosity and discovery, a book of love . . . ?

Probably he will never write it; he has grown too haphazard in his thinking, too undisciplined. (His guts squirm when he remembers the grotesque lectures he used to give at Franklin Heights Com- munity College. Good Christ, how eager those students were to believe him, how readily they idolized him, their flippant, sardonic Professor Mandel!—the closest thing to an "intellectual" they had ever encountered. It is dizzying, the memory of his success. Those adoring young people hypnotized him; there is no other way of explaining it, no other way of comprehending his own delusion. Years of it. Years of applause. Banal paradoxes, trivial insights, simplistic "revolutionary" declarations. He found it remarkably easy to be radical because he knew, all along, that his position in society could not be snatched from him. He could condemn the police state because it protected him, he could jeer at the government because it took no notice of him, or granted him unlimited freedom of speech while taking no specific notice of him. He could reject the past because his students had no awareness of the past and consequently no investment in it, and because it gave him genuine pleasure—to reject the tradition that had, in effect, rejected him. He had been hypnotized, yes. For an extraordinary period of time. And then it had come to an end: one day he awoke. Not long afterward the college itself collapsed, its budget was decimated and a number of its buildings sold to the city, and he had felt no regret at all, only a sense of profound relief. Its collapse was bound up with the collapse of his marriage, and he felt only a bitter, anguished relief about that as well.)

So he takes fastidious, self-querying notes in the ledger. *Is* it true that the truth or falsity of a statement is not inherent in the conditions of life, but rather an impermanent quality, subject to constant modification? If this is true in itself, where are the numerous "truths" of his past? He loved a woman; he ceased to love a woman; he loves another woman now; perhaps someday he will cease to love her: the only constant seems to be the subject *He*. But that too is impermanent. Painful as it is he must accept the fact of his own mortality—his mother died the autumn before, and his father has become increasingly feeble; and Maxine came so close, that desperate, foolish time, to dying. Even Lisabeth who has the appearance of a strong, healthy, contented woman has admitted that the thought of suicide attracted her upon several occasions. But of course, she is quick to say, that was long before I met you.

By the time he and Lisabeth decide to leave Vermont, not so much bored with the countryside as filled with it, satiated, Ted will have scrawled over one hundred pages of notes; he will have completed a kind of outline for a book. Does it matter if he writes the book or not?—the exercise of intellectual curiosity is pleasing in itself. He does things more slowly now. He is no longer rushed, no longer harassed with the attention of others, the need to be *interesting*. (How those students mesmerized him with their admiration!—he still thinks of the queer trick his popularity played upon him, and he wonders if he would be immune to it now. He had not understood before what certain great men meant by angrily rejecting their disciples. He had supposed they were being pathologically modest.)

By the time he and Lisabeth decide to leave Vermont they will have decided, as well, not to marry. "It's just that you're so much younger than I am," Ted says. "God, I can hardly *remember* when I was twenty-seven—isn't that incredible?" She nods slowly and gravely, but her eyes do not fill with tears. A fine, strong *genuine* person, Ted thinks; if only—! But he has begun to feel his age in recent months. And what is most surprising, he has begun to feel fairly content with his age: why has everyone told him that middle age is depressing? If he isn't young any longer he needn't behave as if he were; he needn't pretend. Pretense will be a thing of the past.

Lisabeth has arranged for a job with a mental health clinic in Potsdam, New York, and Ted begins writing letters of application to universities, colleges, and community colleges; he wants very much to teach again, and he is certain that, if he keeps trying, he will be offered a satisfactory position. In the meantime he doesn't mind living a life of relative poverty. The great philosophers and thinkers will be his models once again: why had he ever turned away from them? He plans to remake himself, revolutionize his own personality in terms of what is long-lasting (perhaps even eternal); in a few years he will find himself deeply absorbed in Judaism . . . perhaps as a way of placating his father and yet defining himself against him: for the Judaism that will interest Ted is the mystical strain, which his family has always shunned.

He and Lisabeth will write to each other occasionally, brief impulsive handwritten notes stimulated by memories of their time together in Vermont. As the years pass, their relationship will come to seem more and more idyllic; more nobly romantic. "There are times when I can't imagine why we ever parted," Ted will write, and Lisabeth will write, "You changed my life though I didn't realize it at the time. But I realize it now and want simply to say—*Thank you.*"

Though it is a mild, sunny June day and Maxine knows she should spend it outside—walking, perhaps: she does so little walking now—or seeing about another job (she is a secretary for a small and not very successful firm dealing in trophies and club jackets; she works only three days a week) she decides to go to a neighborhood movie instead. A mistake: the film is a self-conscious western, very familiar despite its attempts to go against the viewer's expectations, and worse of all—truly depressing—is the presence of Marlon Brando, whom Maxine had once admired so much and who is now, in this film, paunchy and hammy and unbelievable and silly, a self-parody whose evident indifference or contempt for himself is almost obscene in Maxine's eyes. Indeed, when he is on the screen Maxine's heart beats with shame, as if she were being forced to see an older member of her family exhibited to strangers' derision—she cannot bear it and leaves early and goes to a nearby bar and has several drinks, keeping to herself, aware of the interest of one or two men but set in opposition to them, bitterly unhappy, resentful of—of what?—Brando's betrayal of his younger self?—of his mockery of her own (and Ted's) idolization?—at any rate she is profoundly depressed. It is a black, inert state, like the one she slipped into some eighteen months before, when she took an accidental overdose of sleeping pills.

She has a few drinks. Not many. She isn't drunk—isn't even close to being drunk. (She could always handle alcohol better than Ted and of course he resented it.) She goes home and immediately dials her friend Fern's number and one of the children answers—must be the boy Terry—how strange, she doesn't even know Terry—has only seen him a few times, really—and he runs to get his mother and Maxine waits, lighting a cigarette, then it occurs to her to pour a few inches of scotch in a tumbler, since Fern is sometimes rather boring—sweet as she is, and Maxine's oldest, closest friend. She waits; Terry is evidently hunting up his mother; she sips at the scotch and finds it oddly tasteless—or is something wrong with her taste buds?—her tongue and the inside of her mouth feel deadened.

"Fern?" she calls. "Fern?"

She waits. Has another swallow of scotch. Carries the telephone to the sofa, passing the kitchen without glancing in—the sink is piled high with dishes, yes, she knows that very well, there's no need to check. Teabags in the sink. Coffee grounds. Toast crusts. Plates from breakfast and last night's dinner and maybe yesterday's lunch and breakfast as well. *"Wisdom comes through suffering,"* Maxine says aloud, lying on the sofa. She laughs. A sudden snort of laughter. "Wisdom . . . suffering . . . Aeschylus. Who the hell was he, spreading such crap? Such biodegradable crap? —Hello, Fern?"

"Hello—"

"Hello, Fern? This is Maxine."

"Yes—"

"Hello? Can you hear me?"

"Yes, Maxine. I can hear you."

For some reason she is irritated at Fern, but she does her best to conceal her irritation. She asks how Fern is, how Alex and the children are, she swings onto the topic of the movie she has just seen—Jesus Christ, how depressing—how truly depressing—*truly*—and tells Fern to be sure not to see it since it would only evoke old painful memories; or maybe she should see it, as a kind of exercise of—of—an exercise of nostalgia—

Fern replies in a voice so faint Maxine can't quite hear. How annoying she is, always mumbling! A bad habit of hers from years ago. Maxine asks if she has a cold—no?—her voice sounds a little nasal.

Fern says that she's quite well.

Maxine asks if Fern might like to meet her for lunch sometime this week in Chicago. They could see the new exhibit at the art gallery, or go shopping, or. . . . While Fern mumbles a reply Maxine lights another cigarette. It seems that Fern is busy this week and most of next: visitors from out of town, something about Linda's school.

Maxine is very disappointed.

She hides her disappointment, though, and asks about Linda. How old is she now? How does she like that new school?

Very well, Fern says. She likes it very well.

Maxine finishes the scotch. It crosses her mind that Ted might be in communication with the Enrights; she asks if they have heard from him recently.

Fern sounds surprised; she says they haven't been in contact with Ted for a very long time.

(In fact the Enrights received a peculiar Seasons' Greetings card from Ted back in January. It was postmarked Los Angeles and Ted's scrawl was practically illegible. "Hey, look at this," Terry said, picking it out of the heap of mail. "Is this some friend of yours? His handwriting's really *weird*.")

Maxine is embarrassed about having asked. She mutters something about Ted behaving so irresponsibly at the end; just going
away, slamming the door on his past like that. Her psychiatrist said
such behavior was juvenile and aggressive, even psychopathic.

Fern, staring at the wall, wonders at Maxine's phrasing. *At the
end?* As if Ted were dead?

Maxine says, sighing, that she is in much better health now, freed
of that confining, stultifying marriage. "It was like a box," she says.
"Like a coffin, Fern. You can't imagine."

Fern murmurs agreement.

Maxine talks for a while, doing her best to be dispassionate and
"objective," analyzing Ted's weaknesses, his reasons for wanting a
divorce, his relationship with his parents. "Especially the mother,
Fern. God! You *can't imagine.*" She sighs again. Fern has the idea
that Maxine is stretched out somewhere, on a sofa or in bed. She is
utterly relaxed, abandoned, slovenly, in a queer way quite happy.
There is something luxurious about her querulous tone. Fern shuts
her eyes against such a vision. She has just returned from a lengthy
luncheon, a bridge luncheon, and she is rather tired—she would like
to take a long lazy bath, she would like to lie down, she would like to
lock herself in the bedroom and cry. (How luxurious, to cry freely
and angrily for a half-hour!) But Maxine is in no hurry. Maxine has a
great deal to say but she is in no hurry about saying it. Her voice slurs
from time to time; no doubt she's been drinking; she drifts onto
topics Fern would rather not hear about—Ted's inadequacies as a
lover and his total inability to deal with finances—"I think the two
are related, don't you?" Maxine asks seriously.

After Ted she discussed, candidly, the gifts and shortcomings of a
recent lover, a man named Tony whom Fern doesn't know. At first it
appears that Maxine met Tony at work, then it appears she met him
in a bar; then it seems that someone, a "dear friend," introduced
them. Tony is superior to Ted in many ways but it would be pointless
to pretend that he's perfect. "He's a long way from *that,*" Maxine
says, suddenly snorting with laughter.

Fern cannot think of anything to say. She doesn't want to inquire
about Tony—she doesn't want Maxine to believe that she is curious
about Maxine's love affairs; she would like to tell Maxine that she's
rather tired, has a headache—but Maxine continues talking, pointing out that she isn't at all serious about Tony—she isn't serious

about anyone—never intends to be serious about anyone or anything again in her life. "I mean, what the hell? It isn't worth it. They
use you and abandon you and that's that, right? —You know I'm
right."

Fern mumbles a meek assent.

(She finds herself thinking of her own lover, her former lover.
Like the others he was the husband of an acquaintance, a woman
Fern's age, in fact a very sweet, pretty woman whom Fern has
always admired. Her name is Thea. Fern likes that name—Thea.
The lover was like any lover, any husband in their circle: nice
enough, really, but ultimately disappointing. Not so intelligent as
Alex, even. Nor so attractive. In his early forties, rather slack-
waisted, with an odd habit of laughing exuberantly at his own
remarks, even when they weren't, in Fern's opinion, very amusing.
Fern supposes their relationship is over: he telephoned several
times, one of the children took a message each time, Fern neglected
to call back. Today at luncheon she and Thea sat near each other and
were no more and no less than ordinarily friendly, so Fern supposes
the husband has not told the wife, nor has anyone else told the wife
though probably—since Lake Forest is a small community—there
were people who knew or guessed. Query: if Thea knows that Fern
has slept with her husband but does not know that Fern knows of her
knowledge, is it possible that the two women, the two wives, can
remain on friendly terms indefinitely? . . . Not, of course, that they
are really friends. Fern has the idea that friendship is past. It was a
phenomenon of her adolescence and young adulthood; and she does
not feel young any longer. Her lovers are not her friends, nor does
she want them as friends. She does not intend to open herself to
them as one must to one's friends; she does not intend to be vulnerable again in her life, all that is past, past. Friendship is a religion in
which she no longer believes.)

" . . . lonely. A well of . . . what is it . . . loneliness. Are you
listening? Fern?" Maxine says querulously.

"Of course I'm listening, Maxine."

There is a moment of offended silence. Then Maxine says in a
louder voice that she is lonely: she isn't ashamed to admit it: she's
lonely. Lonely as hell. It seems that she has been waiting for weeks
. . . for months . . . hoping for a telephone call from Fern, her
closest friend. Hoping for an invitation. Oh not for an evening: not

for one of Fern's precious social evenings! Oh no. Maxine would not
presume. But for an afternoon, for a drink or coffee or. . . . "Look,
am I a leper suddenly? Has Alex written me off too . . . ?"

Fern is shocked. She protests, but Maxine cuts her off.

"All right, all right. I understand," Maxine says cynically. "A
divorcee and all that. . . . I understand."

(Neither woman brings up the fact that the Enrights had not seen
the Mandels socially for years. They met once or twice at restaurants
in the Chicago area, and once at a sea-food place on Lake Michigan
north of Waukegan, but that was about it.)

There is silence for several seconds. Fern begins to speak, and
Maxine begins at the same time. Her tone is contrite; she sounds
suddenly drunk. She is apologizing for possibly having insulted Fern
a while back . . . those remarks she made about Alex's job. . . .

Alex's job? Fern can't remember.

Alex's job, yes. That nuclear power plant or whatever it is. In—
where is it—Saskatchewan—is that how you pronounce it?—up in
Canada. Fairbanks Inc. Some little town contaminated by radiation,
a nuclear dump, something like that, it was in the newspapers for a
while, wasn't it, and Maxine brought it up once: she'd been a little
emotional at the time. (Fern really can't remember. She wonders if
Maxine had meant to confront her with the news, had rehearsed
certain remarks, but then had forgotten about it.). . . . Well, it's a
shame, a goddam shame, that big American capitalists can take
advantage of ignorant people like that, impoverished people; the
worst thing about the situation, the really ironic thing, was that the
citizens of the town got angry at the newspaper reports, not at the
company. How pathetic. . . . But how typical, Maxine supposes;
how typically human. ("I'd better watch myself," she says. "I don't
want to sound like Ted.") Just imagine: a nuclear dump, radiation
contaminating the drinking water, possibly causing cancer, and the
townspeople angry at the *reporters*. Of course it makes sense, a
pitiful sense. If the company moves out the town will go bank-
rupt. . . . But it's terrible that Alex should be connected with it,
Maxine cannot resist saying. After all: *our* Alex.

Fern says that she doesn't think Alex is connected with that particular plant. But her voice is faint and Maxine doesn't hear. Maxine talks
disjointedly about Alex, and about Ted, something about Ann Arbor
again, and then suddenly she is crying. " . . nobody gives a damn,

why should they . . . civilized life . . . they use you and move on and that's that. . . . *Suffering comes through wisdom* or whatever the saying is. . . . Celestial Seasonings. Bastards. Taking advantage. I told him and told him that. . . . Tried to explain. . . . Would he listen? No. Bastard. And you too: gossiping behind my back. I knew all along. Ted knew. Cyn Swanson was a dear friend and *she* told me . . . or was it Annie. . . . Nobody gives a damn. Feel so low. Lonely. Not even drunk. Not sleepy. Wish to God I could sleep . . . I'd like to sleep for three solid days. No interruptions. The hell with the job: see? Let them beg. I'm too good for them. College degree, poems published, should be teaching somewhere. . . . If I took a handful of sleeping pills and went to bed and slipped into a coma . . . if I died . . . if I died and lay in bed and rotted. . . . If. . . . Nobody would give a damn, right? Nobody would give a damn. I know."

Fern tries to interrupt. "Maxine," she says. "Please—"

"*Maxine please!*" Maxine says, mimicking her voice. "The fact is. . . . The fact is. . . . Nobody gives a damn, that's the central fact of our time. Right? Central fact of our time. Ted should've written his goddam dissertation on that."

"Maxine," Fern says shakily, "I wish you wouldn't talk like this. That other time . . . the pills. . . . We were all very upset about you, you know, it was a terrible, terrible experience. What if I hadn't been home when you called? Of course it was only an accident, but. . . ."

Maxine is crying again. "*Maxine please! Maxine please!* Just like Ted. Don't give a damn for anybody else . . . for friendship. The central fact of our time. . . . You're damn right it was an accident, my dear. Don't flatter yourself otherwise."

"Maxine, I wish you wouldn't do this to me," Fern says. "I'm very tired. I could nearly faint, I'm so—"

"Do this to you! My God, what egotism," Maxine says, managing a laugh. "*I wish you wouldn't do this to me!* —Jesus, just listen to her."

"I mean—"

"Talk about egotism: as if someone would commit suicide over *you*. That's really ludicrous, Fern. Oh God. That's really ludicrous."

"Maxine, you know I didn't mean that. I only meant—"

"Go to hell."

"Maxine—"

"I said go to hell! Just like Ted, you're all just like Ted. The thing is. . . . The thing is you don't want love, you don't want to love anyone, don't want . . . don't want to be responsible for . . . for anyone else. Selfish bastards. Lake Forest Country Club: selfish bastards. I'm just a burden, aren't I, a nuisance, something hanging around your fragile little neck like one of those albatrosses or whatever they are called . . . big prehistoric birds . . . huge things . . . hanging around your neck. So you want me to go to hell; you don't give a damn what happens to me. You and Ted and Alex. Selfish bastards. . . . You want me to go to hell, is that it? Is that it?"

"Maxine, what's wrong? I really don't understand," Fern cries. "One moment we were talking, we were just talking about— about— And the next moment you got so angry—"

"Who wouldn't be angry?" Maxine says loudly. "Listen to little Miss Hypocrite! Lies and more lies. Nothing but lies. Ever since your precious husband got that promotion of his . . . ever since you bought that house in Lake Forest. . . . You don't even know how transparent you are! Always saying you'll telephone and then days go by and I telephone instead and one of the children takes a message and you don't bother to call for another week, what do you think that does to me, you little bitch, little lying bitch, dowdy little Fern Enright, do you think you can fool *me*? Your picture taken with those other bitches, benefit or whatever the hell it was for the Chicago Symphony, you don't fool *me*, miss. Not Maxine. Not for a moment. I know you from way back, don't I? Used to tell you how to dress, pick out clothes for you, your taste was pathetic, really laughable . . . used to help you cook. . . . Remember, you begged me to help you in the kitchen, you were afraid of ruining things, you *begged* me to help you. Borrowed my recipe for spaghetti sauce because Alex liked it so. Remember? Remember? Dowdy little Fern, homely little Fern, putting on airs now because her husband makes $150,000 a year poisoning people. . . . You're such a vicious liar, a cruel selfish vicious. . . ."

"Maxine, for God's sake—"

Fern too has begun to cry. She cannot believe what she has heard: for a moment she feels as if she will really faint.

"*Maxine, for God's sake,*" Maxine says. "Why don't you go to hell?"

"I just don't understand—"

"Don't give a damn if I live or die, just like Ted, nobody gives a damn if I live or die, nobody gives the slightest damn," Maxine says loudly. "You know very well what I mean: you understand every word."

She hangs up.

Fern cries, "Maxine? Maxine—?"

She breaks the connection and begins to dial Maxine's number. But she is so nervous she misdials. She starts again, panting. How horrible, how grotesque. . . . What a nightmare. . . . The phone rings and rings and someone answers it but it isn't Maxine: it is a man: a stranger with a Negro accent. Fern apologizes for having dialed the wrong number. She is very nervous now, very upset. (She has a vision of Maxine swallowing a bottle of sleeping pills, washing them down with scotch. The other time, eighteen months earlier, she had called Fern just at dinner time, at seven, and in a voice so faint it was almost unrecognizable she said she'd made a "miscalculation," she was afraid she'd taken too many pills, she had been napping off and on all day and woke around five and felt very, very depressed and took several pills, and dosed off again, and woke, and took some more . . . and maybe she'd taken too many . . . she wasn't sure. . . . Fern had called an ambulance, and the police, and had driven over to Maxine's apartment; unfortunately Alex was out of town that evening, on an overnight business trip to Toronto, so she had to go alone. She had been so frightened of what might happen to Maxine that she'd nearly had an accident. But, as it turned out, Maxine began vomiting as soon as she hung up, and most of the poison was out of her stomach by the time the ambulance arrived, and she was never in really grave danger. Nevertheless Fern had been very upset.)

She dials the number again. The phone at the other end rings. Rings and rings and rings.

Much later she will think: That son of a bitch, Ted. To have left her. To have divorced her. To have moved out of Chicago.

She dials Maxine's number again and no one answers. She is very tired now. Her head is reeling, her hands are clammy, she is trying to think what must be done: trying to remember what Maxine said. It is possible that she has left the apartment. Has walked out, knowing that Fern will call back at once. It is possible that she is in a neighborhood bar at the moment, telling someone about Fern, her dowdy, homely little friend. . . .

"Maxine?" Fern cries.

No one answers.

She hangs up. She goes to the kitchen, drinks a glass of water, presses the cold glass against her forehead. She has a vision of. . . . But no: she must not panic.

Must not exaggerate.

She returns to the phone and dials Maxine's number again, and again she listens to the ringing at the other end. It is maddening, that hideous mechanical sound: she feels her mind is about to snap. "Maxine, please," she whispers. Her face is wet with tears, her body is uncomfortably damp with perspiration.

What will she tell Alex?

(He has said several times already that it might be a good idea for her not to see Maxine again. "I've heard she's drinking too much," Alex says, astonishing Fern—for how does Alex know about Maxine? How does he know about anything?)

She hangs up. Presses her forehead against the wall. Hears again Maxine's drunken ugly voice. *Go to hell. Go to hell. Vicious little liar, cruel selfish vicious* . . .

"Maxine, I don't understand," she says aloud, sobbing.

She tries the number again. Again the phone rings at the other end.

. . . ten, eleven, twelve. Thirteen, fourteen. . . .

And then, suddenly, Fern hangs up.

Linda Enright enters the house by the rear, through the glassed-in porch, bringing with her two girl friends, Cissy and Barbara. Linda is slight-bodied, like her mother, and she has evidently inherited her father's weak eyes. She wears blue jeans like the other girls, and a sleeveless blouse with a sunny, grinning face on the front, and fashionable rimless glasses which are always riding down her nose. She wears her hair long and straight, as the others do; it is a fair, light brown.

"Mother—?"

She has caught sight of Fern at the foot of the stairs, not moving. Fern is simply standing there. Her hand is gripping the bannister but she isn't moving, she appears to be paralyzed, as if listening to something distant. For a moment she does not even seem to be aware of Linda and her friends.

"Mother, is something wrong? Cissy and Barb and I—"

Fern turns dazedly to look at her. Linda thinks—She's been drinking, there's trouble with Father and they're going to get divorced and she's been drinking and—

"Mother, is—is something wrong?"

"Of course nothing is wrong," Fern says slowly. She looks haggard, distraught. Is she drunk? Is that her secret? (She and Barbara know about Cissy's mother, but Cissy doesn't know that they know; at least, she appears not to know.) " . . . nothing wrong. What could be wrong? I was just talking to someone on the phone . . . it wasn't important. Why are you staring at me like that?" Her voice rises peevishly, but when she notices Linda's friends behind her she makes an effort to smile. "No, there's nothing wrong. It isn't important."

"Well okay," Linda mumbles. "I just wondered."

"It certainly is lovely here," Alex says, blinking behind his sunglasses. He is wearing an attractive navy blue sports shirt, white trousers (quite smart, but possibly too sporty for him: he feels rather self-conscious), and hand-tooled leather sandals. "The ocean, the sky, the pelicans, the gulls, even the wind—it certainly is lovely."

"Yes," says Fern, sipping her drink.

"Aren't you glad we came?—on the spur of the moment like this?"

"Yes, that's true," Fern says.

She is staring at the wild, choppy ocean fifty feet below their balcony; her words are not very distinct. Alex isn't certain he has heard correctly. " . . . a change of scene is very important, especially after a shocking experience," Alex says softly. He does not think of Maxine directly: has not thought of her directly at all. He thinks, instead, of a *shocking loss* that must be dealt with. According to a friend of his with whom he plays golf occasionally, the loss must not be allowed to undermine the well-being of the survivors—it must not be suppressed, nor must it be dwelt upon. "And it's really good luck the children didn't mind not coming with us. . . ."

"Did I tell you, I ran into Thea Ferrara in Nieman-Marcus," Fern says suddenly. "I was looking through bathing suits—all on sale— and I heard someone say, *Why it's Fern Enright*, and there was Thea herself. She was looking awfully rested."

"Thea Ferrara," Alex says slowly, frowning. "Oh yes: I know her, don't I? Her and him both."

The week in Miami Beach is a kind of second honeymoon, Alex thinks. He is very pleased with the accommodations (which the company provided). He has no complaints at all. The hotel has a dictation and stenographical service, and he can accomplish a great deal while Fern lies on the beach, or goes shopping with Thea Ferrara, or checks out a possible restaurant for dinner that evening. He must watch his diet, of course, but he feels quite good—quite good.

"It certainly is lovely here," he says.

"Yes," says Fern.

Is There A God Who Cares?—by the merest accident Alex comes across this small, smudgily-printed pamphlet on the beach. He stoops to pick it up, ignoring Fern's disapproval, and as they stroll along the beach he begins to read, and becomes more and more absorbed: Do you want to live in God's righteous new order? Do you want to escape world wars, hunger, disease epidemics, and wanton pleasure-seeking? People who oppose God's rule, Alex reads, would only be troublemakers, so they will not be allowed in the new order.

He finishes the pamphlet, and rereads it.

And then again, secretly, rereads it; and packs it with his clothes to bring back to Lake Forest.

When Ted Mandel meets Fern Enright some years later, in Chicago, they will talk of religion for a while, in that peculiar half-embarrassed way most Americans talk about religion. (But Fern will say nothing about Alex's conversion to Jehovah's Witnesses— she rarely even allows herself to think about it.) Fern has heard of the Kabala, of course, but is forced to admit that she doesn't know anything about it. By this time Ted has become an expert on the Kabala and he talks about it passionately for some time, while Fern listens intently, nodding; the subject gives to their meeting the tone of a profound confrontation. Each is nervous, expectant, a little apprehensive. After all—they have arranged to meet alone at a downtown hotel restaurant, and it soon becomes obvious that Fern has not mentioned the meeting to her husband.

The transition from the Kabala to the fact of Maxine's death is a graceful one, and they talk of her in solemn, frank voices. It is necessary for them to clear the air, of course; to exhibit their sorrow, and their bravery as well. "It cut into me like a knife," Ted said. "I hadn't known I was still so attached to her. . . . It took a long, long time for me to get on an even keel again." Fern agrees, blinking tears out of her eyes: "I felt the same way. I feel the same way." It was a terrible thing, a shocking thing, a pity . . . a tragedy. "But there are evidently suicidal people," Ted says. "I mean their tendency is along those lines. They look for excuses, they practically devour excuses . . . to do whatever it is they must do."

Fern shivers, knowing what he says is true.

They spend some time sifting through their feelings toward Maxine, recounting a number of particularly pleasant incidents—a picnic at Kensington Park, a late-night supper in Ann Arbor, Maxine's characteristic kindness in bringing a bottle of Dewar's Scotch to Alex, as a present, after he had successfully completed his preliminary examinations. Ted tells Fern about the abortion, surprised that she had not known (and half-suspecting that she did and is only pretending, now, to be astonished). Fern tells Ted, hesitantly, about the innumerable telephone calls Maxine made to her and the drinking and the men whom Maxine evidently picked up anywhere she could find them (and wonders, seeing Ted's pained expression, whether she should have brought up such a subject: is it possible that he feels, still, a kind of sexual rivalry?—or did he truly love Maxine at one time?)

They assess their feelings at great length. Their feelings are very enigmatic, very subtle. And Maxine . . . ? What did the poor woman think, what did she *feel?* Both make gestures of bewilderment and resignation. There are those fated to commit suicide . . . programmed in the genes, perhaps . . . and who can prevent them. . . . "If she had only learned to love unselfishly," Ted says. Fern nods in agreement though she does not *quite* understand.

They move on, relieved, to more pleasant topics: news, reminiscing, gossip. Did Ted know about Jerry Hecht . . . ? Divorced. Remarried. And poor Deanna: She had dropped out of sight, evidently. (Yes, it was true that Jerry Hecht had remarried a student of his. How unimaginative, Ted laughs. "It isn't really necessary to *marry* them," he says, mildly shocking Fern.) And what about Darrell Ednie . . . ? He had been working in New York City for a while, but then had gone out West: California, maybe. A kind generous bumbling sort of man, fairly talented but not shrewd enough to make his way in the competitive world of commercial art. A homosexual, obviously. Close friend of the Renekers. (And whatever happened to *them* . . . ? Fern had heard some time ago that they'd been divorced, and that Cynthia had gone to live in London. But since then: nothing.)

"*Was* Darrell Ednie a homosexual?" Fern asks, raising her eyebrows.

"Certainly," says Ted. "He might not have known it back in Ann Arbor but the rest of us did."

"We *did* . . . ?" Fern says doubtfully.

Ted laughs, reassured by Fern's naiveté. Maxine was quite right about her: the woman is charmingly, wonderfully, hopelessly ingenuous.

No one has heard of Darrell Ednie for some years, but Ron Hammersly, of course, has become famous. Notorious. (He had been awarded the National Book Award for fiction but had refused to accept the award. There are no recent photographs of him, he gives no interviews, his entire life is a secret.) Fern has the vague idea that Ron Hammersly writes best-selling novels, so Ted must inform her, courteously, that Hammersly is a writer of *quality;* the critics' darling; an obscure, exasperating, but ultimately brilliant novelist. Fern blinks in amazement. She has the idea—which Ted does not contradict—that Ted has read Hammersly's work, so she listens in attentive silence as Ted speaks of his old friend. Though there were temperamental differences between them, Ted says, he and Hammersly respected each other's intelligence, and they spent some hours discussing in principle the æsthetics of Hammersly's projected novel. "He had envisioned a kind of encyclopediac novel," Ted says. "I suggested that he retreat from active life like a monk, like a mystic, and take with him representative books from our culture—philosophy, science, history, and popular works as well like comics and tabloid papers—and give himself a dozen years or more so that he might create a real masterpiece: something like *Ulysses.* Or *Finnegans Wake.*"

"That's amazing," Fern says. "Remarkable."

"And so," Ted says, laughing wryly, "the man turns out to be the only one of our circle to become famous . . . !"

"He really should have dedicated his novel to you," Fern says.

"I'd hardly expect that from Ron," Ted says. "He was never a very grateful person."

Fern does her best to remember Ron Hammersly. She can recall only a rather ugly young man, strident and uncharming, with a womanish high-pitched voice. And glasses. Or was she confusing him with Darrell Ednie? He had been in love with Annie Quirt for a while. But Annie had ignored him, she'd been involved with someone else. . . . What of Merrill Pritchard? Not a word. Barbara Schiller? Nothing. The Masons? Nothing. (Fern isn't sure she and Alex ever knew a couple named Mason. But she frowns and tries to recall since they seem important to Ted.)

Any news of. . . . Well, there was Annie Quirt: evidently she had had a one-woman show at a gallery in Chicago this past winter (by accident Fern had come across an enthusiastic review of the show in the *Chicago Sun-Times*) and must be living in the area since Fern had seen her, the previous autumn, coming out the Brass Rail with several other people, men and women both, but they hadn't had time to say anything more than hello, which was a pity. (Fern had had the uneasy feeling that Annie hadn't recognized her though *she* had recognized Annie at once.) "She looks the same as ever," Fern says, not quite truthfully. "I suppose she's in the telephone book and I could call her. . . ."

Though Ted is nodding sympathetically he can't remember Annie at first. Then he remembers: remembers suddenly with a pang of emotion. That tall red-headed girl, the artist—how beautiful she had been, and how much Ted had admired her in secret! Ah, he remembers now. Remembers vividly. He had loved Maxine very much of course, in the early days of their marriage; but he had nevertheless daydreamt of Annie Quirt and had been foolishly jealous of her lover, whose name he has now forgotten. Not Ron Hammersly, surely? No: too ugly. But then who? Absurd of him to have been jealous. . . .

It occurs to Ted that Lisabeth had been only a version of Annie, a girl whom he'd hardly known many years ago, and who had not known him at all. Perhaps *she*, Annie, had been the woman meant for him all along . . . ?

"I feel so out of touch with everyone," Fern says apologetically.

"It's inevitable," Ted says with feeling.

As they talk of the past they grow more and more enlivened for some reason, though their friends' faces have become distressingly vague. There was the danger, at first, that Fern would slip meekly into the role Maxine seemed to have devised for her—a kind of younger, dutiful, plain sister, a foil to Maxine's florid self-dramatization; but Fern drinks more now and is consequently freer, and Ted has become skillful at drawing women out. So that danger is avoided.

They are discovering, in fact, that they are very much attracted to each other.

Fern Enright! Sweet little Fern! Maxine had unfairly called her dowdy and boring, and had always been so patronising with her, but Ted thinks she has never looked prettier. She is wearing a knit dress of russet and white, and small golden earrings (might they be genuine gold?) that intensify the stylish golden streaks in her hair. Ted, freshly-shaved, his hair cut and styled only the day before—in reaction to the period of slovenliness he has come through—has a charming habit of gazing into his companion's eyes and then looking down, as if very much moved by what he sees. As they talk it becomes clear that the two of them were keenly aware of each other all along, throughout the years; and the others—Fern's husband, Ted's wife—were merely peripheral, like minor characters in a play. (And what *is* Alex doing these days, Ted wonders. He asks Fern several times and she answers in the most bland, general way—is it possible, Ted thinks, alarmed, that the woman doesn't *know?*)

Fern squeezes his hand impulsively. "It's so *wonderful* to see you again," she cries.

Ted grips her hand hard. He feels, at once, a surge of emotion that is richly complex; far more than merely physical. "Yes, it's a miracle, isn't it? It seems like . . . like a miracle."

Yet he had simply telephoned her and arranged to see her, explaining that he was passing through Chicago on his way to California, to a junior college in Bakersfield. Was she free? For a drink, or maybe for lunch? And she had been free, eagerly free, and so they met at the Palmer House, and spent a very exciting and exhausting three hours together. (Ted is grateful she didn't insist that he come out to their home for dinner: thank God!) Nothing out of the ordinary, really, yet it seems miraculous; they gaze at each other with rapt, glistening eyes.

And then . . .

And then for some reason the moment passes.

Fern glances at her diamond-studded wristwatch and stammers that she must leave. She appears to be suddenly shy, almost frightened. Ted, sharply disappointed, calls for the check. He escorts her out into the bright sunshine where they say goodbye, fairly trembling with emotion, not even daring to shake hands. Ted is very disappointed, but at the same time oddly relieved.

He will have to come visit them soon, of course, and stay for a few days. Maybe at Christmas. —But nothing specific is planned.

And now they back away from each other, smiling. There are tears in Fern's eyes, there are tears in Ted's eyes. She waves, Ted waves. Like children they smile, waving, parting. About to cross the street he calls something after her but she can't hear—and they wave a final time, giddy, delighted, shaken to the very core, blowing kisses at one another like daring children.

"Goodbye! Come back again soon! Will you write?" Fern calls.

Ted nods emphatically, backing away.

Printed December 1978 in Santa Barbara & Ann Arbor for the
Black Sparrow Press by Mackintosh and Young & Edwards
Brothers Inc. Design by Barbara Martin. This edition is
published in paper wrappers; there are 1000 cloth trade copies;
300 hardcover copies have been numbered & signed by the
author; & 50 numbered deluxe copies have been handbound in
boards by Earle Gray & are signed by the author.

Photo: Layle Silbert

Joyce Carol Oates has been called "the best young novelist in the United States today." *All the Good People I've Left Behind* is the eighth book by Ms. Oates to be published by Black Sparrow Press, the others being *The Hostile Sun: The Poetry of D.H. Lawrence* (1973), *The Hungry Ghosts* (1974), *Miracle Play* (1974), *The Seduction & Other Stories* (1975), *The Triumph of the Spider Monkey* (1976), *Daisy* (1977), and *Season of Peril* (1977).

Joyce Carol Oates is married to Raymond Smith, and both are Professors of English at the University of Windsor, Ontario, where they teach and edit the literary magazine *Ontario Review.* They are presently living in Princeton, New Jersey, where Ms. Oates is Visiting Writer at Princeton University for the academic year 1978-1979. Her most recent novel, *Son of the Morning*, was published by Vanguard Press in the summer of 1978.